For Ma

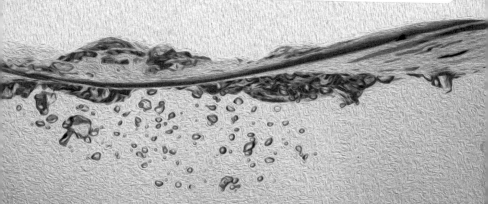

have
One
x

Not the Same River

Anne Lalaguna

Matador
9 Priory Business Park,
Wistow Road, Kibworth Beauchamp,
Leicestershire. LE8 0RX
Tel: 0116 279 2299
Email: books@troubador.co.uk
Web: www.troubador.co.uk/matador
Twitter: @matadorbooks

ISBN 978 1785899 805

British Library Cataloguing in Publication Data.
A catalogue record for this book is available from the British Library.

Printed and bound in the UK by TJ International, Padstow, Cornwall
Typeset in 11pt Minion Pro by Troubador Publishing Ltd, Leicester, UK

Matador is an imprint of Troubador Publishing Ltd

This book is dedicated to the very special people who have supported and encouraged me throughout the long process of writing it. You know who you are and you have my eternal love and gratitude.

'No man ever steps in the same river twice, for it's not the same river and he's not the same man.'

Heraclitus

1

I've hated Thursdays ever since I can remember, thought Dr Maggie Savernake as she hitched the cumbersome dry cleaners' bag over her arm before elbowing her way through the crush of students in the college entrance.

She'd been dreading this particular Thursday for weeks. Two back-to-back lectures in the morning, a staff meeting which would probably take up most of the afternoon, and as if that wasn't enough, a reunion dinner in the evening.

She hung the bag on the back of the door in her office and began unpacking her rucksack. Plenty of room for improvement amongst this lot, she thought grimly as she piled the marked essays on her desk. The second-year students were proving to be something of a disappointment; none of them had reached the promise she'd predicted. It looks as though none of them has done any work at all during the summer, she thought.

The first weeks of the new academic year were always a trial. The responsibility to inspire her students weighed heavier on Maggie's narrow shoulders than on many of her more cynical colleagues. Teaching was a great deal more than just a profession as far as she was concerned. It was her whole life, all she had ever known for as long as she could remember. Whenever she was asked why she had chosen it, her answer was always the same: 'I don't think I ever had a choice. It's imprinted in my DNA.'

She glanced at her watch. In spite of leaving home early,

there were only five minutes to spare before her first lecture was due to start. Feeling uncharacteristically anxious, she picked up her files and checked through them again before she reached the door. Eight of the new intake had signed up for her Shakespeare's Sonnets option. Perhaps my pet subject is gaining in popularity after all, she thought as she made her way quickly to the lecture room.

Less than an hour later, she was ending the lecture in her time-honoured fashion, by reciting the final verse from one of the Sonnets. This morning she had chosen number 148.

O cunning Love! with tears thou keep'st me blind,
Lest eyes well seeing they foul faults should find.

Maggie laid the last page of her notes down on the desk. Number 148 was the Sonnet that Jack Millfield had sent her when they were students. Is that why I chose it today? I wonder if he will be there tonight. She smiled. He's probably married with grown-up children by now. It's hard to imagine Jack with a family.

A polite ripple of applause forced her attention back to the present. The students were getting to their feet, chatting and laughing as they shuffled towards the exit.

Maggie switched off the back projector and put her notes inside a blue cardboard file labelled Shakespeare's Sonnets – Year 1, in her neat, round handwriting.

Dust particles were floating in the beams of thin sunlight falling across the empty chairs opposite. The air was heavy with a potent blend of cheap body spray and youthful sweat. In a few more weeks they will be challenging me on every detail, she thought. It was the lively exchange of ideas which she enjoyed more than anything else about her work, always insisting that her students taught her as much, if not more, than she ever managed to instil in them.

The large white face of the clock high on the wall above her head signalled that there was still half an hour to go before her class with the second years. That's definitely going to be a test of my patience, might be a good idea to have a coffee first, she thought as the tantalising aromas from the cafeteria reached her nostrils.

She hurried to join the noisy crowds jostling around the counters, cheerfully acknowledging the waves and smiles from some of the more familiar faces, with her spirits lifting. It was a huge relief to be back after the long summer recess. This year it had been more of a test of endurance than a holiday. After a self-imposed, month-long retreat to the British Library to finish some urgent research, she had been irrationally disappointed to discover that most of her friends had disappeared to sunnier climes.

Now, armed with a cup of steaming black coffee, she scanned the tables in the refectory, and was delighted to see two familiar faces on the far side overlooking the quadrangle: Rose Cooper and David Moreton. Rose had been a friend since they were students and was now a colleague, and David was an old family friend and a retired colleague. Academia is an incestuous profession, she thought as she wove her way through the tables towards them. Everybody knows everybody.

'I didn't expect to see you two this morning. I thought you didn't have any classes on Thursdays, Rose,' she said.

David stood up, dwarfing her. His smile accentuated the wrinkles in his weather-beaten face as he bent to give her a peck on the cheek.

'I'm going to return some books to the British Library and then I'll stay there until I come back here to change. I've left my stuff in Joe North's room.'

'And I'm on my way to a ridiculously expensive hairdresser near Portland Place and then I'll brave the crowds in Oxford Street to find something to wear,' said Rose.

Maggie touched the untidy knot of curls on the top of her

head. 'This mop defeats every hairdresser I've ever taken it to,' she said sadly.

'It suits you, and it's a stunning colour,' said Rose. 'Why would you change it? Anyway my shopping spree is a reward from me to me after being lumbered with both kids for the whole summer while my ex rolled around on a Mediterranean beach with his new tart. Frankly, I deserve it.' She stood up. 'I'll leave you two to chat. See you later.'

Maggie turned back to David. 'I've got ten minutes before my next lecture. What's all this?' She patted the papers on the table.

'My trip to Chile. I was going to ask one of the Admin people here to cast an eye over it before I take it to the Embassy.'

David gathered up the sheets. 'Is there more bureaucracy involved in organising these trips than there used to be? Or is it me? Am I getting too old?'

'Yes to the first. Definitely no to the second. Although launching yourself into the depths of Chile again might be a tad ambitious.'

'What, at the ripe old age of seventy-five, you mean? Go on, say it! Don't spare my feelings,' he laughed.

'I didn't mean it like that.'

'Yes you did. You know you did, and you're probably right. But the desire to learn never leaves you, even if everything else fails.'

He covered her hand with one of his. Maggie saw that the bones were clearly visible beneath the mottled, papery skin and looked away.

'I can't just sit around here waiting for the final curtain to fall. You wouldn't want to condemn me to that, would you?'

'Of course not! But couldn't you at least find a research student to help you with some of the more challenging bits? There must be quite a few who would kill for the opportunity. I could ask around for you.' David's wounded expression made her feel guilty.

'I'm only trying to make your life easier,' she added.

'This will be my last trip. To Chile, anyway,' David said.

'You're hopeless. And you're raising the bar very high for the rest of us. God knows what I'll be doing when I'm your age.'

'You're not doing so badly. Your father would've been very proud of what his girl's achieved.'

Maggie said nothing. She couldn't remember her father ever showing any interest in what she did.

'After listening to Rose telling me about what her two kids get up to, you were a model child in comparison,' David said.

'I'm from another generation, David. In any case, I didn't get the opportunity to be anything else. The school my father sent me to was horrendously strict. It was more like a detention centre.'

David laughed. 'Don't exaggerate. But I have to agree that things have changed. Apparently Rose's daughter is already on the pill.'

Maggie raised her eyebrows.

'Really? That must have happened this summer. I would've thought that fifteen is a bit young, but what do I know? Bringing up a teenage daughter must be an enormous challenge, especially for a single parent. I don't know how Rose copes. Her son Seb is pretty wild too. I'm glad that I haven't got any children.' She sipped her coffee. 'What about your trip? When are you leaving?'

'Not sure.'

Maggie's look of exasperation prompted him to add, 'Don't worry, I'll send you a postcard.'

She scraped the bottom of the cup with the tiny plastic baton which served as a spoon. David was the last tenuous link she had with her dead parents. Although she didn't see much of him anymore, losing him too was something she didn't want to think about.

'If I get all this paperwork ready now,' David said, opening his briefcase, 'it'll be one less thing to worry about when the time comes. Anyhow, enough about me. What have you been up to over the summer?'

'Guess.'

'Working? Why am I not surprised?'

'I was doing some research, except I didn't have to cross the Atlantic to do it. And by the time I'd finished, all my friends had escaped to the sun and left me to twiddle my thumbs in soggy old London.'

'And whose fault was that?'

'Mine. I know. It's not all bad news though. I did manage to have a few days in France with Diana and her new husband. I don't think you ever met her, did you? She was a RADA graduate who came to do a bit of part-time lecturing here two years ago. We used to take students on theatre visits together. She had a friend at the RSC who wangled some great reductions.'

'I think I did meet her at one of the Christmas parties here. Short and dark. Vivacious. A bit like Rose, only slimmer.'

Maggie nodded. 'Her new husband is a tall blonde Viking with a beard. They make a striking couple. She met him when she was on holiday with her sister. She called it, *un veritable coup de foudre*,' Maggie laughed. 'Apparently, it means being struck by a bolt of lightning.'

'God, what does that feel like? Have you ever...?' David's eyes were mischievous.

'No! Never!' Maggie exclaimed in mock outrage, then added as an afterthought, 'OK, maybe once. A long time ago. When I was a student.'

She turned abruptly to gaze at the quadrangle.

'They're trying to start a family. Diana's the same age as I am. She told me that a woman's fertility drops like a stone as she approaches forty.' She paused. 'Not sure how I feel about that.'

David watched her carefully. 'How was France?'

'France?'

'You said you were in France, remember?'

'Oh, yes. The weather was good, and there was plenty of delicious food and wine. We seemed to spend a lot of the time laughing.'

'Sounds awful,' David said drily.

'Diana's the polar opposite of me. Very extroverted and uncomplicated. I suppose that's why I get on so well with her. They've asked me to go out there for Christmas,' Maggie said.

'And will you?'

'Not sure.'

'Did you meet any nice men while you were there?'

'No, I wasn't looking, David. I'm still licking my wounds from the last one, thank you very much.'

Maggie swirled the last dregs of coffee around in the bottom of her cup. Don McPherson had been a salesman for an international academic publisher. She'd met him at a conference. He was twelve years older than her, newly divorced, with two very temperamental teenage sons. In spite of his obvious unsuitability and repeated warnings from friends, it had taken her almost two years to accept the fact that the affair with Don was never going to develop into anything more than the occasional joyless weekend whenever he happened to find himself in London on business.

Maggie's cheeks burned at the memory. 'I seem to be a very poor judge of character,' she said. 'Don McPherson was the second mistake since I moved to London ten years ago.'

'Only the second in ten years?'

David wagged an admonitory finger. 'You're not getting enough practice, my girl. You need to put those books away and get yourself out there.' He pointed at the quadrangle.

'Diana and Lars suggested that I go out to look for *it* because *it* won't come looking for me. Whatever *it* is,' she said with a hollow laugh.

'I agree,' said David.

He nodded at the quadrangle, now teeming with students.

'There must be at least one man out there who would meet your rigorous standards?'

'Oh, for heaven's sake,' she said impatiently, 'Quite apart from the professional ethics involved, I haven't quite reached the stage of being one of those desperate, middle-aged women who chase younger men, thank you very much. In any case, from now on, I'm definitely going to avoid anybody even remotely connected with academia.'

'I didn't mean the students or the staff. Heaven forefend! I meant in the big wide world beyond this campus. You need to get yourself out there more often. I think that's how they put it today, don't they?'

Maggie shrugged and pushed her chair back. David meant well, but the implied criticism had stung. Was he suggesting that she was turning into a dried-up old spinster?

'We need to decide where we're all going to meet up tonight. Rose and I thought we could go in a cab to Knightsbridge.'

'Ah yes, the famous reunion. I'm hoping that some of the old tutors will be there. Have you heard anything?'

'No. Only that it's been organised by the Old Students Association,' said Maggie. 'Frankly, I'm not looking forward to it.'

'Why? It'll be fun finding out what everyone's been up to.'

'Fun? Hardly,' she said. 'They'll all be happily married with at least two or three children each. Where does that leave me? Single, still unattached and much too close to the dreaded four zero.' She picked up her bag and files. 'I don't understand why it's being held in London, either. If they'd held it in York, it would have been much easier to refuse.'

'They've probably discovered that most of you live or work in or around London now.'

'How?' Maggie looked genuinely surprised.

David frowned. Was she being deliberately obtuse?

'By searching the internet, of course. That's where I would

start. Wouldn't you? I don't know why you're complaining. It's a black tie do, in a very posh hotel in the best part of London. The food and the wine will be excellent.'

'Which explains the exorbitant price of the tickets,' she said.

'Well, I can't wait. I'll be downstairs in the main reception, suited and booted by six thirty.'

Maggie grinned. 'I am glad you're coming. It'll probably be the last chance I get to see you before you leave.' She blew a kiss in the direction of his cheek. 'See you at 6.30 then.'

David watched her slight figure disappear in the throng of students leaving the cafeteria. She's got no family, no partner and she's close to forty already. He shook his head sadly. She's totally alone in the world, apart from me and a few close friends. Why don't young people realise how quickly time passes?

2

Two and half miles away, in a luxurious new block of offices just off Knightsbridge, Jack Millfield lay sprawled in his high-backed leather chair, with one leg hooked casually over the armrest. He looked as though he had been thrown there from a great height. The bilious hue of his handsome face bore graphic testimony to the fact that the second cup of strong black coffee had made no discernible difference to yet another epic hangover. He was still wearing the same clothes that he had worn the previous day; the expensive grey three-piece suit and the black shirt were a lot less pristine and the knot of his co-ordinated silk tie rested untidily in the middle of his chest.

A discreet tap on the door heralded the arrival of Valerie Cook, his formidable and soon-to-be-retired PA. Jack eyed her warily as she approached. With the immaculate dark blue skirt and a mountain of post expertly balanced against the impressive bosom which was firmly encased in a startling lime green jacket, she conveyed an air of intimidating efficiency. Jack detected the unmistakable scent of disapproval as her calculating, pale blue eyes swept over his dishevelled appearance and her nostrils twitched as she inhaled the unmistakable stench of stale alcohol.

'Mor – ning,' she trilled with forced cheerfulness.

Jack found the pause between the two syllables even more annoying than usual.

'Caffeine not doing the trick, I take it?' she said with what Jack misinterpreted as a note of triumph.

He maintained a mutinous silence. His ears were still throbbing painfully from the auditory assault they had received a few hours earlier in a nightclub somewhere in South London. He couldn't remember exactly where or even what it was called now. Both my eardrums are probably perforated, he thought miserably, stone deaf at the tender age of thirty-eight.

Valerie was setting the pile of post firmly in the centre of the blotter with a stare that Jack said could freeze a leg of lamb at fifty paces.

'There are several complaints about the new dog food ad. Did you catch it, last night?' She eyed him suspiciously. 'No? I thought not, somehow. You won't be pleased to hear that there are several people threatening to report us to the RSPCA.'

She gave a scornful snort before adding, 'The usual collection of moronic do-gooders who can't tell the difference between fact and fiction. I wonder how many of them have actually seen a real-live dog using a knife and fork?'

Jack cradled his head in his hands moaning softly and praying that she would either leave quickly or shut up.

Val didn't seem inclined to do either as she patted the pile of post again. It wobbled precariously as Jack squinted at her between his fingers and contemplated the significance of her apparently obsessive compulsion to fuss whenever she came anywhere near him. She was staring over the top of his bowed head at the glorious panoramic view of Hyde Park, framed in the huge tenth-floor window behind him. 'It's a beautiful day outside,' she observed with a kind of determined optimism.

'What?'

'It was a statement, Jack. Not a question. I don't expect a reply,' she said tartly.

Jack swivelled his chair around to look out of the window and then swivelled it back with a deep groan. The low autumn sun had pierced his retinas. Now I'm blind as well as deaf, he thought.

Val was flicking through the pages of her notebook, apparently searching for something. He sensed that it was a delaying tactic; a lecture of some sort was imminent. He braced himself. Although he complained about her constant nagging, he knew that her crude attempts to elicit a reaction from him in the mornings hid a deeply felt concern. She'd rebuked him several times recently about arriving at the office with a hangover and even threatened to talk to his father on one occasion. Jack wasn't unduly worried; Sydney Millfield had rarely shown any genuine paternal concern for him after his parents divorced when he was nine years old. Since then, 'keeping an eye on Jack' seemed to have become an integral element of Val's daily routine, and although he was reluctant to admit it, Jack found it comforting to be reminded that there was still somebody who cared about him. For a brief moment, he wondered how he would feel when Val finally retired to that newly purchased flat overlooking the sea on the south coast.

When she lowered her spectacles from where they were balanced on the top of her short grey curls to study him more carefully, Jack groaned and covered his face. When she looked at him with that potent mix of disappointment and reproach, she reminded him of an elderly housemaster who had wasted many fruitless hours berating him about his studies and wasting his father's money.

'For God's sake, Val, give me some space, will you? I've got a raft of meetings today and I'm trying to get myself into gear, which is not easy with you standing over me like the avenging angel,' he pleaded in a hoarse voice.

Val's lips compressed as she turned to leave. 'Don't be such a child, Jack. You've still got fifteen minutes before the first meeting and, if I may say so, you would do your liver a lot more good if you drank some water instead of all that appalling black coffee.'

Jack stuck out his tongue as she closed the door before turning his attention to his computer screen and scrolling through his diary.

'Fuck! The York reunion! It's tonight! Fuck. I'd completely forgotten,' he yelled, sitting bolt upright as he hurled a stream of colourful abuse at the screen before leaning forward to rest his throbbing head on his blotter in exhausted silence.

There was a discreet tap on the door and Val's head reappeared. 'I've had your navy dinner suit cleaned. It's hanging in your locker in the men's room with a new shirt,' she said.

Jack raised bleary eyes. 'My God, woman, you're a bloody mind reader. I'd completely forgotten about it.' He groaned loudly. 'I really don't want to do this. It's too short notice. I need time to gear up.'

Val tutted impatiently and closed the door behind her before advancing towards his desk again.

'What are you talking about? It's not short notice, Jack. We talked about it and I sent your acceptance months ago. Look at the date of the entry in your diary.'

She jabbed a finger at the screen; it read 25th June 09.00am.

Jack pouted. 'But I'm driving down to Newquay to surf with Josh on Saturday and we'll be leaving at silly o'clock. I've got to get some decent shut-eye before then.'

Val shook her head. 'Saturday is two days away. If you get an early night on Friday, you'll be fine for the drive down to Cornwall. In any case, you'll be sharing the driving. You ought to go to the dinner, Jack, it will be a chance to meet some of your old friends. Show your professors that you've managed to make something of yourself.'

Jack snorted. 'What? Tell them that my father bailed me out after they kicked me out of uni? Then gave me a job when I was on the skids? That's really going to impress them. NOT. In any case, I haven't kept up with any of them, apart from Dominic Goldman and I've only seen him a couple of times in the last few years.' He paused. 'The only other person... is a girl. Someone I was...' His voice trailed off.

'A girl? Now there's a surprise. Well, that's another good reason to go, Jack. Let's face it, an old students' reunion dinner will make a nice change from your usual unsavoury choices.'

He grimaced again as she closed the door quietly behind her, wondering who he would appoint in her place after she retired. She'll have to be at least forty years younger, for starters, he thought, and preferably someone who can't even spell the word nag. What did my father used to say about interviewing secretaries in the old days? 'Yes, very nice, love. Can you type?' Jack wondered if his father had used those words when he interviewed his mother for the job as his PA. He waved a finger at his invisible parent. 'Naughty Dad. That sexist attitude wouldn't get you very far these days. We have to be a bit more subtle now, even if our basic attitudes haven't changed, whatever the Women's Libbers might tell us.'

Jack sighed as he looked at his computer screen. There were several more exhausting hours to get through before the reunion. Let's hope I'm still alive at the end of all this, he thought.

3

Jack trudged wearily towards the men's room to shower and change. Since his recent promotion to Creative Director, he seemed to spend all his working hours either smoothing the ruffled feathers of the prima donnas in the art department or massaging the fragile egos of the account managers.

It hadn't taken him long to discover that the creative side of his newly elevated status was virtually negligible. In fact, he had the sneaking suspicion that his father had handed him a deliberately poisoned chalice before he retired after selling the business to a much larger company. The heady halcyon days of his time as a copywriter when he'd spent many happy hours inventing ridiculous straplines for bath cleaners or baby food, liberally interspersed with extended visits to the local pub or the betting shop, were long gone.

Jack finally emerged, miraculously revitalised, wearing the newly cleaned dinner suit and recently purchased shirt. Val was already in her outdoor coat and swinging a bunch of keys impatiently in one hand as she waited for him. She watched him with barely contained admiration as he approached, walking jauntily down the long blue-carpeted corridor with the athletic ease of a ballroom dancer, in spite of his ruinous lifestyle. He had the short, sinewy build of his father and the arresting colouring of Lucinda, his mother, with the same pale, ash blonde hair and cobalt blue eyes fringed with dark lashes.

Val frowned. Jack looked thinner; the elegant navy blue silk jacket hung much more loosely on him than it had the last time he'd worn it.

He spun on the heels of his expensive Italian evening shoes as he reached her, his eyes teasing as he held out his arms to her in a mock invitation to dance.

'Well? Did I clean up alright, boss?' he asked confidently.

She nodded.

'You didn't need to wait for me, Val. I'm quite capable of locking up by myself, you know.'

She brushed an invisible hair from his lapel. 'That's better,' she said.

'Thanks... Mum.' He waltzed away with an invisible partner towards the lifts.

'If I had been your mother, Jack, your life would have been very different, and you know it!' she called after him as she pulled the office door closed.

'That's my tragedy,' he said softly as he held the lift doors open for her.

A large crowd of people had already gathered on the pavement outside the entrance of the hotel which was just over five minutes' walk from his office. Jack made his way determinedly through the reception towards the bar, then, acting on his well tried and tested theory that it was much better to plan ahead when competing with a large thirsty crowd, he ordered himself two very large dry Martinis and found a space at the end of the counter.

He drained the first glass in one before turning to survey the increasingly animated and boisterous scene. Everybody seemed to be yelling with delight and kissing everybody else, at least twice. Jack began to feel like the lonely passenger left abandoned at the airport arrivals gate. It was just as bad as he had predicted. He didn't recognise anybody. That's what marriage and two point five kids does for you, he thought bitterly as he glanced around the faces. It changes you beyond recognition, and not in a good way, judging by the state of this lot. Jesus, they all look so old. So tragically grown up and self-satisfied. My God, this is so fucking depressing.

As he turned back to the bar to retrieve his second Martini, a sudden peal of laughter rang out and the hairs on the back of his neck stood on end as the years between fell away.

He stared incredulously at the reflection in the huge Art Deco mirror behind the bar. Maggie? Maggie Savernake? It *was* Maggie Savernake. Her long, curly auburn hair was twisted up into a knot on the top of her head, with unruly tendrils escaping on all sides. Jack's eyes narrowed and he put his glasses on.

She was slimmer than he remembered, but it was definitely her. An intriguing, pre-Raphaelite vision, with a delightful laugh which erupted occasionally, breaking through that armour of reserve and offering a tantalising hint of another Maggie, hidden deep beneath the cool exterior.

He remembered how he made her laugh when they were students. It wasn't easy, with her natural inclination to be grave and introspective. He recalled telling her once that when she smiled it was like the sun appearing from behind a cloud. He cringed at the memory. Had he really been that crass, that cheesy? Flashbacks of the times they'd spent together were exploding in his head like fireworks.

Maggie was talking to two men, one of whom Jack recognised. He'd been a lecturer in the English department at York when they were students. The other was a very tall, silver-haired man with a deep tan. Both of them looked as though they were well past retirement age.

Jack sipped his drink slowly, unable to take his eyes off the long white column of Maggie's throat rising from a deep V neckline. Was he imagining the tantalising glimpse of those small, almost forgotten breasts? He felt a lurch deep in the pit of his stomach. She's hardly changed.

He stood motionless, willing her to notice him. When she finally glanced in his direction there was a flicker of uncertainty in her eyes, then a shy smile and a nod of recognition. Jack bowed solemnly, raising his glass in salute and Maggie turned back to her companions with the colour rising in her pale cheeks. Jack's heart was hammering in his chest. It was an uncanny replay of the first time he set eyes on her in 1986. She was the only girl he'd ever met who forced him to make the first move.

As he began to weave his way through the tightly packed crowd towards her, he realised that she was watching him and holding out her hand in greeting.

'Jack.'

'Maggie.' He lifted her small hand with its short, unpainted nails to his lips, searching her face, wondering if she remembered any of the times they'd been together.

They stared at each other for a brief moment until a shrill cry rang out.

'Jack! Big, bad Jack Millfield! Well, *you* haven't changed one little bit, have you?'

Jack stiffened and Maggie smiled ruefully.

The owner of the voice was standing directly behind him, clinging onto the arm of a tall man with an apologetic, long-suffering expression on his face. The woman's free hand was resting protectively over a very advanced pregnancy bump which strained beneath a voluminous, tent-like creation, patterned with eye-popping, scarlet flowers on a white background. Matching red patches of excitement on both her cheeks seemed to glow under the lights.

Jack noticed that her pupils were dilated, almost covering the irises. She looks demented, he thought. Is that what pregnancy does to women? He had no idea who she was, but his smile didn't waver.

'Don't tell me, I have. Changed, I mean.' She paused, clearly expecting Jack to disagree. He stared back at her with a fixed smile.

'Oh, come on, Jack, you *must* remember *me*. Chrissie. Chrissie Winterton. Well, Chrissie O'Donovan, now.' She gazed up proudly at the man shifting uncomfortably from one foot to the other beside her.

'And this is my husband, Kevin, and this,' she said, patting the bulge with evident pride and satisfaction, 'is Master Patrick Kevin O'Donovan, due to join us in three days' time. He's number four son!'

Her voice had risen to an alarming crescendo. There was an audible intake of breath from the people around them. All eyes were now focused uneasily on the undulating scarlet flowers.

'Hi, O'Donovan Number Four,' Jack said, clicking his heels and bending to salute the bulge.

The ironic gesture was received with a few suppressed sniggers and the two red spots on Chrissie's cheeks spread quickly to the rest of her face and neck.

She responded with a sarcastic drawl.

'I shared rooms with Maggie in the first year. You know, when you two had the big breakup.'

Jack saw an unmistakably malicious glint in her eye. It was impossible to tell what Maggie was thinking.

'That was a very long time ago,' he said slowly as he scanned the faces around them, trying to decide which of the men might be with Maggie.

The sound of a gong and the croaky tones of an elderly waiter broke the awkward silence.

'Ladies and Gentlemen, dinner is served.'

The crowd turned like an ebbing tide and began moving towards a large table plan set up on an easel outside the dining room. Jack's uncertainty about Maggie's partner was answered when he noticed that a tall, silver-haired man had put a hand in the middle of her back as he steered her towards the easel.

Maggie glanced over her shoulder. 'Are you coming?' she asked with a warm smile and the muscles in Jack's stomach clenched. My God, you really are something else, he thought as he followed behind them, his eyes fixed on her slim legs.

Unable to resist the overwhelming urge to stand close to her, he peered over her shoulder at the table plan.

'Partner or... sugar daddy?' he whispered with his lips almost touching her ear.

Maggie's hazel green eyes were blazing when she turned and Jack felt another surge of excitement.

'Neither. A very dear family friend.'

She turned back to the easel and before Jack could say anything else, the very dear family friend was tapping the plan with his spectacles case.

'You're on table 5, Maggie, and I'm on table 6. They're on the far side, we'll have to go through the other door. Come on, I'm starving. It feels like a century since the coffee this morning.'

Jack watched them walk away. The easy manner between them sparked a sudden rush of envy in him. He turned back to the plan, searching for table 5.

Dr M. Savernake. Doctor? Why was he surprised? She had been the top student from day one in 1986. It was the rare combination of her impressive intellect, stunning good looks and endearing naivety which had made her such an irresistible challenge.

Jack was filled with disappointment when he discovered that he had been put on a table at the opposite end of the dining room, and once seated, soon realised that it was what he immediately dubbed 'the Losers' Table'.

He was one of two men and six women who, presumably, had all come without a partner. Worse still, he had been placed with his back to the dining room, which made it virtually impossible to see Maggie.

He toyed with the idea of asking one of his fellow diners

to swap places, but decided that he couldn't think of an even vaguely credible reason for making such a peculiar request.

The first few agonising minutes were spent with his face hidden behind the menu, desperately trying to decide which, if any, of the women sitting at his table he might have had sex with while he was a student. The relief was overwhelming when he decided that he didn't recognise any of them, except the smiling, plump brunette sitting directly opposite him in a revealing scarlet dress. She looked vaguely familiar. Reading upside down, he managed to decipher the name on the card in front of her: Rose Cooper.

He studied her covertly for a couple of seconds. *No, I don't remember a Rose. In any case, I think I would have remembered that.* His eyes wandered admiringly over her impressive *décolletage.*

Rose was giggling girlishly at something the man sitting next to her had said. *She's a desperate divorcee and if you play your cards right, you could be in there tonight, pal, no problem,* Jack thought as he forced his eyes back to the menu.

He swivelled around on the pretence of surveying the room and found Maggie watching him. He nodded and raised a hand, and she smiled. A woman at Maggie's table noticed the interchange between them and whispered something to her neighbour. Jack bit his lip and turned away; it was hopeless. If he crossed the floor to speak to Maggie now, it would attract a lot of attention and he knew that she would hate it.

The rest of the meal passed agonisingly slowly while he listened politely to the two women on either side of him comparing notes about their jobs and their various failed relationships since leaving university. He wondered vaguely why so many unattached women felt the need to boast about failed relationships. *Was it a badge of honour? Or a vindication of the perfidy of men as far they were concerned? Women are so different from men,* he thought. *We only boast about our successful conquests.*

He ate virtually nothing and drank far too much while skilfully evading all his dining companions' attempts to engage him. He was very relieved when they finally abandoned their interrogations and continued their discussion across him.

As far as Jack was concerned the evening was proving to be marginally worse than a disastrous experience he'd had with a dating agency dinner party which Val had organised as a surprise birthday present when he was thirty.

By eleven o'clock, most of the guests had begun to leave, including Rose Cooper and her newly acquired admirer. Jack watched them with a sharp pang of jealousy as they walked away, still laughing and holding hands.

He turned to scan the fast-emptying dining room. There was no sign of Maggie or her companion anywhere. The elderly professor who had been in the bar with them was now drinking a glass of brandy and deep in discussion with the wine waiter.

They've left early to avoid the rush, he thought as he watched the rowdy guests moving towards the cloakrooms. Why the hell didn't I go across and speak to her during the meal? Why was I so worried about these idiots, anyway? I'd put money on the fact that most of them didn't even recognise me, let alone remember my name.

By the time he reached the street, there wasn't an empty cab to be seen anywhere. Angry and oblivious to the November chill, he turned his collar up and decided to walk along Knightsbridge towards Hyde Park Corner, then through the park to Bayswater Road, convinced that the exercise would clear his head and calm his jangling nerves. Meeting Maggie again after so many years had disturbed him. When their eyes met in the bar it had felt like two naked wires touching inside him.

'Too bloody late, mate.' He spat the words out angrily as he strode beneath the skeletal trees lining the path, kicking the dead leaves and sending them floating up into the air before fluttering back down again like confetti around his feet.

He had never forgotten the sex he had had with Maggie; it was aeons away from the overwhelming emptiness he experienced after the countless, alcohol-fuelled encounters with so many nameless women since. Jack's mouth twisted. Perhaps time had distorted his memory? Could the sex with her really have been that good? Was anything, especially sex, ever that good?

He raised his head and stared thoughtfully along the shadowy path into the distance. It would be interesting to find out. But how to find her now? Start with the internet, mate, he thought. How many Dr Maggie Savernakes can there be?

The roar of traffic signalled his arrival at Bayswater Road, which was still very busy in spite of the late hour. Jack stood on the curb with his arm raised until a cab eventually slid to a halt in front of him. Then, huddled in the back seat, he stared wistfully at the deserted streets speeding past the windows.

The breakup with Maggie had been the precursor to a catalogue of disasters, culminating in a drunken argument with a tutor over an examination mark, for which he was rewarded with a permanent suspension.

Jack recalled his father's reaction to his sudden and unannounced return to the family home. The rage didn't last. Sydney Millfield went for his perennial solution: when in doubt, just throw money at it.

Jack was swiftly dispatched to spend a few months with his mother, Lucinda, in the south of Spain, where, predictably, after a few short weeks, he managed to get himself arrested for bringing a small amount of cannabis across the frontier after a riotous weekend in Morocco.

Jack shuddered inwardly as he recalled his brief incarceration in the Spanish jail. The authorities had eventually decided to let him go with a severe caution when his father agreed to fork out another exorbitant sum.

Several unsuccessful temporary jobs had followed, until Sydney eventually succumbed to Val's tireless entreaties, and against his better judgement, agreed to let Jack join Millfield Advertising as a junior copywriter. Where, much to everyone's surprise and relief, Jack finally found his *métier*. His prodigious talent for shameless 'blagging' had become his salvation.

After only three years he was promoted to a senior position with an eye-watering salary and all the perks that were an integral element in the life of an executive in a very successful London advertising agency.

Jack grinned. Maggie would be impressed, he thought as the cab came to a halt outside the exclusive block of luxury apartments overlooking the ponds on the edge of Hampstead Heath. He leaned forward, holding out the money to the driver. She's bound to be on Google.

Inside the flat, he went straight to his computer and less than a second later, there she was: Dr Margaret Savernake, PhD, senior lecturer in the English department at London University. There was a small photograph of her with an impressive list of publications.

Christ, she must have a very understanding husband or partner, Jack thought. He pushed an impatient hand through his hair as he studied the numerous titles. What have I got to show compared with this? His eyes searched the page again. There was an email address and a work telephone number.

Jack sat there staring at the photograph of Maggie for a long time.

'No harm in giving it a try,' he whispered finally as he typed a brief message and pressed SEND.

'After all, what's the worst that can happen?'

4

On her way home in the back of a black cab, Maggie was lost in thought; she'd known that she was being watched long before she saw Jack in the bar. She'd read somewhere that it was a primitive, self-preservation mechanism, a long-forgotten animal instinct, a natural warning that a predator was near. She frowned at the unfair metaphor. Jack might have been persistent when we were students, but he was hardly a predator, and even if he was, I was a very willing prey, let's face it. A faint surge of excitement ran through her. Long-buried memories were beginning to surface.

Beyond the driver's shoulder, she caught a glimpse of a poster on the back of the stationary bus in front of them, depicting a scruffy dog with a napkin tied around his neck. He was brandishing a knife and fork in his front paws and salivating over a large plate of dog food. Maggie grinned at the comical expression on its shaggy face; the spiky blonde top knot reminded her of the way Jack wore his hair when they were students.

The cab was crawling forward metre by metre and Maggie closed her eyes, leaning back against the seat. She'd been completely bowled over by Jack's energy and enthusiasm, his carefree attitude to everything. It was such an exhilarating contrast to her own. She remembered the night when he'd thrown stones at every window in her hall of residence and woken everybody up, including three female tutors. On another occasion, he'd got down onto the floor under the tables in the refectory during supper and crawled about until he eventually grabbed the knee of a very distinguished visiting female professor from Harvard, mistaking it for hers. Maggie giggled as she recalled the elderly woman's outraged screams when Jack's grinning face had surfaced next to her thigh with the tablecloth draped around his head like a cowl.

There were other memories too. Maggie's colour rose. Jack was always very warm and affectionate. Constantly touching her, putting his arm around her, and everybody else for that matter. He told her that it was a trait that he'd inherited from his French grandmother. She'd never met anyone like him and fell head over heels in love for the first time in her life.

While they were together they were either laughing or making love, often at the same time. She called him 'Tigger' because he reminded her of the irrepressible character in *Winnie the Pooh* by A. A. Milne; the book had been a childhood favourite, the only present that her father had ever given her.

The cab had ground to a halt again and Maggie's smile faded. It was too good to last, of course. After a few intoxicating months, the very qualities that had attracted them to each other had become irreconcilable differences. Her desire to focus on her studies and get a good degree and Jack's single-minded pursuit of a hedonistic lifestyle were a doomed combination. Small disagreements escalated into arguments, then the arguments became fierce rows and her work began to suffer. Her tutors complained, Jack accused her of putting her studies before him and she accused him of being petulant and unreasonable.

She caught the eye of the cab driver watching her in the rear view mirror and looked away, imagining that he could read her thoughts. She put a hand on the back of her neck. Jack had been standing so close behind her when they were looking at the table plan that she could feel his breath on her skin. She remembered turning to find herself staring into his eyes. The cobalt blue irises and thick, dark lashes were startling, even behind the rimless spectacles he now wore.

Maggie shivered and pulled the collar of her coat up around her chin. Has Jack changed? He looks different. He looks older, more mature. A small smile played around her lips. A mature Jack Millfield? That really would be a change.

The cab had stopped again. Yet another traffic jam. The whole of London seems to be out tonight. Why didn't Jack come over during the meal? Did Chrissie's tactless outburst put him off? Maggie shook her head. Same old Chrissie. She's been indiscreet since she was born. Marriage and all those children hasn't changed her.

Maggie moved impatiently on the worn leather seat; the journey was interminable. She glanced anxiously at the meter and checked her purse. She had enough cash as long as there were no more holdups. She settled back on the seat as her mobile phone rang. I bet that's Yuki asking for more reassurance before her *Viva*. It was a serious mistake giving that girl my number. When students get to their finals, they seem to assume that I run a twenty-four-hour counselling service.

At last, the cab was turning into the familiar, litter-strewn side street near the British Museum, where Maggie lived. She bent to retrieve her bag from the floor and took out her purse again. I'll email the poor girl before I go to bed. Then hopefully she'll get a decent sleep before the *Viva* tomorrow.

Maggie locked the front door of her flat on the top floor, kicked off her shoes and, still wearing her coat, went straight to the computer with a loud yawn.

She sent a suitably sympathetic and soothing reply to the anxious student, and then scanned the rest of the mail. Jack Millfield's name caught her eye at once and with a surge of excitement she opened it.

'Hi, great to see you again. Drinks next week? Any evening except Monday. Jack Millfield x.'

Maggie's heart was racing. He must have got my email address from the university website, she thought and smiled. Trust Jack. Drinks next week? Why not? We didn't get a chance to catch up tonight and I'd like to know what he's been doing. She hesitated, fingers poised over the keyboard. It's only a drink. Get a grip, Maggie. Remember what they've all been saying to you. You need to get out more. She took a deep breath and began typing quickly.

'Why not? I could do Thursday. M'

Minutes later, the reply pinged into the inbox.

'Great! Knightsbridge Stn, next Thursday 7.15. J x'

5

As Maggie hurried towards Knightsbridge underground station, she noticed that there was more than one entrance. She grinned. It reminded her of the time when she and Jack had got confused about an arrangement to meet in London on their way back to university after a long weekend spent separately with their 'families'.

They'd passed more than an hour frantically searching for each other as they travelled backwards and forwards between Swiss Cottage and St John's Wood, finally coinciding when she spotted him standing on the up escalator as she was travelling down on the other side. She'd yelled out his name and watched, laughing helplessly as he began his perilous descent against the upward tide of irate commuters.

And here we are again, all these years later, she thought with a lurch of excitement as she saw Jack standing on the corner of Sloane Street, anxiously scanning the faces of the passers-by.

'I'm here, Jack. I'm sorry I'm late,' she said breathlessly as she approached him.

He leaned forward to skim her cheek with his lips. 'There you are! I'm such a fool, I'd forgotten that there is more than one exit. I thought I'd missed you. Like that time in St John's Wood or was it Swiss Cottage, do you remember?'

'Both, I think,' she said, feeling ridiculously pleased that he'd remembered.

'Which way did you come?' he asked.

'I decided to walk to Warren Street, then I took the tube to Green Park and walked the rest. It all took much longer than I expected.'

'I was beginning to think that you'd stood me up. Do you still want to have a drink or shall we eat instead?'

He sounded uncertain, almost diffident. Not at all like the Jack she remembered.

'I'm really sorry. I had no idea it was so late. I'm hopeless with time.'

Jack took her apology as an acceptance. 'There's a little place I know about seven minutes' walk from here,' he said as he took her elbow. 'Do you still like Italian?'

Maggie nodded, acutely aware of the warmth of his hand through the fabric of her raincoat sleeve.

'The place I have in mind is usually quiet. We've got a lot of catching up to do,' he said.

Maggie stopped to gaze at the window display of a small boutique, and they stood side by side, regarding the two faceless mannequins dressed in brightly coloured ball gowns and baroque masks, reminiscent of the Venice Biennale.

'When they don't show the prices, it usually means that they're very expensive,' Maggie whispered.

'They are very pricey,' Jack said, 'although it doesn't seem to damage their business.'

'How do you know?' Maggie swung around to look at him.

'I work over there.' He was pointing at a tall office building. An army of cleaners was clearly visible, moving slowly from room to room with their equipment.

'We're on the tenth floor. My room is on the other side, overlooking the park,' Jack said.

'Is that why you chose to meet in Knightsbridge?'

He looked wounded. 'No. Not at all, I chose it because I

thought that you might like it, and I know most of the watering holes in this neck of the woods.'

He guided her past a crowded bar and stopped in front of an equally crowded restaurant.

As they stepped inside, the manager came forward to greet Jack like an old friend. Jack whispered something and the man's knowing dark eyes swept over Maggie with practised and unashamed interest before leading them to a small table in a secluded corner.

Jack took Maggie's raincoat and handed it to the manager.

'What did you say to him?' she asked in a low voice as they sat down.

'I told him that this is a very special occasion,' Jack said casually as he surveyed the other tables.

Maggie glanced at the manager who was talking to another customer. 'What on earth will he think?'

'Who cares what he thinks? We've got a table, and that's all that matters.' Jack was waving at a blonde girl sitting with a crowd of people on the other side of the restaurant. She blew a pouty kiss at him. Maggie could feel the girl's critical eyes as she picked up her menu.

'What would you like to drink, Maggie? What about a champagne cocktail to start?' Jack was holding two fingers up to the manager and nodding.

'I don't think I've ever tasted a champagne cocktail,' Maggie said, remembering the lemonade shandies they used to share when they were students, and wishing she had the courage to ask for one.

'Really? I've never met anyone who hasn't had at least one champagne cocktail. What about birthdays?'

Maggie shook her head.

'What have you been doing with yourself all these years?' he asked with mock sarcasm.

Maggie was securing the escaping tendrils of her hair. 'I

came straight from work. There was no time to go home and change.'

Jack's eyes softened. 'When you do that with your hair it reminds me of when we were students,' he said. 'You look fantastic. I came straight from work too.'

Maggie glanced at the elegant dark grey chalk-striped suit, pale pink shirt and tiny rosebud in his buttonhole and said nothing as she brushed a hand across her black corduroy skirt.

'These people have nothing else to do with themselves all day except get ready for the evening's entertainment,' he whispered from behind his menu as the waiter placed their drinks and a small plate of green and black olives on the table.

Jack lifted his glass. 'And after all the effort they've made, none of them looks as beautiful as you.'

Maggie's cheeks burned as she took a cautious sip from her glass. He could still make her blush.

'You won't want to drink anything else after this,' Jack said as he removed his spectacles and cleaned them carefully with his serviette. 'I can't believe that we're actually sitting here, together again after so many years. It's magic.'

'It's a long time,' Maggie said and picked up her menu, avoiding his eyes. 'What do you recommend?'

'I'm sorry?'

'What would you recommend? To eat?'

'What do you prefer, mademoiselle? Fish or meat?'

'I don't eat meat.'

'Right,' Jack said, his eyes fixed on the menu.

'I'm not strictly vegetarian, I do eat fish,' she added quickly.

'OK. That increases our options a bit. There are quite a few fish dishes here. Or I could ask them to make you something?' He looked up. 'We should have gone to a vegetarian restaurant. There are several around here.'

'I thought we were just going to have a drink. I'm sorry. But I love Italian food. They always have plenty of vegetarian options.'

She was relieved to see the waiter approaching with his pen poised above a small pad.

'*Signorina?*'

'I'll have the *Risotto ai Porcini*. Thank you,' Maggie said firmly.

'Signor?'

'I'll have the same.' Jack smiled at Maggie. 'I can do veggie. No problem.'

'And to drink?' The waiter looked expectantly from one to the other.

'Maggie?' asked Jack.

'You choose; I don't know much about wine.'

'OK, we'll have a bottle of the *Trebbiano Bianco 2003*, and two more glasses of this.' Jack tapped his empty champagne flute and Maggie put her hand over hers, which was almost full.

'Not for me, Jack, I've got to work tomorrow. I'm not much of a drinker.'

'OK, no more champagne, just bring the wine.'

Jack waited until the waiter was out of earshot. 'We should have done this on Friday or at the weekend, then it would have been a lot more relaxed. I didn't think it through properly,' he said.

Maggie touched the single white flower in the centre of the table with a nervous finger trying to ignore an unsettling sensation of *déjà vu* that had just come over her.

'Well? What have you been doing with yourself all these years?' Jack's voice was gentle.

She looked up. 'Me? Oh, the usual. Working,' she said without looking at him.

'Just working?' He looked sceptical.

'I know. It sounds very dull.'

'Oh, it's definitely not dull, Maggie. Quite the opposite. According to your web page you're a dazzling star in the academic firmament. Even a philistine like me knows that you can't write that much stuff without working very hard.'

That must be how he found my email address, she thought, recalling David's comment about finding people on the web.

'Not really. It was more a case of settling for the security of something that I already knew well and felt comfortable with,' she said. 'I've never been the adventurous type. When I got my doctorate, York offered me a part-time research position, and I stayed there until I moved back to London permanently in 1996 when my dad's health deteriorated.'

She took a small sip of the wine. 'You were much braver when you jumped into the deep end.'

Jack threw back his head and laughed. 'Brave? Hardly. I was a complete bloody idiot,' he said. 'And I didn't jump. I was pushed. I was chucked out of uni for punching one of the tutors. I deserved everything I got. You must have heard about it. I was completely off my head all the time I was there. Wasted.'

Maggie was shocked by the bitterness in his voice. 'It was all a long time ago, Jack. No point in beating yourself up about it now. We all did crazy things when we were young,' she said gently.

'You were right to give me the elbow, Maggie. I was a hopeless case for years,' he said.

She was relieved to see the boyish grin return.

'That's a first. I don't think I've ever admitted that to anyone, apart from to myself, in the middle of the night,' Jack said.

Maggie was struggling to reconcile Jack's memories with her own idyllic version of their time together.

The long silence that followed was broken by the waiters arriving with their steaming plates of risotto. One offered freshly grated parmesan and ground black pepper as Maggie inhaled the tantalising aromas.

'This smells absolutely delicious,' she murmured,

Jack picked up his fork and they ate in silence for several minutes until Maggie asked, 'What are you doing now, Jack? Where do you work?'

Jack picked up his glass and sat back in his chair.

'Guess. I'm working for my father's old company, Millfield Advertising. He sold it to a large American agency when he retired and I was part of the deal.'

Maggie ignored the resentment in his voice. 'Really? Doing what?'

'Advertising, of course,' Jack said with a mirthless laugh. 'Convincing people to buy stuff they don't need and can't afford. In other words, we help big companies to screw the consumers for lots of money. I think there's a word for it.'

He swallowed the contents of his glass, picked up the bottle and held it over Maggie's. She covered the glass with her hand again.

'Not for me, Jack.'

He shrugged and refilled his own.

'I don't know much about advertising. I suppose you get to meet a lot of glamorous people. Celebrities and suchlike?' she said brightly.

'The old man made me start at the bottom. He thought I needed a bit of healthy humiliation after the fiasco at uni.'

He picked up his glass and drank again before adding with a brittle smile, 'It's not all bad, though. Here I am, fifteen years later, the new Creative Director of Millfield Advertising. So there you go. Who gives a monkey's?' Maggie's look of admiration prompted him to add, 'Oh, it's not as interesting as you might think. I spend all my time in endless meetings and signing pieces of paper. The creative bit is virtually non-existent.'

Maggie watched him empty his glass and felt a sudden rush of sympathy. He looked sad and disillusioned.

'The money's good, though. I guess that's something.' Jack turned to scan the nearby tables.

'It's the same everywhere, including academia,' she said. 'The higher you climb up the ladder, the more time you spend in meetings. I managed to avoid it by opting to do research and writing.'

'I've noticed!' he replied with a grin as he swallowed the last forkful of risotto.

'You made an excellent choice, Maggie, the rice was delicious. You ought to choose my meals for me every night. Or, are you married and choosing someone else's now?'

'No.' Maggie kept her eyes on her plate.

'Engaged?' he persisted.

'No.'

'Have you ever?' His eyes were searching her face.

She looked up and took a small sip from her glass.

'Have I ever what? Been married or engaged? No. Have you?' She forced a smile to hide her irritation.

'I've been close, twice. I retired just before the final bell, each time. Phew!' Jack mopped his brow, with another mirthless laugh.

'Why?' Maggie asked curiously.

'It never felt... I don't know, right. What about you?'

'Me? Oh, the usual.' Her hand was back on the table decoration, stroking the petals of the flower.

'What does that mean?' he asked quietly.

Maggie shrugged.

'It's difficult to believe that you haven't been engaged or married at least once since we last met. A beautiful, intelligent woman like you.'

'You're very kind. I suppose it's because I haven't met anybody that I wanted to do either of those things with,' she said.

'Does that include me?' he whispered, both arms on the table, leaning towards her.

'I thought we were talking about...since we were together.'

'The time we spent together meant a lot to me, Maggie.'

Jack's hand had closed over hers on the table. It felt warm and somehow familiar.

She pulled her hand away. 'Don't, Jack.'

Jack's hand lay palm upwards, abandoned and waiting.

'Why? I've never felt like this about anybody else, Maggie. Seeing you again the other night just stirred it all up again. I haven't stopped thinking about you.' His voice was choked with emotion.

She could still feel his touch on the back of her hand.

'It was a long time ago, Jack. We're very different people now. We've both changed, we're... older.'

'But that's precisely why we can go back. Because we've both grown up. It didn't last before because we were too young to understand what we were doing. Now we're older and wiser.'

Maggie picked up her fork and prodded the remains of her meal.

'My risotto's cold,' she murmured as unexpected tears pricked the backs of her eyes.

Jack didn't take his eyes off her.

'I didn't mean to upset you, Maggie. Let's talk about something else. What about hobbies?'

Maggie looked up. 'Hobbies? No. Do you?'

'I like surfing. I was supposed to be driving down to Newquay with a mate this weekend. But he cancelled. His partner hates the water and anything connected with it. She thinks I lead him into trouble.'

'I don't remember you being interested in sport.'

'I wasn't in those days. I had other, less healthy, interests. Played a bit of rugby for a bit. Not anymore. I'm too scared of getting hurt these days. Now I go to the gym, like everybody else.' He patted his stomach.

'What? Every day?'

Jack snorted. 'Nah. Not even once a week. Things keep getting in the way. You know what it's like.'

The waiter cleared their plates away and Maggie looked at her watch. It was close to eleven and the tables were emptying.

'Oh my goodness, it's so late. I've got an early class in the morning. I must go home.'

'Eleven? Already? God, that's gone quickly.'

Jack sprang to his feet, signalling to the waiter for the bill.

Outside on the pavement he pointed at the traffic.

'This is going to be difficult. Where do you live?'

'Near the British Museum.'

'OK. That's roughly in my direction. I'm in Hampstead. We could share a cab. Let's start walking towards the station.' He took her arm, signalling at every cab that passed and cursing loudly when they didn't stop.

'Why don't we just get on the tube, Jack? It'll be a lot less stressful and much cheaper,' Maggie suggested, checking her watch again.

The tube train was packed and Maggie strained to keep herself upright as Jack rocked against her each time it came to a sudden, screeching halt.

'Sorry,' he whispered, his cheek brushing hers. Maggie breathed the pungent citrus notes of his cologne, focusing her gaze on a map of the underground.

The train slowed to a halt, the lights flickered and they were plunged into darkness. Maggie's skin prickled when she felt Jack's breath on her neck and his hand touching hers on the handrail.

The lights came on for a couple of seconds and went off again, and a hoarse voice began to chant.

'Why are we waiting, why are we waiting.'

There was a burst of raucous cheers from a group of youngsters when the lights finally came on and the train groaned and creaked like an old sailing ship as it began to inch forward.

Maggie noticed a small scar above the corner of Jack's mouth.

'Rugby,' he whispered as the signs for Russell Square flashed past the windows.

'This is my stop, Jack. Thanks for a lovely evening. It's been…'

The rest of her words were lost as she pushed through the crowd to get to the doors.

'I can't leave you to walk the streets of Bloomsbury alone at this time of night.' Maggie jumped at the sound of Jack's voice behind her. 'One of the Mummies from the museum might jump out and ravish you,' he said as he took her arm again.

'Jack. There's no need, honestly. You're going to make yourself very late. You have to work too.'

'It's OK. It'll be easier to find a cab in this part of town,' he said and any further discussion was futile as they were carried along by the queue of passengers rushing impatiently towards the exit.

Once at street level, they turned into Southampton Row in the direction of Great Russell Street, passing overflowing waste bins and silent sleeping forms huddled in shadowy doorways. A large dog raised its head and growled.

'A dog must be a great comfort when you're out here all night' Jack said.

'Not just as a companion, they keep them warm as well.'

Maggie had stopped in front of a plain black door, sandwiched between two shuttered shop fronts. Jack leaned backwards to peer up at the unlit windows above their heads.

'This is where I live,' she said, turning to face him.

'Easy commute,' he said, hands thrust deep into his trouser pockets and the collar and lapels of his jacket turned up against the cold as he hopped from one foot to the other. 'Brr, it's cold.'

Maggie smiled, remembering how they'd stood outside her halls of residence, whispering to each other for hours on end. 'Let me come up, Mags. I'll be very quiet. Please.' Jack had begged her so many times.

She unlocked the door quietly and stepped into the dimly lit hallway.

'I won't ask you in, Jack. It's late. The neighbours might complain.'

Jack's lips were a comical, upturned U of disappointment.

He pointed at the ancient rusty bicycle leaning against a pile of old cardboard boxes behind her.

'Yours?'

'Certainly not,' she giggled. 'Thank you, Jack, it was… nice.'

'It was more than nice,' he said, moving forward with his eyes on her mouth. Maggie took a step backwards.

Jack held up his mobile phone.

'We need to exchange contact details,' he said with a smile, 'Give me your phone and then we can type it all into our address books. It's quicker than dictating.'

Maggie hesitated for a fraction of a second before she handed her phone to him, watching admiringly as he began typing quickly with both thumbs.

'Don't forget to give me all your email addresses as well as the phone numbers, home and work.' He said, glancing up at her.

She handed his phone back to him and watched as he checked what she had typed.

He pressed it to his lips.

'Now we'll never lose each other again,' he said.

6

'I want to see you again. When? J x'

Maggie stared at the text message and put her mobile back on the bedside table. She lay back on the pillows with one arm covering her eyes. She had slept very badly. The evening spent with Jack had disturbed her more than she dared admit. There were several moments when she'd looked into his eyes and almost believed that they had somehow managed to travel backwards in time; that they were students again and all the years between had never happened.

She got out of bed and went to open the curtains, staring down into the street below. It was already busy with traffic and the early morning commuters. She rested her forehead against the cold glass, watching as her breath formed a small patch of condensation. She drew the initial J in the middle and stared at it for a moment before rubbing it out guiltily. You're being ridiculous. It was a long time ago. We're very different people now.

And yet, and yet. It had felt so right when his hand was on her elbow as they walked home. The memories of their intimacy had flooded into her mind every time he'd touched her, even accidentally, reawakening long-forgotten emotions and sensations that she thought had gone forever. She'd longed to invite him upstairs.

She turned to look at the alarm clock beside her bed. It's

almost time to leave for college. I'll talk to Rose before I call him. I can't think straight now.

Although Rose had also been at York at the same time as Maggie and Jack, it was not until she joined the staff at UCL that Maggie and she had become friends. Rose was a divorced mother of two unruly teenagers and Maggie was full of respect for the way that she fought to overcome the odds stacked against her. She believed that Rose knew a great deal more about life than she did herself.

As soon as they had sat down with their sandwiches and coffee, Maggie held up her phone.

'Look what I received from Jack Millfield this morning. What shall I do?'

Rose's dark eyes scanned the message. She looked bewildered.

'Why are you asking me? Did he upset you last night?'

'No.'

'Did he make a pass at you?'

'Not exactly.'

Rose exploded with laughter. 'Not exactly? I'll take that as a yes.'

'No, he didn't make a pass,' Maggie protested quickly. 'At least not in the way you mean. It's just that I don't know whether he's…'

'Whether he's what? Gay? Married? Transgender? What?' Rose sounded impatient.

'Whether he's changed,' Maggie said, shamefaced.

'Changed? What do you mean, changed? When I saw him the other night, he looked almost the same as he did when he was a student. Men make me sick. They don't age like we do,' Rose said, then realising that Maggie wasn't joking, she added, 'He's a lot better dressed than he used to be and he's lost weight. Oh yes, and he was wearing glasses.'

She laughed. 'Sorry, Maggie. The truth is, I don't remember much about Jack, or anybody else at uni for that matter. I was out of it for most of the time. Happy days.'

Rose gazed around the crowded cafeteria with a nostalgic expression and then back at Maggie.

'Are you really worried? That he's married, I mean?'

'He said that he isn't. But how do I know whether he's telling the truth or not?'

'Tell me about it,' said Rose as she began removing the unappetising slices of limp cucumber and lettuce from her cheese sandwich before taking a large bite.

'If he'd told me that he was married, we wouldn't be having this conversation at all. I've already learnt that lesson,' Maggie said hotly.

Rose snorted. 'You mean that shitty salesman? What an arsehole he was. But Jack's not like him, Maggie. You know Jack. And so what, if he's changed? We've all changed. Even you, kiddo,' Rose spoke through a mouthful of sandwich. 'I'm certainly not the same person I was twenty years ago. In any case, what are we actually talking about? He's only asked you for another date. What's wrong with that? You ought to count yourself bloody lucky.'

'Is that supposed to be one of your back-handed compliments?'

Maggie couldn't help smiling. Rose was making her feel more confident already.

'Don't be so suspicious, Maggie. Poor Jack. You ought to be flattered that he's still interested in you after all this time. Christ! That's what I call a compliment.'

'Yes. But what about all the rows we had when we were at uni?'

'He was just a kid then and so were you.'

Rose paused, studying Maggie's solemn expression. 'Well, perhaps not all of us. Some of us were never kids,' she said.

'What do you mean by that?'

'Nothing. My advice is go for it, Maggie. Go for it while you still can!'

Rose scrunched her empty sandwich packet in one hand, drained her coffee cup and stood up.

'And on that note, I'll leave you. I've got a meeting at 2.30 with the external examiner. Call me tonight after you've spoken to him. And if you decide not to see him again, let me know. I might have a go myself.'

'Rose!'

Maggie looked shocked and Rose walked away shaking her head in despair at her friend's lack of humour.

Maggie telephoned Jack on her mobile while she was walking home.

He answered immediately. 'Maggie?'

She could hear the sounds of music and loud laughter in the background.

'Have I called at a bad time?'

'No. I'm having a drink with a few colleagues,' he yelled cheerfully.

'I got your text. I was teaching, I couldn't reply.' Her voice faltered on the lie.

'Don't apologise. Are you at home?'

'No. I'm walking down Tavistock Place. Can you still hear me? There's a lot of traffic.'

'Just about. How's everything? Did you sleep well?'

'No.'

She caught a glimpse of her smile reflected in the window of a passing car.

'I was hoping that you would come out and choose my dinner for me again,' Jack said.

Maggie stopped in the middle of the pavement, oblivious as pedestrians tutted and pushed past her.

'Maggie?'

'Yes.'

'What about tomorrow? Saturday? I could come to your place at seven?'

'This Saturday? Tomorrow?'

'Yes, tomorrow. This Saturday.'

'At seven?'

'Yes, Maggie. Tomorrow at seven.'

Rose's words echoed in her head. 'Go for it, while you still can.'

'OK. Tomorrow, at seven. Ring the bell and I'll come down.'

'Great.'

Maggie could hear a woman's voice. 'Jack, we're going! Coming?'

'OK. Give me two minutes.' A long pause and then Jack said, 'Sorry about that. I've got to go. See you tomorrow at seven.'

Maggie left a message on Rose's answerphone.

'Hi Rose. It's Maggie. I took your advice. I'm meeting him tomorrow night. Wish me luck.'

7

When the doorbell chimed at ten minutes to seven, Maggie was ready. She pushed up the heavy sash window and leaned out to see Jack standing on the pavement below. She was relieved that he had opted to dress casually.

'Do you want to come up?'

He craned backwards, one hand shading his eyes from the glare of the street light. Maggie could see that he was holding a bunch of white roses behind his back. She pressed the buzzer, fastened her hair more securely and went to wait for him on the landing.

Jack came bounding up the stairs, whistling tunelessly. As soon as he realised that she was watching him, he clung to the banisters, hauling himself up the final flight, hand over hand, panting and wheezing theatrically, finally falling to his knees at her feet, offering her the flowers.

She giggled. 'Thank you. They're lovely. Come in and sit down for a minute.'

Jack stood in the middle of the room, nodding.

'This is exactly what I imagined your flat would be like,' he said.

'What do you mean? Untidy?'

Maggie tweaked a cushion.

'No, not at all. It's very... nice.'

He waved at the bookshelves.

'What an impressive collection. A proper library. You can almost smell the knowledge. Wow, not airport paperbacks either.'

Maggie bristled.

Jack was reading aloud from the spines. 'Bacon, Marlowe, Webster, and Kyd? Thank God there are a few names here that I recognise. McEwan, Attwood, Mantel and the illustrious bard, Will.'

He picked up her leather-bound copy of the Sonnets, flicking through the pages. 'I suppose you know them all by heart.'

Maggie detected a faint ring of sarcasm. 'I inherited a lot of the books from my father,' she said defensively as she went to fill the washing-up bowl with cold water for the flowers.

Jack was examining a large framed print of a landscape by Claude Monet leaning against the old fireplace when she returned.

He touched the eclectic collection of ornaments jostling for space on the shelf above it. 'Yes, I like it. It feels... very ... comfortable,' he said, with his back to her.

Maggie smiled to herself; comfortable was a polite way of saying cluttered.

'It's a squeeze. I've got a lot of books,' she said. 'The flat's much too small, really. I only stay here because it's so close to the college and I don't like travelling on public transport.'

'No telly?' Jack sounded surprised. 'Or do you watch in bed?' He glanced at the open bedroom door.

'No, I don't have a TV,' Maggie said quickly. 'I'm usually too tired to do anything but sleep after work. There doesn't seem to be any point in spending the money on an expensive thing like a TV that I'm never going to watch. In any case, as you can see, I'm a bit pushed for space. Where would I put it?'

She took her raincoat from the back of the armchair and Jack moved to help her.

'Do you live by yourself?'

She turned to look at him. 'Yes. Why do you ask?'

'Just wondered.' He sounded amused as he leaned forward to examine another print hanging next to the door.

'I let a room to a colleague for a few months, to help with the expenses after the landlord put the rent up. But it didn't work out. She wanted her boyfriend to move in as well. I thought that three was too many to live in such a small space. There are only two bedrooms and I'm a bit precious about having my own space. I'm well past the student pad thing. I suppose I'm getting old and crabby.'

Jack held the front door open for her. 'Not at all. I agree with you. I like my own space too.'

Once they were downstairs in the street, Jack tucked her hand into the crook of his arm.

'Right, I've been giving this evening a bit of thought, and I wondered how Hampstead might grab you? I've booked a table for eight o'clock. We could take a cab, or the tube, whichever you prefer.'

'You've booked a table in Hampstead?'

'Don't say it like that. Have you got a problem with Hampstead?'

'No, of course not. It's just that I can't remember the last time I was there. I sometimes have supper with my friend Rose Cooper and her children in Kentish Town, but that's about as far north as I go.'

'Rose Cooper? Where have I heard that name before?'

'She was at York when we were there. In the year above us. She's small with very short dark hair. Very bubbly and vivacious.'

'Oh yes. I know who you mean. She sat at my table at the reunion thing. She seemed to be enjoying herself quite a lot, if you know what I mean?'

He winked suggestively.

Maggie ignored him. 'It'll be interesting to see if Hampstead's changed since the last time I was there,' she said.

Half an hour later they were strolling along the crowded pavements of Hampstead High Street and it didn't take long for Maggie to realise that Saturday night in Hampstead Village was the same spectacle that it had always been. All the bars and restaurants were packed to capacity with the rich and famous of North London.

'Well?' Jack asked when Maggie's eye was caught by the paintings in the window of a small art gallery. 'What's the verdict?'

'I couldn't afford any of them!' she said sadly.

'Not the paintings, Hampstead!'

Jack rolled his eyes in mock exasperation.

'Oh.' She blushed awkwardly. 'Sorry. It feels more crowded and noisier than I remember. It's probably me. I don't go out in the evenings very often.'

She could feel Jack's hand in the middle of her back as he steered her across the road towards a crowded pub.

'I've booked the table for eight. We've got time for a drink before we eat. What would you like?' he said over his shoulder as he elbowed his way towards the bar.

Jack returned holding two large glasses of white wine high in the air. 'You did say white, didn't you?'

Maggie took the glass wordlessly; she'd asked for something non-alcoholic.

'How's that old family friend of yours?' Jack's mouth was close to her ear against the deafening noise. His cheek brushed against hers as he leaned in again. 'The guy who was with you at the dinner?'

Someone shoved past Maggie as he fought to get to the bar, pushing her hard against Jack and spilling her wine. She reached for the back of a nearby chair to steady herself, blushing furiously and brushing at the stains on her raincoat.

'David? Why are you asking?'

'Just wondered. He looks like a nice chap.'

'He's going to Chile to do some research. Social anthropology.'

'Still working then?'

'He's retired but he likes to keep busy,' she said.

'Quite right too. It's quarter to eight, we've got time for one more before the restaurant. Do you want to stay here, or there's a very nice wine bar just up the road?'

'I don't mind,' she said.

Jack put his empty glass on a window sill and Maggie put hers, which was virtually untouched, beside it.

Outside in the street, Jack shivered and zipped up his leather jacket. The temperature had dropped noticeably.

'Perhaps we'll go straight to the restaurant instead,' he said as they hurried across the road.

Maggie watched as the manager checked the list of reservations, shaking his head while Jack remonstrated angrily. They were attracting the attention of the diners at nearby tables.

Several minutes passed until the manager eventually pointed to an empty table, next to the door marked STAFF ONLY, with an apologetic lift of his shoulders.

'I'm sorry, sir, there's been a mix-up with the reservations. My colleague put you down for nine o'clock. This table is all that I can offer you.'

Jack turned to Maggie impatiently, 'What do you think?'

'Let's take it,' she said quietly.

Once they were seated, their faces were barely half a metre apart. She was forced to angle her knees to avoid bumping his.

'I think we can call this intimate, don't you?' he said, peering at her over the top of the menu.

'Definitely.'

'There's been a mix-up with the reservations. Apparently somebody had written nine instead of eight in the book. I was livid.'

'It doesn't matter, we're here and we've got a table.'

'This place wasn't my first choice, the one I wanted was fully booked. I should have organised it earlier.'

Jack held the menu at arm's length to maximise the light from the small candle in the middle of the table.

'I can't read a thing.'

'Where are your glasses?'

'That's the other problem. You'll never believe it, I've left my glasses and my mobile phone at home.'

He put the menu down on the table with a sigh. 'You'll have to choose for me.'

He loosened his scarf, revealing an open-necked shirt. Maggie caught a glimpse of the deep tan on his neck and chest.

'Which do you prefer, fish or meat?' She asked with her eyes firmly back on the menu.

'Pasta and plenty of it. I don't care what it's with, I haven't eaten properly since the meal we had on Thursday.'

'But that was two days ago. Why?'

She was shocked.

'Oh, stuff keeps getting in the way. It doesn't matter. You choose. I'll have whatever you're having.'

'What about the spaghetti putanesca? It's made with anchovies, olives and tomatoes.'

'Sounds delicious. We'll need a good robust red to go with anchovies.' He signalled to the waiter, who had been watching them from a discreet distance with his hands clasped behind his back.

Maggie watched as Jack expertly twisted the pasta around his fork, remembering the plates of spaghetti they had shared when they were students.

Was that why she'd chosen spaghetti? Was it conjuring up the same memories for him?

'That's better,' Jack said when he finally sat back for a breather, dabbing his lips with the serviette.

The waiter refilled their glasses and Jack raised his, 'Thanks for coming out with me again.'

'Don't say thank you, Jack. I've enjoyed it.'

They held each other's gaze for a second before Jack picked up the menu.

'Are you going to have a sweet?'

'No, I couldn't.' She looked at her watch. 'Oh my God, it's nearly eleven o'clock. I've missed the last tube, haven't I?'

Jack roared with laughter. 'Of course you haven't. But you're not travelling on the Northern Line tonight in any case, my darling. It's Saturday.'

'Why not?'

'It'll be heaving with football supporters and clubbers. I'll call you a cab. Come on.'

Before she could say anything, Jack reached for her coat and signalled to the waiter for the bill.

It was raining heavily when they got outside and the traffic was at a complete standstill. Maggie shivered in the sudden chill as they took shelter under the restaurant's awning and Jack put his arm around her shoulders.

'Look, my place is only ten minutes' walk away, seven if we run. I'll call you a cab from there, my office has an account with a mini cab firm in the City.'

'You can use my mobile.' Maggie began searching in her bag.

Jack snorted. 'Don't bother. I can't even remember the name of the company, let alone the number. My PA deals with all that stuff for me. I'm pretty sure that she put the number on my mobile. But my mobile is lying on my bed where I left it, probably with my glasses.'

He was knotting his scarf around his neck and zipping his jacket up, and hopping from one foot to the other.

'It's the first time I've forgotten my phone for months. I was too busy thinking about meeting you.'

He put his face very close to hers, they were almost nose to nose. Maggie tried to ignore the wafts of vanilla and spice from his aftershave. Jack took her hand. 'Come on, it'll be a damn sight warmer at my place than standing around here getting saturated.'

By the time they arrived at the heavily smoked glass doors leading to the elegantly appointed hallway of the small block of flats on the edge of the Heath, they were both very wet, breathless and laughing.

A wide circle of reflections from a large crystal chandelier danced across the highly polished parquet floor. Maggie wiped the dripping strands of hair from her face as she thought of the shabby entrance of the house where she lived. She wondered what had gone through Jack's mind when he saw it.

'I'm on the first floor, it's not worth taking the lift.'

Jack was standing at the foot of the carpeted staircase, holding his hand out to her with a boyish grin.

'Come on, let's burn off a few more calories.'

Maggie stood back as he unlocked the dark mahogany front door on the first floor.

'Welcome to my humble abode.' His pride was obvious.

The vast open-plan area was furnished in a dramatic monochrome scheme. A huge black leather sofa faced a wall of pleated white gauze panels covering smoked glass doors which led out onto a wide balcony. Another sofa faced an enormous television screen. On the far side, there was a long dining table with eight high-backed chairs in front of an open galley-style kitchen with gleaming stainless steel units and black granite worktops.

The entire area was lit by spotlights in the ceiling and the floor, highlighting displays of black glass ornaments and several impressive indoor plants. There were no books or magazines anywhere.

Maggie was speechless. My entire flat would fit into this room, she thought.

Jack took off his jacket and threw it down onto a sofa, before sliding the glass doors open and gesturing to Maggie to follow him out onto the balcony.

'Come on, it's not raining too hard now.'

They stood together, leaning on the stainless steel balustrade, staring across at the shadowy outlines of trees on the Heath.

'Well? What do you think?'

Maggie noticed the haze of golden stubble on his chin when she turned to look at him. It had been a permanent feature when they were students. She remembered how it felt much softer than it looked. She tore her eyes away.

'It's amazing,' she murmured, before realising that Jack hadn't waited for her reply; through the gauze curtains she could see him taking a bottle of champagne out of the fridge.

As he walked towards her holding the bottle and two glasses in one hand, Maggie's head began to swim; she felt dizzy and wondered if the cold air had affected her. She went inside to sit on the sofa.

'Not for me, Jack. I've already drunk too much. I really must go home. Will you call your cab company, please?'

She swallowed nervously. Her mouth felt odd; it was difficult to frame the words properly. Jack stared at her and quickly put the bottle and the glasses down on the coffee table next to his spectacles. He muttered something under his breath and put them on with a grin.

'I'll go and get my mobile.'

He disappeared through a door, reappearing seconds later with the phone clamped to his ear.

'OK. Call me as soon as you have one. Thanks.'

He tossed the phone down on the sofa.

'Idiots! A wet Saturday night in Hampstead and guess what? Nothing available. They said it'll be about twenty minutes.'

He picked up the bottle of champagne again and twisted it to release the cork, which shot high into the air and hit one of the spotlights with a loud crack. The wine gushed out and spilled onto the floor. He filled both glasses with a froth of bubbles.

'You can manage one little one, surely?' he said as he held the glass out to her.

Maggie shook her head and smiled.

'Go on! It's a special one. Vintage.'

She took the glass reluctantly and Jack sat down next to her, clinking his glass against hers.

'Here's to us,' he whispered, leaning forward.

Maggie took a small sip. 'I wasn't joking when I said that I've had too much, I feel a bit light-headed.'

'We've only had one bottle. Anyway, what's wrong with being light-headed?'

He stretched his arm along the back of the sofa behind her.

'And the drinks before and now this.'

She took another sip, enjoying the sensation of the champagne fizzing on her tongue. She leant back against Jack's arm and gazed around the room.

'You must have a marvellous view from the balcony in the daytime. It's facing south, isn't it?' She waved her glass, ignoring the wine splashing onto the floor.

'West, it's facing west,' Jack said. 'You get the best view from the top of Parliament Hill.' His arm was around her shoulders. 'On a clear day you can see as far as the South Downs.'

'Parliament Hill? That's near where Rose lives,' said Maggie as she turned to look at him. Their faces were almost touching.

'Rose?' Jack said, his eyes holding hers.

'You know, Rose. The one I was telling you about. She lives near Parliament Hill.'

Maggie peered at her watch, tipping her glass and spilling more wine.

'Sorry,' she said frowning at the floor. 'It's nearly midnight. Must go, Jack.'

Jack scrabbled along the sofa for his phone, dialled the number to give them a reminder, rolling his eyes at Maggie as he listened to the reply.

'OK. Let me know as soon as… thanks.'

He drained his glass and put it on the floor, before tightening his arm around Maggie.

'You look as though you're waiting to see the dentist,' he said.

Maggie giggled, 'Why?'

'I don't know. You've still got your coat on. As though you're ready to spring into action. Isn't that what they call the fight or flight syndrome? It's supposed to be a sign of being nervous.'

'Oh,' she smiled sleepily.

'Are you?'

Jack pulled her against him.

'What?'

'Nervous?'

'Should I be?'

'Of course not. You already know everything there is to know about me. I don't think I've changed, have I?'

He took the glass out of her hand and put it down on the floor next to his before removing his spectacles and pulling her close.

'You haven't changed, Maggie. You're still the most beautiful woman I've ever met,' he whispered as he started to kiss her, softly at first and then more urgently.

Maggie closed her eyes. Her head was spinning again; she was slipping into a vortex, helpless and unable to resist when she felt Jack's impatient hands loosening the belt of her raincoat.

8

Jack's breathing slowed to a steady, even rhythm as he rolled onto his side, away from her. He was fast asleep.

Maggie lay there, listening and staring up at the ceiling. She was filled with a deep sense of loneliness and something very close to desolation. A tear rolled slowly down her cheek and she shivered as a draught of cold air from the balcony cooled the little beads of moisture on her warm skin. She reached for a section of the duvet and rolled onto her side. There was almost a metre between them on the wide bed.

Two hours later, she woke to find Jack lying spread-eagled beside her and still snoring loudly.

Trying to ease her aching back, she changed her position. Jack mumbled incomprehensibly and rolled towards her, pinning her to the mattress with a heavy leg, while his eyes remained firmly closed.

Maggie wriggled away from him and stood up unsteadily as she gazed in dismay at the trail of discarded clothes on the floor. The empty champagne bottle and glasses were lined up accusingly next to the sofa. She picked them up and took them to the kitchen as fleeting images from the previous night began to surface.

After collecting her clothes and checking that Jack was still asleep, she went to seek refuge in the bathroom, studiously avoiding her dishevelled reflection in the huge wall mirror.

She had been standing under the comforting cascade of warm water for several minutes, when she heard Jack's voice.

'Maggie, Maggie. You OK? What's going on?'

She turned the water off and wrapped herself in a large towel before opening the bathroom door, to see Jack sitting on the edge of the bed, still naked and polishing his spectacles with a corner of the duvet.

He put them on with exaggerated care to look at her, his face wreathed in a delighted smile.

'Morning, gorgeous. Why did you get up so early? I was beginning to think you'd left me without saying goodbye.'

He massaged his head roughly with both hands, leaving his hair standing up in a comical blonde halo.

'I've got to go home,' she said, not daring to look at him, and closing the door quickly to shut out his protests.

Once she had dressed and tidied her hair, she re-emerged to find Jack still sitting on the edge of the bed, waiting for her. He frowned, head tipped quizzically to one side.

'I'm going home,' she said.

Jack leapt to his feet and crossed the room, pulling her roughly against him, one hand under her sweater, stroking her back and pulling at her bra strap.

'Oh no you're not, Dr Savernake. It's Sunday, remember? What about the plan we made last night?' he mumbled, his face buried in her neck.

'What plan?'

She pulled away from him.

'We're spending the day together.'

He smiled as he watched her rearranging her clothes.

'I've got a terrible headache, Jack. I never drink like that. I must go home. I've got a lot of marking to do. I need to change my clothes.'

Maggie recited the list without looking at him, her voice tremulous.

Jack stroked her cheek. 'Don't stress, sweetie. I'll drive you.'

She glanced at the alarm clock on the shelf behind his bed. 'It's very late. I must go.'

She walked into the lounge, holding her shoes in one hand, with Jack in pursuit and still naked.

'Wait, Maggie. Please. Just let me jump in the shower, five minutes max. Promise. Then I'll drive you. Be a good girl and go and make some coffee.'

Maggie bristled instinctively as she watched him disappear into the bathroom. His buttocks were very white against the rest of his deep golden tan. She averted her eyes, momentarily distracted as she struggled to marshal a rush of conflicting emotions – mostly shock at the realisation that she had slept with Jack, overlaid with a deeply troubling sense of guilt because she wasn't sure how she felt about him.

Maggie stared at the bathroom door, listening to Jack whistling in the shower. Rose had told her to go for it. Is this what she meant? And why did she have this horrible feeling that she had just made a mistake?

She heard Jack turning off the shower, and went to prepare the coffee.

Less than half an hour later, he was leading her towards a silver sports car, gleaming under the overhead lights in the underground car park.

'I hardly ever drive it,' he said with what sounded like pride. 'It's the latest model. What do you think?'

'I don't know what to say. I don't know anything about cars. It looks very expensive.' She assumed that that was what he wanted to hear.

'It is. Very,' Jack said with a distinct note of triumph as he opened the passenger door for her, 'and very fast too.'

They drove out into the thin, wintry sunshine in silence. Maggie glanced sideways briefly and looked away. Jack was concentrating on the traffic. It was the first time she'd seen him clearly in daylight since they were students. The stubborn set to his jaw was still there.

'I don't shave at the weekends, if that's what you're looking at,' he said, rubbing the stubble on his chin, without taking his eyes off the road.

Maggie said nothing as he negotiated through the traffic in Chalk Farm and the bustling crowds thronging the stalls in Camden Market.

They had almost reached the Euston Road when she said, 'I was actually thinking that sometimes I see the Jack I remember and at other times I see another, different Jack.'

He glanced sideways. 'What? Like some kind of Jekyll and Hyde weirdo? Thanks.'

Maggie realised that she had annoyed him.

'No. I didn't mean it like that,' she said quickly. 'It's just that this all feels… a bit odd. I'm not quite sure what happened last night.'

Jack took his left hand off the steering wheel and squeezed her thigh, then slid it up her leg very slowly, his eyes on the road.

'What do you mean odd and you're not sure what happened? That's not very flattering.'

His hand was at the top of her leg now, stroking gently, fingers probing. Maggie clamped her thighs together and Jack returned his hand to the steering wheel with a grin.

She stared blindly through the windscreen. The awful truth was that she couldn't remember much of what had actually happened after he had kissed her on the sofa. She had a vague memory of him arguing with the porter when he rang Jack's doorbell to announce the cab had arrived after they had ignored the intercom. She had been crouching behind the door, giggling helplessly, when Jack opened it a fraction. They were both naked.

Maggie's cheeks burned. How absurd they must have sounded to the astonished porter. How had she let herself get that drunk, that reckless? She couldn't even remember whether Jack had used a condom or not. Why had she let it happen?

The shocking recollections were still running through her head when the car came to a sudden noisy stop. They were a few metres from her front door.

'I don't think you can park here,' she said quietly as Jack turned the engine off.

'It's Sunday, we're OK for a couple of minutes.' He glanced in the rear view mirror before turning to face her.

'Now, listen to me, Maggie. It was bloody wonderful, last night. How can you say that you're not sure what happened? I'll tell you what happened, Maggie. Everything bloody happened. Everything. And it was just like it was before, only much, much, much better.'

He touched her face, tracing her features.

'This is our second chance. We'll do it differently this time, more like grown-ups.'

He tipped her chin and put his mouth on hers, pushing his tongue between her lips. He drew back, his eyes boring into hers.

'We both know this relationship has no legs. But neither of us is looking for commitment or all the crap that goes with it anymore, are we? We're both old enough to know it ruins everything, especially the sex.'

One hand was on her thigh again. Maggie moved to retrieve her bag from the foot well and placed it on her lap. She was finding it difficult to breathe. The cramped interior of the car was claustrophobic: it felt like a trap.

'Why can't we just lie back and enjoy it, before all the bits start dropping off?' Jack sniggered as he checked his hair in the rear view mirror, teasing strands into place.

'You sound like Rose,' Maggie said flatly.

'Rose?' Jack laughed. 'That doesn't surprise me, at all. By the way, did she get it on with that bloke she was all over like a rash the other night? The bald, geeky one?'

'No idea.' Maggie gripped the door handle.

'And I bet you wouldn't tell me, even if you did,' he said. 'You women stick together. Sisters under the skin and all that. It's all a bit more civilised, these days,' Jack continued, staring thoughtfully through the windscreen. 'You girls want your independence. Don't you?'

He turned to face her. 'I'm right behind you on that one. It lets us guys well off the hook.'

Maggie said nothing as Jack studied her face, the pallor of her cheeks and the dark circles under her eyes. He patted her hands gripping the strap of her bag.

'You're not much of a party girl, are you?' he said more gently. 'That hasn't changed either.'

He leaned across her to open the passenger door and she shrank inwardly as his arm brushed against her chest.

Jack straightened up in his seat, one hand on the steering wheel.

'I'll call you next week when you've had time to recover from the Millfield treatment,' he said.

Maggie eased herself out of the low passenger seat onto the pavement, relieved that he'd made no attempt to kiss her. It had started to rain again. She closed the car door and pulled her hood up over her hair as she ran towards the familiar black front door and turned to glance back.

Jack was looking at his mobile phone. He put it down on the passenger seat next to him, then started the car with a thumbs-up sign in her direction.

The powerful engine echoed in the empty street as he drove away and Maggie closed the front door quietly behind her.

9

Just over a month later, Maggie woke with a start from a recurring dream. She was trapped somewhere dark and narrow, struggling to reach a flickering light held high in the air by a tall, unrecognisable figure in the distance.

She shivered and ran a hand lightly across the cold skin of her abdomen. Still nothing. No cramping, no dragging pains, no backache. Nothing.

Her period was late for the first time in twenty-six years. She stared up into the darkness with a flashback of a freezing winter morning in the boarding school dormitory, when she'd woken to find her pyjama trousers soaked with blood. She recalled the paralysing embarrassment and humiliation she'd felt as the blood trickled down her legs onto the floor and the other girls crowded around, sniggering, with shocked, frightened faces. Then another memory, the stunned expression on the sad, grey-bearded face of her father when she'd gone home the following weekend.

'My period has started, Daddy,' she'd announced with a mixture of pride and adolescent diffidence.

Felix Savernake had frowned with what looked like disapproval and left the room in silence. It was the first and last time Maggie had tried to confide in him.

She moved restlessly on the uncomfortable divan bed and wondered, not for the first time, whether the responsibility of bringing up a daughter by himself had been the cause of his fatal depression.

Unconsciously, her hand was back on her stomach. In spite of the unhappy memories, thinking about the past was infinitely preferable to thinking about the present. How could she admit to anyone that she had been so drunk that she couldn't remember exactly what had happened in Jack's flat? That she had gone to bed with a man she hadn't seen for years? A stranger, to all intents and purposes. She hadn't even been able to bring herself to tell Rose when she'd begged for a blow-by-blow account.

'There's nothing to tell, Rose. I went straight home in a cab.'

'Yeah, yeah, yeah, Maggie. I'm sure you did.' Rose had replied.

Maggie groaned, burying her face in the pillow as she recalled Rose's knowing expression.

Now her period was two weeks late. Three hundred and thirty-six long hours late; she was consumed with dread and fear.

She'd been trawling the internet at every opportunity, desperately searching for explanations. She had been prepared to consider any possibility except the obvious, until yesterday when, unable to bear the stress and uncertainty any longer, she'd taken a bus to a large supermarket on the other side of town. Somewhere safe from the prying, inquisitive eyes of her students or colleagues.

Maggie could feel a spasm of cramp developing in the icy toes of her right foot. She swung her legs over the side of the bed, working her foot up and down on the cold wooden floorboards to relieve it. She stared down at her narrow white feet, absently examining the toenails one by one, unaware that she was delaying the awful moment of truth, until the pressure in her bladder became impossible to ignore. It was an insistent reminder of what the young girl behind the counter in the supermarket pharmacy had told her, with all the careless joviality of youth.

'For maximum accuracy, you need to use this first thing in the morning, dear. When you open your bladder? Know what I mean?'

Had that girl raised her voice deliberately when she said 'bladder'? Maggie had been mortified by the barely concealed amusement on the face of a girl who looked younger than most of her first-year students.

The fluorescent numbers on her ancient alarm clock told her that it was already six-thirty. She groaned as she stumbled into the small bathroom, clutching the packet and trying to ignore the flutters of apprehension in her chest as she read the instructions one more time.

It looks very straightforward, she told herself, just pee on the stick and wait for a second blue line to appear. What could be simpler?

With her bladder now on the point of rupturing, Maggie straddled the toilet and bent down to peer between her legs, with the blood pounding in her temples. This was definitely not the best position to adopt with another migraine lurking somewhere in the back of her skull.

She watched with revulsion as the stream of urine splashed onto her fingers for two or three seconds, until she was satisfied that the stick was wet enough.

'There's always a first time for everything,' she whispered to the wretched reflection staring back from the rust-spattered mirror.

'Anyway, this is only a precaution. It's all going to be absolutely fine,' she said loudly, in a fruitless attempt to drown the uneven thudding inside her chest as she held the stick up to the light. Was that blue line there before?

'Yes, that's the marker line, you idiot, there has to be a second one.'

She was suddenly overcome with an insane desire to laugh at the absurdity of it all.

'My God, I can't believe I'm actually doing this. At thirty-eight years of age.'

Her index finger and thumb were turning white with tension

as she gripped the stick. She stared more closely. No change. A shuddering sigh of relief escaped her dry lips.

'There you are. No change. A false alarm. Thank you, thank you, thank you, God,' she whispered as she moved to toss the stick away.

One foot was already on the pedal of the waste-bin under the hand-basin when she noticed the second, very faint, blue line appearing. She stepped backwards and held the stick up to the central ceiling light with a trembling hand. There was no mistake. There was a second blue line and it was getting darker and more distinct as she looked at it.

Maggie's legs had turned to water. She collapsed onto the old rush laundry basket in the corner with the bile rising in her throat. No. No. No. This isn't true. It can't be happening. There must be a mistake. It's impossible.

She ripped the crumpled instructions out of the packet.

'If you're pregnant, the amount of human Chorionic Gonotrophin or hCG rises rapidly in the early days and weeks, and the home pregnancy test can detect this in your urine... if you don't know when your next period is due, wait at least nineteen days after you last had unprotected sex...'

Wait nineteen days to do it again? But that's almost three more weeks. I can't wait that long. No, wait a minute, it's nineteen days now. It's more than nineteen days since I was with Jack. She scanned the paper again and tossed it onto the floor.

Why am I reading this? I know when it happened. My period is two weeks late and it has never been late before. Full stop. End of story. This is ridiculous. It's pitiful.

She stared at the stick on the floor, with the two clear, blue lines. There was no mistake. How could there be? She'd known for days that the test was only ever going to be a confirmation of what she'd already begun to suspect and then dread. She hadn't been able to admit it because that would have made it feel more real.

Now, the evidence was there on the floor in front of her, irrefutable and terrifying.

Maggie was shivering so hard that her teeth were chattering. She went back to her bedroom and stood there in her crumpled, faded pyjamas, staring bleakly at the bed as panic swept over her. I must deal with this quickly. Now. Before anybody finds out. She dropped onto the bed, knees doubled up, hugging herself. Thoughts racing. I'll have to go to the GP first. John Sullivan, it must be John Sullivan. Let's hope he's still working there. John will help me; he was Dad's GP. He'll know what to do.

She went back to the bathroom, and bent to retrieve the thin white stick from the floor. The second blue line was much darker and clearer in the daylight which was now streaming in through the small window. Maggie threw the stick into the bin and washed her hands three times, in quick succession.

She dressed in a daze, collected her files, shoved them into the rucksack and put on her coat, moving like a robot, instinctively seeking some kind of refuge and solace in the familiarity of her daily routine. It was Thursday again and another full day lay ahead of her, even though it was the last week of term. She had a seminar to go to and the students would be waiting.

Outside, the traffic seemed to be much heavier and noisier than usual. Christmas shopping was reaching its usual frenzied crescendo.

Maggie's thoughts were far from festive as she strode through the crowds, with the image of the little white stick dancing in front of her and a mocking voice in her ear.

'Getting pregnant by mistake doesn't just happen to socially deprived teenage girls. It happens to stupid, middle-aged women like you, who drink too much and lose their reason.'

A newspaper man, wearing a set of plastic reindeer antlers on his head, stepped out in front of her with his customary greeting. He stared after her, open-mouthed with the newspaper in his outstretched hand as Maggie walked straight past him, without a second glance.

'Blimey, what's got into her? Boyfriend not treating her right, or what?' He offered the rejected paper to the man behind her.

Maggie had almost reached the main gates of the college when a sickening thought brought her to an abrupt standstill. Jack. What about Jack?

She'd been ignoring all his attempts to contact her. When he'd driven her home the day after they'd slept together and made the extraordinary suggestion of a 'no commitment relationship', she had been deeply shocked and humiliated. Jack had changed. He was not the same man and she had made a terrible, tragic mistake. Maggie stared blindly ahead of her. Should I tell him? Will he want to know?

Students were pushing past her, through the gates. A voice yelled, 'Nearly Christmas, Dr Savernake,' and brought her crashing back to the present.

Hardly aware of what she was doing, she took her mobile out of her pocket and typed quickly.

'I am pregnant. MS'

When she heard the customary buzz of excited voices behind the closed doors of the lecture hall, Maggie faltered, then took a deep breath. She lifted her chin, pushed the door open and made her way quickly to the front.

She slipped off her jacket before realising, too late, that she had buttoned her white shirt unevenly during her distracted departure. She picked up her notes quickly, in a vain effort to cover the oversight.

'First, I apologise for my late arrival. I forgot to set my alarm.'

A couple of inaudible comments from the back row were met with a hard stare as she went on, 'This morning we are comparing the roles assigned to women in the comedies and tragedies of William Shakespeare. Sean, perhaps you would like to start us off?'

10

Jack Millfield was lying on his bed, flat on his back with his mouth wide open, like a dead starfish stranded on a beach. He was snoring raucously. Even the piercing scream of a car alarm somewhere in the street outside didn't penetrate his contented oblivion.

It was only when the sun reached his face that he finally began to stir. Must have forgotten to close the blinds last night, he thought as he yawned, stretching his arms above his head and sending his spectacles, the alarm clock and a couple of magazines crashing to the floor and sliding under the bed.

Jack yawned again and leaned over to get them, where he discovered, too late, that when his head was lower than his feet it produced a sharp shooting pain in the right hand side of his neck.

With the alarm clock still annoyingly out of reach, he gripped the bed with flexed legs and feet and made a determined lunge, eventually emerging with the clock held triumphantly aloft as he wriggled back across the mattress, shouting, 'Gotcha!' as he squinted myopically at the time.

'Shite, nine o'clock. Thursday. Shite.'

He leapt out of bed and went to the window, pulling back the opaque gauze panel and standing there, naked, to admire the magnificent panorama for which he had paid a small fortune. In the far distance he could just make out the tallest buildings in the City of London, already shrouded in a smoky yellow veil of pollution, before noticing, too late, that a group of elderly female dog walkers, dressed in bulky anoraks and unflattering woolly hats, were staring up at him, open-mouthed and clearly scandalised.

Jack clicked his bare heels and saluted with a dazzling smile before grabbing a corner of the long gauze panel in a hopeless effort to preserve his masculine modesty.

The three women turned their backs in synchronised disgust and stomped away, and Jack shrieked with delighted laughter. I'll be the main topic of conversation at their coffee mornings for at least a week after this display of masculine perfection, he thought.

He peered at his reflection in the long mirror in the bathroom and stuck out his tongue. The colour reminded him of a piece of driftwood on Fistral Beach. He closed his mouth quickly and jabbed the digital shower controls before turning his face into the deluge, absorbing the reviving moisture through every thirsty pore as he mentally regurgitated and examined the events of the previous night's entertainment.

Those cocktails were a real killer, he thought with a smirk of satisfaction. The Mojitos were particularly messy. Was that my idea or Jason's? He spat out a mouthful of shampoo and shook his head like a wet dog, spraying out a halo of sparkling droplets. At one point Jason was laughing so hard that he'd lost his balance and fallen off the stool. Jack laughed out loud while he massaged the lemongrass shower gel into his skin. He could hear the distant trill of his mobile heralding the arrival of a new message.

'Go away! Who the hell is that? Can't a guy have a shower in peace anymore?'

Then, unable to resist finding out, he grabbed a towel and went to retrieve the phone from the bedroom, squinting at the message.

'I am pregnant. MS'

Jack peered closer, like someone trying to interpret a particularly obscure code.

'MS? MS? Who the…?' He gulped, almost dropping the phone. 'Christ. Maggie Savernake? No. It can't be.'

He read the message aloud, slowly, enunciating carefully, 'I am pregnant. MS'. But how? When? And more important, why the hell is she telling me? I haven't seen her for weeks.'

He threw down the phone, watching it bounce across the bed, disappear over the far edge and clatter onto the polished floor.

'For fuck's sake. I don't need this today. I've got to be in Knightsbridge by ten thirty,' he yelled as he careered around the bed and stubbed his toe painfully on one of the large wooden ball feet.

He flicked impatiently along the rails of colour co-ordinated shirts and suits, grabbing things indiscriminately; twenty minutes later he was racing down the hill in the direction of the underground station, with the desperation of a criminal escaping from the scene of a crime.

He skidded to a halt in front of a small van selling coffee and grabbed his customary double-shot macchiato, swallowing it in eye-watering mouthfuls before joining the rest of the commuters shoving their way unceremoniously through the barriers.

After fighting his way onto the first tube, he found himself sandwiched uncomfortably between the doors and the stained yellow tie of a large man who was sweating profusely. He watched with morbid fascination as the streams of sweat coursed slowly down the man's face and soaked into the grimy collar of his crumpled shirt.

The heaving sea of bodies ebbed and flowed around Jack at each station until mercifully, Yellow Tie was replaced by a young woman with her coat unbuttoned, revealing a vertiginous neckline. Sadly, Jack was in no mood to register the improvement in the view as he tried to process the implications of Maggie's text message.

Even if she is pregnant, she'd have to prove it's mine, he thought, wincing at his own treachery. Don't go there. Don't consider it. Not even as a remote possibility. It can't be true.

He tore his eyes away from the girl who was now smiling. I must talk to Maggie before I start making any assumptions. She's probably just having a laugh. Yes. That's it. This is her warped female sense of humour, her way of getting my attention again. It's got to be. I'll text her when I get out of this cattle truck.

Jack changed trains at Leicester Square; fighting his way through the crush of bodies like a man in a daze. I knew she'd see the sense of my suggestion, eventually. Though God knows why it's taken her all this time to make up her mind, he thought. Yes, that must be it. She's decided that she wants to go along with it and she's just trying to get my attention. Panic over.

He was still smiling when he shoe-horned himself into the claustrophobic Piccadilly Line train. He turned his thoughts to inventing a credible excuse for his late arrival at the office and the meeting with the new client. He imagined Val's implacable expression when he told her that his alarm clock had broken. Dragon Lady will be breathing fire, he thought.

Once he was above ground, he stopped outside the elegant windows of Harvey Nichols and took out his phone.

'Call me tonight, at home. J'

He pressed SEND with a surge of excitement.

*

The day passed agonisingly slowly, in spite of Jack buoying himself up with regular doses of strong black coffee and half a prawn mayonnaise sandwich, which had been delivered by a very tight-lipped Val. Her mood hadn't thawed since he arrived. The snack had been accompanied by a few very curt words of advice.

'Caffeine on an empty stomach is a very bad idea. How many more times do I have to tell you?'

He watched her put the plate on the desk with a disapproving clatter. I wonder what she would say if I told her about Maggie? he thought. It was very tempting: if only for the amusing prospect of her scandalised reaction.

His mouth twitched. No, Jack. Very bad plan. In any case, Val's got no sense of humour. She definitely won't see the funny side of it.

Val had turned at the door. 'The new copywriter is waiting to show you his stuff for Davidson Baths. Buzz me when you're ready for him.'

The meeting was not a success. Instead of presenting his ideas for selling a new range of baths and shower suites, the fresh-faced young graduate spent more than ninety minutes arguing with Jack about the inconsistencies of the syntax in the brief he had been given.

Jack decided that the double first from Cambridge, which had figured so largely on the young man's CV, was a distinct shortcoming. He made a mental note, scribbling on his blotter as the man left: 'Avoid All Graduates'.

A similarly frustrating session with the director of the media department followed. He was more interested in whining about his wife's post-partum lack of libido than presenting Jack with a coherent strategy for the sites of the hoardings for a new lingerie campaign.

Jack scribbled, 'Avoid Media Department' under his previous note.

He poured himself another cup of coffee before going to the boardroom to chair a marathon three-hour meeting, mostly refereeing a bitter battle for budgets between two of the most pompous account managers in the company.

By the time he had finally convinced them both that it was time to go home, it was close to seven-thirty. It was only then that he realised he hadn't received a reply from Maggie.

He resisted a very tempting invitation to the pub next to the office from an attractive young woman in the accounts department. Val had suggested he interview her as a possible replacement.

'We're off to The Saddlers, do you want to join us for a quick one?' she said.

Jack hesitated, fighting the temptation to accept. A large drink was exactly what he needed.

'I'd love to, but I've got some important stuff to catch up with.'

The eyes below the glossy fringe softened alluringly

'Another time maybe?' she whispered.

'Oh, absolutely!' Jack said, watching her long smooth legs as she crossed the reception. Make a note. Speak to Val tomorrow about offering her the job. She's perfect. I wonder if she can type.

As soon as he arrived home, he went straight to the kitchen to pour himself a very large glass of red wine, swilling it around his teeth before swallowing. His stomach complained noisily, reminding him that half a prawn sandwich was the only solid thing that he'd eaten in the past twenty-four hours.

He threw a frozen ready meal into the microwave and flicked on the TV where a game show was in full swing. Jack hurled a couple of lurid insults at the grinning presenter before punching the Off button on the remote control.

The so-called 'Mediterranean Risotto with a Salsa of Sun-Dried Italian Tomatoes' bore no visible resemblance whatsoever to the colourful illustration on the packet when he took it from the microwave. It was tasteless and disgusting.

'Bastard advertisers,' Jack hissed with unwitting irony as he swept the half-finished food into the waste bin and went to open the doors to the balcony to clear the air before flinging himself down on the sofa.

He watched the opaque gauze panels swinging gently in the

cold draught for several minutes before being drawn back outside to stand on the balcony where he could just make out the lights of North London twinkling through the trees; the eerie yellow haze they cast up into the night sky camouflaging the stars.

He stood there a long time, listening to the distant rumble of traffic. It was a soothing counterpoint to the resounding silence in the empty rooms behind him. He shivered in the cold night air, massaging his aching eyes with his forefinger and thumb before returning to the sofa.

It's nine-thirty. Why hasn't Maggie called?

He remembered the first time he set eyes on her. 'Who's that?' he'd asked the man standing next to him in the students' bar.

'That's Maggie Savernake. Not bad, eh? Well out of your league, mate. She's destined for much bigger things.'

Jack looked at his watch and stood up again. Why hasn't she called? Perhaps she didn't get the message. He went to pour himself another glass of wine and a sudden wave of retrospective embarrassment swept over him as he remembered his ridiculous show of macho bravado to his rugby friends, all those years ago.

'Too many glasses of a rather dubious Rioja and we were soon deep in lust. She didn't stand a chance.'

He grinned at the memory of the admiration and envy on their faces as they listened.

It was more than an hour later when he felt the mobile phone vibrating in his pocket. He yanked it out, bellowing, 'Maggie! What's going on? Are you alright?'

'Jack? Is that you?'

It was his mother, Lucinda's voice. Bloody hell, why's she ringing at this time of night?

'Mum? Everything OK?'

'Are you alright, Jack, you sound upset. Who's Molly and what's the matter with her?'

'Maggie,' corrected Jack tersely.

'Maggie, Molly, Milly. Whatever. I can't keep up with you and your women, Jack.'

His expression hardened when he heard her tinkling laugh. 'I thought you were in Spain,' he said.

'I am, darling. I'll be in London for a couple weeks. I...'

'I can't talk now, Mother, I'm busy. I'm waiting for another call.'

'Alright, Jack, there's no need to speak to me like that. It's simply to let you know that I'll be arriving on the 18th. Before I go, are you in London for Christmas?'

'I don't know. Call me on the mobile when you get here. I've got to go. Sorry.' He put the phone down. Christ, that's all I need. My bloody mother, on top of everything else.

When the phone rang for the second time an hour later, Jack was engrossed in a new war game on his computer.

'Jack?'

'Maggie, I've been waiting for you to call for hours. Are you OK?' He grimaced. What kind of a stupid question is that?

'No, I'm not alright. I'm pregnant.' Her voice shook.

Jack feigned surprise, playing for time. 'What? Are you sure? But you're on the pill, aren't you?'

'No, I'm not. I don't know how this happened. I don't remember much about what happened after we arrived at your flat.'

Jack frowned. What the fuck was she suggesting? 'What are you going to do?' he asked after a long pause.

'What do you mean, what am I going to do?'

A muscle twitched in Jack's jaw. 'What are you going to do?' He repeated the question as though he was speaking to an obstinate child. His meaning was unmistakable. When Maggie didn't reply, he added casually, 'Any idea who the father is?'

The words were out of his mouth before he could stop himself. He knew they would hurt her and he didn't care. He had a sudden irresistible desire to step away.

The ensuing silence seemed to stretch into infinity, and then he heard a click as Maggie put the phone down.

Jack sat motionless, staring at the phone in his hand for several minutes. I can't leave it like that. I must make her understand. See things from my point of view. He dialled her number.

'Maggie, try to understand. I just can't deal with this.' He was breathless. 'I don't want children, I don't even *like* children. They're just not on my radar. They're not part of my plan.'

He paused, waiting for her reaction.

Silence.

Jack could hear her breathing. 'And I have to say that I assumed that you were on the pill, otherwise…'

He couldn't finish the sentence. It was a total lie. The truth was that he hadn't given a thought to birth control that night. It was the very last thing on his mind, and hers, apparently. She'd giggled uncontrollably and very irritatingly, at the beginning. At one point he'd thought she was getting hysterical. It had almost ruined everything. Jack raked a nervous hand through his hair. Not quite, though. A man has to protect his reputation, after all.

He stood up and went to stare at his own reflection in the darkened glass of the window, holding the phone against his ear. 'Look, as far as I am concerned, this really is *your* problem, Maggie. My advice is, get rid of it, sweetie.'

Then, in a feeble attempt to inject a little sympathy he added, 'It's best to be honest, then we all know where we are, right?'

The phone was sliding through his sweating fingers. He tightened his grasp, waiting, listening to the long drawn-out sigh at the other end before Maggie said in a flat voice, 'Why am I surprised? I don't know why I bothered to say anything. I just thought that you should know.'

'But you'll get rid of it, right?'

She put the phone down.

Jack wondered whether it was worth calling her back again.

He shook his head. What was the point? There's nothing more to say. This is her problem.

He went into the kitchen to pour another large glass of wine, filling his mouth with the full-bodied Rioja and trying to drown nagging feelings of unease mixed with anger and resentment. What was all that stuff about not remembering what happened? What kind of a ball-breaking remark was that to make to a man after a night of unbridled passion?

11

When Maggie tried to arrange the appointment to see Dr John Sullivan it had taken a great deal of persistence with a very unsympathetic receptionist.

'We have no appointments with Dr Sullivan until after Christmas. Dr Chatterjee has a slot at 8.30 next Wednesday, the 20th. You could have that one, if it's urgent.'

The woman sounded as though she didn't care whether Maggie took it or not.

'No. Thank you. I want to see Dr Sullivan. Only Dr Sullivan.'

'Can I ask why you want to see Dr Sullivan?'

'No you can't. It's personal.' Maggie blinked back tears of frustration.

There was a long silence followed by the sound of fingers tapping on a keyboard.

'I've squeezed you in at 4.30 this afternoon. It'll have to be quick, we're very busy.'

'I'll take it. Thank you.' Maggie was making rapid mental calculations. I'll miss the Christmas drinks. Who cares? They probably won't even notice.

*

Although John Sullivan had officially retired, he was still working as a locum on an occasional, part-time basis and Maggie had been one of his patients since she moved back to London.

His face lit up as she entered. 'Maggie, how nice to see you. It's been a very long time. What can I do for you, so near to Christmas?'

Maggie took her place on the chair next to his desk and his smile was quickly replaced with a look of concern.

'Maggie?'

'I've got a problem. I don't quite know how to say this.' She paused. 'I've made a mistake. A terrible, stupid mistake. I was very drunk. I can't remember exactly what happened and I'm not on the pill. It was only once. I didn't think you could get pregnant that easily. I'm thirty-eight, practically menopausal, for God's sake!' Her voice broke as the words poured out and she covered her face with her hands. 'I want a termination, John. Now. As soon as possible.'

John Sullivan removed his glasses and leaned back in his chair with a heavy sigh.

'When was your last period?'

'Seven weeks ago. I'm three weeks late. My period's never late. It's always been like clockwork. That's why I did a pregnancy test yesterday. It was positive. I couldn't believe it. I made one stupid mistake. I don't want this.'

She punched a clenched fist into her stomach. 'I don't want it. I don't want it. It makes me feel soiled and dirty, as though he's dumped something inside me,' she sobbed.

John Sullivan frowned and drew some paper tissues from a box on his desk and pushed them into her hand.

'Try to keep calm, Maggie.' He waited until she was quiet. 'Now, I have to ask you this. Did he force you?'

Maggie raised a shocked face. 'Are you asking whether he raped me? No. I know him. I met him when we were students, years ago.'

'But you said you can't remember what happened.'

'I can't but I am sure that he wouldn't do anything like that.'

'Is he your partner?'

'No. We had a short relationship when we were students and I met him again recently at a reunion and we went out a couple of times for a meal.' She sighed. 'We got very drunk on the second date. We went back to his flat to get a mini cab number. There was a lot of traffic. It was raining. He'd left his mobile at home.'

'Have you got a partner?'

'No. Why do you keep asking me? I haven't got a partner, and the man I slept with is not my partner. He wants me to get rid of it. He blames me. He said he thought I was on the pill.'

'And you're not?'

She began to cry again. 'No, I am not on the pill. I said that. I haven't been in a relationship for two years.'

She dabbed angrily at her face with the soggy ball of paper tissues. She wasn't making any sense. She sounded hysterical. John would think she was out of her mind.

'And you're absolutely certain that you want a termination? It's not just that this man wants you to have a termination?' He looked intently into her face.

'Of course I'm certain. This was an appalling mistake. I don't want anything to do with him. I don't want to see him again, ever. I must put an end to it. Can't you give me a pill or something? Anything. I'll do anything. Whatever it takes.'

Maggie looked distracted and desperate.

John Sullivan was drawing circles on a notepad, round and round, grinding the tip of the biro into the lined paper until it ripped under the pressure. He put the pen down and looked up, sadly.

'Alright. I think that I've known you long enough to know that you mean what you say, Maggie. I'll have to do a quick physical examination and a couple of tests first.'

He picked up a calendar on the desk. 'When did this... happen and when was your last period due?'

'I slept with him on the 11th November, my period was due about two weeks later, the 24th or 25th. I did the test yesterday.'

The old man was studying the calendar.

'And today is the 15th December. It's not too late for the morning-after pill,' he said, 'but you should have come to see me earlier.'

Maggie's face was white. 'Don't tell me that. I know. I thought that my period was going to start. I really believed that it would. I didn't think you could get pregnant that easily. I didn't think I could be that unlucky.' She paused, looking away. 'No, that's not quite true either. Oh, I don't know, John. I'm so ashamed and frightened. I hate him and myself and all of it.'

John Sullivan was watching her, his faded blue eyes full of sympathy.

'Don't worry, it's still very early.' He stood up slowly and patted her shoulder as he went to wash his hands and make the necessary preparations for the examination.

His thoughts were on his old friend, Professor Felix Savernake, Maggie's father. He was relieved that Felix was no longer alive to see his daughter's present predicament.

He sighed heavily as he dried his hands on a paper towel and tossed it into the bin, watching Maggie's reflection in the mirror above the basin. With her shoulders bent and her head bowed, she looked defeated. How on earth did an intelligent, mature woman like her manage to get herself into such horrendous difficulties?

Social mores may have changed since I started practising medicine, he thought, but human frailty is as big a mystery as it always was.

Less than ten minutes later, with all the tests completed, Maggie watched and waited impatiently as he began to type a letter on the computer with two arthritic index fingers.

At last, he turned to face her as the printer whirred beside him. 'Well, Maggie, you're definitely pregnant. It's still very early days and we've got two options: a chemically induced abortion or a minor surgical procedure under general anaesthetic. In your particular case, I would recommend the second. I think it would suit you better, particularly because you live alone. The first option is where drugs are used to induce the abortion and may involve risks, like excessive bleeding, infection, allergic reactions or an incomplete abortion.'

Maggie gulped and nodded. 'I would definitely prefer the surgery,' she whispered.

'I'm going to call a friend of mine who is a consultant at a private clinic in West London. If you would like to wait outside for a couple of minutes?'

Half an hour later, Maggie was walking towards the underground station with a letter in her bag signed by John, confirming that the termination would take place on Friday 22nd December and would be carried out under a light anaesthetic, and she would be able to return home later the same day. John insisted that he would visit her after she returned from the clinic, because she had been adamant that she would not be calling on any of her friends for help or support.

12

After last year's debacle in the Japanese restaurant, Jack had chosen the venue for the annual Lunch with Mother a little more carefully. He was hoping that the understated luxury of the Edwardian hotel in one of the most expensive streets in Knightsbridge would meet with her approval. He was half an hour late and barely acknowledged the salute of the doorman as he ran up the wide, carpeted steps and past the discretely decorated Christmas trees.

He spotted Lucinda immediately, sitting in a straight-backed armchair on the far side of the lounge, head tipped at a flattering angle with her long slim legs crossed to show them to advantage.

She was a striking figure, tall and elegant, with her silver blonde hair drawn away from patrician features and secured in the nape of her neck with a narrow black velvet ribbon. She wore a very pale sage green silk dress with a long, matching pashmina stole draped in folds over each shoulder. Jack thought it would have looked theatrical and affected on anyone else, but his mother carried it off to perfection.

He brushed a nervous hand across the lapel of his new suit, and checked his reflection in a huge baroque framed mirror as he passed. The only thing he had inherited from his mother was her colouring; everything else was pure Millfield.

He stood for a moment watching her with grudging admiration and pondering the extraordinary contradictions of their relationship. Two human beings, inextricably joined by one of the closest links that one individual can have with another and yet so far apart, with very few shared experiences or memories.

The thing that he regretted most was that they had none of that easy familiarity, the private jokes and secret language that he witnessed and envied between his friends and their parents. How could there be? Lucinda had lived abroad since she had divorced his father. He had never forgotten the time when he overheard her discussing her plans on the phone.

'And I've even managed to solve the Jack problem. He's going to board at his father's old school, that's how I got that monster to pay for it. Two birds with one stone, darling.'

Jack could still hear the echoes of her laughter as she put the phone down.

Less than a week later, he was delivered like an unwanted parcel to the public school in the West Country, a month after his seventh birthday.

From that moment on, his only contact with Lucinda had been restricted to the rare occasions when she returned to England and came to the school to take him out for what she described as a special treat, which invariably consisted of a very uncomfortable afternoon tea in an expensive teashop.

She usually arrived with at least one of her friends and spent the entire afternoon gossiping about people and places he knew nothing about.

Standing watching her in the hotel lounge now, thirty years later, Jack realised that nothing had changed, the only difference being that the so-called special treat was on him.

Lucinda was on her feet waving excitedly. She looks like a political leader on an official visit, waving at the punters, he thought sourly as he stepped forward to greet her, kissing her dutifully on both cheeks and inhaling wafts of her expensive perfume.

'Jack darling, after all this time. Happy Christmas.'

She held both his hands and leaned back to look at him. 'Let me fill my eyes with you. Tell me all your news,' she gushed, smiling proudly at the curious onlookers.

Jack shook his head, embarrassed by her exaggerated display of maternal affection.

'Let's eat, I'm absolutely famished.'

Lucinda laughed, linking her arm through his as they made their way towards the dining room.

'I haven't stopped thinking about you since we spoke on the phone. You sounded so worried. What has that wretched Molly done to you, my darling?'

'Maggie,' corrected Jack, wearily.

'Women are always trouble, darling. Take it from me.' She gave a little girlish giggle.

Ain't that the truth, he thought as the waiter led them to a reserved table by the window. Less than five minutes had passed since they'd met and Jack could already feel the tension tightening the muscles across the back of his neck.

They studied their menus in silence for several minutes, exchanging surreptitious glances across the table. Jack had just settled on the grilled sea bass with a green salad when his mother said she liked the look of it. He promptly changed his mind, full of irrational resentment at the betrayal of his genes.

When the waiter arrived to take their order, Jack chose the pan-fried John Dory, which he'd never really liked, and an indulgent and very pricey bottle of Chateau de Puligny-Montrachet as a personal consolation prize.

That'll make up for the food, he thought, and couldn't help feeling secretly pleased when he noticed Lucinda's nod of approval.

'Are we celebrating something, darling?' she asked in a conspiratorial whisper as they clinked glasses.

'No. Absolutely not. I just thought it would go well with the fish. They have a particularly good cellar here.'

He tried to ignore her eyes watching him suspiciously as they savoured the wine.

Lucinda sighed loudly. 'Oh Jack, please tell me what's wrong? I always know when you're hiding something from me.'

His jaw tensed. Her words reminded him of a school vacation long ago when he was sent out to Spain to spend the summer with her. She'd challenged him after he had helped himself to some money she'd left out for the housekeeper. He remembered how he'd looked up into those penetrating blue eyes and been terrified that she could read his thoughts.

'Jack, did you hear what I just said?'

He picked up his glass and smiled.

'I knew there was something wrong when we spoke on the phone. I know you, Jack.'

He rotated the stem of his glass between his thumb and forefinger and said nothing. You're like a bloody terrier dog after a rabbit. We meet once a year for about an hour. I make that roughly thirty hours in total that we've actually spent in each other's company since you sent me away to school. The fucking post-boy in my office knows me better than you do. How the hell can you possibly claim to know me?

'I'm certain it's something to do with that girlfriend of yours, Molly, Maggie or whatever you call her.'

Jack looked across at her, incensed by her implicit assumption that she had some kind of divine right to have an opinion about anything connected with him or his life.

The words were out of his mouth before he could stop them. 'Maggie thinks she's pregnant.'

The colour had drained from his face. It was the first time that he had articulated the word since Maggie's phone call. He looked more shocked than his mother.

Lucinda's eyebrows rose.

Jack was staring as though he'd never seen her before. What had possessed him to tell his mother, of all people? What was he trying to do? Shock her or impress her? Giving shape to the word pregnant had somehow made it seem more real, more terrifying. Panic was overwhelming him; he could feel his restraint slipping away.

'This is her fault. Maggie's fault. She knew we were never going to have that kind of relationship. Children were never going to be part of the deal,' he said.

Lucinda put her knife and fork down and dabbed the corners of her mouth with her linen serviette.

'What on earth do you mean when you say deal, Jack? I don't understand. What kind of relationship do you have with this woman?'

She moved her cutlery, lining up the knife and fork into the six o'clock position on her plate. Jack watched in bemusement. I don't believe this; I don't think she's understood a fucking word I've said.

'It's quite simple, Mother, I had a plan, my life was going to be bloody perfect and she has ruined it. And, it's got absolutely nothing to do with me.'

'In that case, why are you so upset?' The amusement in his mother's voice only served to reignite his fury.

'I've told her to get rid of it.' Jack was bouncing the tines of his fork rhythmically against the edge of his plate.

A flicker of irritation crossed Lucinda's face.

'But you've just said that it's got nothing to do with you. If that is the case, what right have you got to say anything to her?'

Jack drew figures of eight on the tablecloth with the tip of his index finger, lower lip protruding stubbornly.

'It is yours, isn't it?' she added quietly.

Jack glanced at the nearby tables as though he had just realised that they weren't alone. 'I can't handle it… I can't deal with it.' He said.

He pushed his plate away, causing it to collide with the silver cruet. 'This is all so fucking pointless. Why am I telling you? Just forget what I said.'

Lucinda stared at him. He was more like his father than ever. She knew it was futile trying to deal with the intractable Millfield temperament. Jack's inherited the worst of both of us, she thought.

'No problem, Jack.' Lucinda's smile didn't reach her eyes.

There was a long awkward silence which was suddenly broken by Jack crashing his fist on the table.

'What do you mean no problem? Of course there's a fucking problem, Mother. I told her to get rid of it, but how do I know that she will? She won't speak to me.'

Lucinda jumped and several heads turned in their direction.

'There is no need to shout, Jack. Calm down. She may not even be pregnant. Women's plumbing can be... how can I put it? Women's plumbing can be very unpredictable and unreliable. How old is she?'

Jack punched his temples in exasperation. 'Oh, for fuck's sake. What's her age got to do with anything? She's thirty-eight, like me. OK? You don't understand. This is not about her, it's about me.' He jabbed at his chest with a finger. 'I can't deal with it.'

Lucinda was examining her immaculate nails. If the girl decides to keep the baby and it is Jack's, I'll be a grandmother. What a ghastly prospect.

'How long have you two been together? I've got a vague memory that you mentioned a Maggie when you were at uni, or am I getting confused again?' she asked.

'Yes, we were together, as you put it, when we were students. I met her again recently at a reunion. That's how we...' He groaned loudly, drumming the table with his fingers. 'What the hell difference does it make now?'

Waiters were clearing their plates, brushing the tablecloth and topping up their glasses. Jack ordered coffee and they waited, studiously avoiding direct eye contact.

After several minutes Jack asked, 'So, have you got anything planned while you're here?'

He didn't register the disappointment in her face.

'I haven't given it much thought. The weather is miserable. I might go and stay with friends in Scotland.'

'I shouldn't think the weather will be any better up there.'

They waited in silence while the waiter poured their coffee, and then Lucinda said, 'Would you like me to talk to her, Jack?'

'You? How would that help? What do you think you could possibly say or do, that would make any useful contribution to this God awful mess?'

'I could talk to her. Take her out to lunch or something. Does she work?'

'Of course she bloody works. What kind of an idiot question is that? Contrary to what you might like to believe, Mother, most people do work nowadays. They don't all lead a charmed life, like you. Maggie is a university lecturer. She's a high-profile academic.'

He wondered why he sounded so defensive. Was he hoping to impress his mother with his conquest? Bathe in some of the reflected glory of the brilliant Dr Savernake?

'What? I don't believe it. Jack Millfield with a blue stocking? But that's not your usual style, darling, surely? What is she? One of those ghastly women with thick ankles, hairy armpits and hidden talents in the bedroom?'

Jack leapt to his feet, pushing his chair back, snagging one of the legs on the thick pile carpet. His handsome face was contorted with rage.

'OK that's it, I've had it. I can't take any more.'

Lucinda raised an imploring hand. 'Jack, please don't go, I was joking.'

Jack didn't hear her; he was almost at the desk, waving his bank card at the waiter.

Lucinda caught up with him outside on the steps of the hotel, where he stood, stony faced, waiting while the commissionaire waved down a black cab.

She touched Jack's sleeve. 'Don't be angry, Jack. I was only trying to help.'

He jerked his arm away in disgust. You always have to finish on the high ground, don't you?

Jack pressed a £20 note into the commissionaire's hand and helped his mother into the cab. He was shocked at how thin and fragile her arm felt through the sleeve of her coat. There seemed to be no flesh on her at all.

'Goodbye, Mother. Have a good Christmas.'

'Thank you for lunch, Jack, it was lovely to see you again.'

She kissed her fingers and touched his cheek lightly through the lowered window before the cab moved forward. Her high cheekbones were accentuated in the shadowy interior; she looked sad and unexpectedly old.

'I hope things work out for you, Jack. You know where I am if you need me.'

Jack watched the cab disappear into the traffic. She's probably ticking my name off her latest To Do list already, he thought as he rolled his head on his shoulders to ease the muscles in the back of his neck.

He scrubbed unconsciously at the spot on his cheek where he could still feel the touch of her fingers, trying to erase the last trace of her as he had done so many times before.

He looked at his watch; there was still an hour and a half before his next meeting. Hyde Park was beckoning irresistibly.

13

Jack crossed the road, weaving his way expertly through the fume-laden queues of traffic, towards the tall iron gates.

Once inside, it felt as though he was stepping into another world. He walked slowly at first, eyes devouring the vast expanses of greensward. He quickened his pace, imagining each step was taking him away. Away from his mother, away from Maggie, away from all the chaos they had made of his life.

At the edge of the Serpentine, he stood still for a moment to enjoy the view. The traffic was barely audible.

In spite of the chilly December air, he sat down on an empty bench to watch the passers-by, mostly office workers like himself, escaping for a much-needed breath of fresh air. There were a few shoppers, loaded with Christmas purchases, and plenty of tourists busy with their cameras, studying maps.

Jack watched a couple of male ducks challenging each other, flapping their wings and rising up out of the water, each one trying to get his head higher than the other. They were arguing over a female who seemed to be completely oblivious to the furore she had caused as she swam lazily away from them.

I know how you feel, mate, he thought as he watched the two drakes swim off in search of another female.

Jack was still grinning to himself when a fresh-faced young woman sat down at the other end of the bench, one hand clamped firmly on the handle of a large old-fashioned carriage pram.

She affectionately smoothed the baby's neatly brushed hair and planted a kiss on the tip of his tiny nose. The baby grimaced and wriggled away from her touch, his attention caught by two small children chasing and hitting each other with paper carrier bags bearing the Victoria and Albert Museum logo. The baby was clearly entranced with their antics.

The young woman began tapping out a message on her mobile phone and soon the children were being summoned to follow their exhausted-looking parents along the path.

The baby watched them recede into the distance and turned away, his attention caught by Jack. He scanned Jack's face as though memorising every feature in microscopic detail. Jack didn't move, trapped in the unblinking stare before finally trying to break the spell, pulling a comical face and sticking out his tongue.

The baby started, his soft lower lip trembling ominously and his clear, blue eyes wide and bright with tears.

Jack was horrified. He waited, hardly daring to breathe for what felt like an eternity, until the baby's apprehension was replaced by a sudden, captivating, toothless smile and a deep, infectious giggle which bubbled up from somewhere deep inside the tiny body and he began to laugh uncontrollably.

Jack marvelled at the miraculous transformation; it was the first time he had ever interacted with a baby.

Then, unable to stop himself, he began to laugh too, in a joyful moment of shared intimacy with the little stranger; until suddenly, unexpected tears began to course down his cheeks and he jumped up and strode away, with the baby's disappointed eyes following him.

14

The week between her visit to the GP and her appointment at the clinic was the longest and most difficult of Maggie's life as she counted the days, marking them off the calendar hanging in her little kitchen, like a prisoner waiting for her release.

In spite of her unshakable resolve to go through with it, she was tormented by feelings of guilt and increasing apprehension about what lay ahead of her, and full of resentment towards Jack who had started bombarding her with messages, all of which she had ignored.

The Christmas invitations from friends and colleagues had been difficult. Rose, in particular, insisted that she spend the Christmas break with them in Kentish Town.

'Please, Mags. The kids are going to their father's on Boxing Day. I'll make us a nut roast and then we'll get drunk and watch a film together. Go on. You know you want to. We always have a laugh.'

Maggie had wavered momentarily; it was tempting, but she couldn't risk it.

'I think I'm coming down with gastric flu or something. I'm aching all over, I was planning to spend the weekend in bed,' she'd lied, avoiding Rose's searching brown eyes.

'Don't be ridiculous. You must come. We'll look after you. We can't leave you alone, if you're ill. Can we?'

Maggie smiled. 'I'll see how I feel, nearer the day.'

David had been much less of a challenge. When he phoned to say that he'd found a cheap ticket to Valparaiso on a Merchant Navy cargo vessel, which was due to leave Southampton on the 20th, she'd struggled not to sound relieved.

'Oh well, I can hardly compete with Christmas spent crossing the Atlantic and feasting at the captain's table, can I?' she'd joked.

'It's not that, you know it isn't,' David protested. 'This is a bargain that's too good to miss.'

On Thursday 21st December, Maggie decided to use the time to prepare for the long weekend ahead: she would do some food shopping in the morning and then make a quick visit to the college after lunch to pick up some books and check any post which might be waiting for her.

Although the university was officially closed until early January, she knew that there would be a skeleton administrative staff and the usual security people on the campus.

After spending an hour or so in her room on the first floor she went to the library to collect her books and check a few references. After listening to long expositions about the two librarians' plans for Christmas, Maggie eventually left for home much later than she'd anticipated.

It was already dark and raining heavily when she got outside. Maggie looped the strap of her rucksack over her shoulder; it was heavy with the books which she was hoping would provide her with a distraction during the difficult days ahead.

As she went through the gates, she nodded briefly to the security man, huddled in his anorak and laughing loudly into his mobile about the number of pints he'd apparently drunk at a Christmas party the night before.

Half way down Gower Street she suddenly became aware that someone was walking behind her and getting uncomfortably close. She increased her speed with her heart beating fast and her legs trembling. She didn't dare to turn around. This is when

I get mugged, like Rose last year, she thought in the split second before she felt a hand grab her arm just above the elbow.

She swung around, terrified, to see Jack's face glaring back at her.

'Jack! What the hell are you doing? Let go of my arm, you're hurting me!' she cried as she tried to free herself, wincing as the pressure of his fingers increased.

'Why don't you answer your fucking phones?'

Maggie was paralysed. His face was almost touching hers, and his teeth were bared as he spat the words at her.

'I've changed my mind. I want you to have the baby. I want you to have my baby. Do you understand?'

He shook her arm, emphasising each syllable. His saliva splashed across her face and she tasted the unmistakable tang of alcohol. The bile rose in her throat and with a supreme effort she shook her arm out of his grasp and moved around him in a bid to escape.

He lunged at her again. 'Don't walk away from me.' His voice was low and menacing.

Maggie shook her arm free again and took a step backwards. A couple passed, glancing at them curiously but they didn't stop.

'Stand still, for fuck's sake! Stand still, will you?' Jack snarled as he grabbed a handful of her coat.

She swung the heavy rucksack at him and while he was temporarily disorientated, seized her opportunity to run, turning into a small side street in a blind panic before realising, too late, that it was deserted.

Jack was behind and reaching for her again, one hand on her arm and the other tearing at her hair.

Maggie screamed, 'Leave me alone! Go away! It's over! It's finished!'

He tightened his hold, gasping, 'Oh no it's not.'

'It is. It's too late!' Tears of desperation were streaming down her face.

Jack paused for a split second, drew back, frowning as her words sank in.

'You've done it already, haven't you? You've got rid of it? You've killed my baby,' he growled.

Maggie was panting, struggling for breath as she realised what he was saying. *He thinks I've had the termination already. He's trying to blame me.*

'I did what you told me to do. I got rid of it. You told me to get rid of it, remember?'

She watched, mesmerised as the colour drained from Jack's features. She didn't notice his arm raised to punch her hard in the face.

She gasped, swaying under the impact and staggered backwards with her arms wind-milling helplessly as she slipped on the wet pavement, struck her head on the curb with a sickening thud and everything went black.

Seconds later, she heard shouting and feet pounding towards her. She opened her eyes and looked up to see three shocked faces staring down, their hands reaching out to help.

Maggie closed her eyes again, groaning softly.

'Are you alright, love? Did he take anything?'

'Oh my God, that bastard hit her. Look at her face.'

Maggie opened her eyes, struggling to focus. She touched her face gingerly then stared at the blood on her fingers.

The two men helped her get to her feet and stood either side, supporting her while the young woman picked up her rucksack.

'You're very pale, wouldn't you be safer sitting down while we call the police, you might have concussion or something?' she said peering anxiously into Maggie's bruised and rapidly swelling face.

'They could take forever, in this weather,' observed one of the men wiping the rain from his face with his sleeve.

Maggie glanced fearfully up and down the street. There was

no sign of Jack. One of the men muttered, 'Don't worry love. Bastard legged it when he saw us. He's long gone.'

'Bloody men,' the girl added as she put the rucksack between her feet and lit a cigarette, exhaling the smoke through her teeth with an angry hiss.

Maggie reached down to brush ineffectually at the mud stains on her trouser legs.

'Thank you. I'm fine. Honestly,' she whispered.

'Good thing we left the pub when we did,' one of the men said.

'You ought to let a doctor have a look at you. We could take you to the A&E, it's only up the road,' suggested the girl.

'No, no. I don't want the police or the hospital. I can walk from here. I'll be alright. Honestly. Thank you very much. Thank you.'

She brushed at the mud stains, fighting the tears, heaved the rucksack onto her shoulder and began to walk unsteadily towards Gower Street, leaving her rescuers staring after her, shaking their heads in disbelief.

Half an hour later, Maggie was studying her reflection in the cracked bathroom mirror. The damage to the right hand side of her face where Jack had punched her was much worse than she expected. The skin had been broken and a livid bruise was developing. Her right eye was almost closed. There was a throbbing ache in the back of her head and her left hip and knee were very sore.

As the full horror of what had just happened began to sink in, the shock took over. Jack did this. He attacked me in the street. He punched me. How could he do that? How did he know that I would be in Gower Street tonight? Has he been following me? Was he waiting outside the college? Was he outside the flat?

She turned on the tap and splashed cold water on her bruised features, wincing and searching deep into her swollen eyes. I provoked him by making him think that I've already had the termination. That's why he hit me. I lied to him. She reached for the towel. Why should I feel guilty? What difference does it make? In a few hours it will all be over anyway. Why should I care what he thinks? Now he knows it's over, he'll leave me alone.

As she leaned across to hang the towel on the rail beside the hand basin, a cold shiver passed through her and the room began to spin. She could feel beads of sweat breaking out as she hung on to the basin in a desperate attempt to stay upright. The muscles in her lower back felt tight, locked in a spasm.

I must have pulled something when I fell, she thought abstractedly as she groped to turn off the cold tap.

A crippling shaft of pain shot up through her pelvis and she screamed out in agony, clutching her abdomen with both hands as a second, much stronger, pain followed.

Maggie was doubled up with her arms wrapped tight around her ribcage, she was panting hard when she felt the unmistakable warm liquid trickling down the insides of her legs. She watched in horror as the shocking crimson puddle formed on the worn black and white linoleum at her feet and her legs buckled as she groped frantically in the pocket of her raincoat for her mobile phone.

15

John Sullivan arrived at Maggie's flat a few minutes behind the ambulance team which he'd summoned as soon as he put the phone down after her call.

'Did you see his face? Would you recognise him if you saw him again?' he asked urgently as he bent over her, stroking her head.

'No, it was dark,' she replied with her eyes closed, terrified that he would detect the lie which had sprung instinctively from her lips. 'I don't think so.'

'No more questions,' she heard the female paramedic say as she was bundled into a blanket and carried down the stairs on a chair.

*

Maggie was woken by the sound of a woman's voice calling her name and gently patting the back of her hand.

'Maggie, Maggie, wake up. I've brought you a cup of tea.'

The smiling face of a pretty young nurse swam into view as Maggie forced her eyes open and struggled to sit up, looking around in bewilderment.

'Where am I? What time is it?'

The nurse was rearranging her pillows.

'It's Friday and it's ten o'clock and someone has sent you

some beautiful flowers,' she said, pointing at a huge display in a basket on the windowsill.

'Look,' the nurse said as she held out a small card.

Maggie took it.

'Hope all is well. See you later. John.'

She fell back against the pillow as helpless tears rolled slowly down her cheeks. The nurse made a clucking noise with her tongue and patted Maggie's hand soothingly.

'Don't cry, Maggie. Mr Faulkner will be in to see you later.'

Maggie sipped the tea slowly as nightmare images from the previous night flashed through her head in a bizarre collage; they were shocking and horrific.

Jack's face looming out of the shadows, his arm raised to hit her, the feet of the people pounding along the pavement towards her. John Sullivan's shocked expression in the ambulance, the paramedics, and the blood. So much blood.

She closed her eyes, haunted by Jack's face, distorted with hatred.

He hit me, he knocked me over. He made me lose the baby. It was his fault. Not mine. He did it. He did all of it. Her jaw trembled. How ironic. The baby that nobody wanted had slipped away by itself. Disappeared. Gone. Returned to nothingness. It was almost as if it knew it wasn't wanted. Where is it now? What have we done?

She covered her face with the sheet and wept bitterly until she fell into an exhausted sleep.

A long time later, she was woken by a rap on the door. A tall, cheerful-looking middle-aged man appeared, dressed in an open-necked blue shirt with the sleeves rolled up above his elbows and a stethoscope swinging jauntily around his neck. The plastic-covered identity card pinned to the breast pocket of his shirt bore the name Michael Faulkner, Consultant Obstetrician.

'Hi,' he said as he approached the bed. 'How's things? Apart from the face?' He grinned as Maggie tried to sit up.

'A bit uncomfortable, but OK,' she said, with her swollen eyes focused on the lemon yellow bedcover which she was gripping with both hands.

'That's what we like to hear,' he said briskly. 'Oh and you'll be glad to know that there are no bones broken. You were very fortunate. Just a bit of a golf ball on the back of the skull. Nothing too serious.'

He lifted her chin with his index finger, and leaned in closer to examine the bruising on her face.

'Yep,' he pronounced finally, 'the bump on the back of your head and this bruising will take a while to disappear, but the rest of you,' his eyes swept down the bed cover, 'is back to square one,' he coughed, 'so to speak.'

The colour rose in Maggie's cheeks but she said nothing as the consultant picked up her wrist with his eyes on his watch.

'I've had a chat with John Sullivan. He rang about thirty minutes ago. I told him that everything went very well. You had a miscarriage last night. Hardly surprising, under the circumstances.' He cleared his throat again. 'But you were booked in for a termination today at the private clinic where I work, so I guess everything's worked out, one way or another.'

He unhooked the clipboard on the end of her bed, scanning the notes.

'It was all over by the time you were admitted last night. The only complication was that you had lost a lot of blood, so we had to give you a bit of a transfusion. Oh, and we did a quick ultrasound on your uterus, just to make sure it was all clear. Oh, and a scan on the skull. You missed all the fun,' he added with a small laugh. 'All you need to do now is make an appointment to see John for a check-up in a couple of weeks or so.'

Maggie kept her eyes down. She was surprised by the apparently casual, offhand manner in which the doctor was describing one of the most terrifying and shocking experiences she had ever been through.

'John's very fond of you. He said he's known you since you

were a kid.' Michael Faulkner was scribbling on the notes with a black ballpoint pen.

'He used to be my father's GP. I was very lucky that he came straight over or I don't know what would have happened. There was so much blood. I freaked out. I was pathetic. I dread to think what he thought of me.'

Michael Faulkner patted her shoulder clumsily. 'Not at all. He's very sympathetic. We all are. You've been through the mill, Maggie.'

She watched him walk to the door.

'I'd better get on,' he said. 'John will come in at lunchtime to drive you home. My advice is take it easy for the next two or three days and you'll be right as rain in no time. By the way, Happy Christmas.'

16

Maggie was discharged in the afternoon with a small supply of painkillers and a handful of booklets about post-operative care and birth control.

Once John Sullivan had seen her safely up the stairs to her flat and repeated his colleague's advice about taking things quietly over the weekend, he picked up his coat and prepared to leave. As he passed her desk he noticed that the telephone landline had been pulled out of the connection socket on the wall.

'Why's this phone disconnected?' he said, eyebrows furrowed.

'People ringing up to sell stuff or asking me to take part in a survey,' Maggie said quickly.

John Sullivan bent to push the cable firmly back into the wall socket.

'Use the answerphone to monitor calls, Maggie. That's what it's for. It's definitely not a good idea to be completely cut off when you're on your own and just out of hospital.'

'I have got a mobile, John,' she reminded him quietly.

'I know. But you should leave the landline on as well. Mobiles have a bad habit of running out of charge. I'll call you later on tonight.'

After he left, Maggie wrapped herself in a fleece blanket and sat in the armchair, her eyes drawn to the dark patch of sky just visible above the buildings opposite. It gets dark so quickly at this time of the year, she thought sadly; her initial euphoria at being home seemed to have faded with the daylight. Now all she could feel was a throbbing pain in the back of her head and an unfamiliar sense of loneliness and vulnerability.

She turned her head to look at the reconnected phone, lying silent on the corner of her desk. Is it over, really over?

Maggie dozed uneasily in the chair before finally summoning enough energy to climb into her bed in the early hours of Saturday morning.

The piercing sound of the landline woke her at eight o'clock. It was John Sullivan asking for an update on her condition and offering to make a second visit. It took her a while to convince him that she was feeling much better.

She didn't mention the terrifying nightmare she'd had when she woke up in a cold sweat after dreaming that she'd found a tiny baby screaming inside a box.

'Thank you, John. You're very kind. Now go and enjoy your Christmas with your family. I'm fine, really.'

When the phone woke her for the second time, Maggie was confused to find the room lit only by the faint glow of the street lights outside.

'It's ten past eight. I've been asleep for hours,' she said to herself as she pushed the long strands of hair off her face, and picked up the receiver.

'Maggie. It's me, Jack. Look, I'm really, really sorry about the other night. I was well out of order. I didn't hurt you, did I?' He gave a nervous little laugh. 'We need to talk. What about coffee?' He was talking quickly, slightly breathless. 'I don't know what came over me the other night. I was drunk. Completely off my head, as usual. You know me, sweetie, always going off on one.' He sniggered again. 'Anyway, that's enough about me. You and I need to talk. What about tomorrow? Yes, tomorrow. Sunday. Sunday's good for you, isn't it?' He paused. 'You still there?'

Maggie flinched as she touched the lump on the back of her head. 'Don't ring me, Jack. It's finished.'

'What do you mean, finished?' He sounded genuinely surprised. 'Don't be silly. Of course it's not finished. You're pregnant with our baby. How can it be finished? This is the beginning.'

'No, Jack. There is no baby. Leave me alone.'

She put the phone down, shivering. She pulled her dressing gown from the bottom of the bed and draped it around her shoulders as the phone rang again. She lifted the receiver. 'Leave me alone, Jack.' Her voice was barely a whisper.

'You don't mean that, you can't mean it. We are having a baby. You told me that we're having a baby.' He whined the last word like a small child.

Maggie had a vision of the look of hatred on his face when he hit her.

'No, we're not having a baby. There is no baby.' It was difficult to frame the words through her quivering lips.

There was a short pause and then Jack began to yell hysterically. 'No! No! You bitch! You can't do that. Not without my permission. It's illegal.'

Maggie slammed the phone down and fell back against the pillows with her arm covering her face. I didn't do it. You did it. You killed the baby when you hit me. The doctors said so. You killed the baby. She rolled onto her side and closed her eyes. What difference does it make what he thinks? It's over. The baby's gone.

The next time the phone rang Maggie didn't pick it up. She lay there, listening to the stream of invective coming from the answer machine until Jack ran out of breath or the tape was full. She wasn't sure which happened first.

There didn't seem to be any oxygen left in the room. Maggie was finding it difficult to breathe as she lay there, curled up in a foetal position with her hands clamped over her ears. She felt as though she had been punched again. The red light was flashing on the answer machine and a voice in her head was telling her, 'Get up and wipe the tape. Wipe it clean. Delete every trace of Jack from the phone, from the computer, from everywhere. Do it now.'

Once all his messages had been deleted, she disconnected the landline and switched off the computer and the mobile. Then she had a shower and changed her nightclothes and went to sit in her father's old leather armchair with her eyes closed.

The traffic in the street outside had almost stopped; there were no sounds coming from the flats below hers.

Maggie listened to the silence for a long time, trying to steady her breathing. But she could find no peace as the fears began to surface. Jack's face loomed behind her closed lids, leering and taunting her. What will he do next? Will he come here? Perhaps he's here already, standing in the street outside this building.

She got up to peer through a gap in the curtains. The street below was empty. The windows in the buildings opposite were in darkness. She tiptoed around the flat, checking that all the windows and the front door were securely locked and bolted before she finally climbed back into bed.

She was woken up by the sound of the street door being slammed hard. The green fluorescent numerals on her alarm clock told her it was 2.30 in the morning. Maggie listened to the sound of footsteps slowly ascending the stairs, hardly daring to breathe. The voice in her head taunted her once more. Jack has tricked one of the neighbours into letting him into the building. He's going to knock on the door at any minute.

She got out of bed and tip-toed across the room to stand with her ear pressed against the cold wood.

The footsteps stopped on the floor below, a door was opened, then several voices whispered 'Merry Christmas' followed by a lot of muffled giggling and doors closing. Maggie listened as the keys were turned and the bolts were slid into place. Then silence.

She waited, shivering in her nightclothes for several minutes, before she allowed herself a deep sigh of relief and returned to her bed. It's Christmas Eve. I forgot. It's Christmas Eve. I'll have to remember to turn the phones back on tomorrow morning. Rose is bound to call me, and David, if he can get a line. Maybe Diana and Lars too.

By lunchtime on Christmas Day, after convincing a very insistent Rose that the GP had recommended another couple of days of rest to be sure that she was over the virus, she spent the rest of the day trying to decide how to stop Jack.

Changing her telephone numbers and her email addresses was the obvious solution, but it would be difficult to achieve in practical terms. All her contact details were listed on the university website. She couldn't see how she could ask the people in Admin to remove her name from the site without giving them a plausible explanation for doing so. It's probably one of the conditions of my employment, she thought.

17

After repeatedly declining the invitation to Rose's annual New Year's Eve party with the excuse that her viral infection was not quite over, the days passed quickly for Maggie as she made her preparations for the new term.

She was feeling stronger each day and was relieved to be back at college. The bruising and swelling on her face had almost disappeared and she had surprised herself about the ease with which she had been able to lie about being mugged by a stranger and the virus.

Although her elaborate subterfuge had engendered a good deal of sympathy from both friends and colleagues, it had done nothing to ease her increasing anxiety caused by the escalating harassment from Jack.

She disconnected her landline and switched off her mobile phone and her computer every night, in a vain attempt to sleep. But each morning when she switched everything back on, there was an endless number of voicemails, texts and emails from him. Maggie deleted them and told herself that she ought to be grateful that he was restricting himself to messages.

She had convinced herself that she was coping, unaware that her newly acquired habit of checking that the doors and windows in her flat were secure was fast becoming a compulsive obsession. On three occasions, she was half way up Gower Street on her way in to college when she decided to return home to check that her front door was closed and locked.

During February she had two panic attacks. Once in the middle of the night when she woke up in a cold sweat, with her heart racing so fast that she could hardly breathe. It had taken more than an hour for the symptoms to subside but by the following morning when she realised that she felt better, she decided to ignore it.

Maggie had never been fond of socialising; consequently, her repeated refusals to invitations, using a variety of ambiguous excuses about the pressure of work, a migraine or some other unspecified malaise, were accepted without question.

She began to spend all her free time in a corner of the British Library, telling herself that she was getting on with research while subconsciously counting the days until the month-long Easter break when she had eagerly accepted another invitation to visit Diana and her husband in Sweden for two weeks. She was hoping that her absence might result in Jack losing interest in tormenting her.

Diana and Lars welcomed her with open arms, cheerfully accepting her heavily edited version of the attack and virus without question. Even her vague excuse about leaving her mobile behind wasn't questioned.

'I think we could all do with taking a digital sabbatical once in a while,' Diana said, 'You could be starting a trend, Maggie.'

Diana and Lars went out of their way to entertain her for two glorious weeks, in a generous bid to make up for her miserable Christmas, and Maggie returned to a very wet London feeling much stronger and more optimistic.

But her newly found confidence was short lived. When she opened the front door of her flat, the light was flashing ominously on the answer machine, and when she pressed Play the tape was full. They were mostly messages from Jack, some begging her to meet him or speak to him, others were threatening and abusive.

He sounded desperate, confused and often extremely drunk.

It was half an hour before she removed her jacket, closed the curtains, switched on the lights and double locked her front door.

She knew that the obvious solution would be to report Jack to the police, but she was fearful. They'll want to know everything. They'll say that it's my fault. I know they will. They'll say that I asked for it.

She kept remembering the time when two of her female students told her about a mutual friend of theirs who had been raped. They had gone into shocking detail about the intimate nature of the questions the police had asked.

Maggie shuddered as she deleted all the messages and disconnected the landline. There were more than thirty emails from him on her computer which she deleted without opening, before disconnecting the internet.

18

The war of nerves rumbled on for several more weeks, until the situation was brought to a head one day when Maggie returned home to find an envelope for her in the rack on the ground floor.

There was no postmark and only her name scrawled across the front in biro. It was from Jack and she realised with horror that it had been delivered by hand.

Although it contained the usual accusations and threats, the thought that he had been standing outside the building where she lived seemed infinitely more frightening.

That night, she spent more than an hour checking and rechecking that the front door of the flat and all the windows were double locked. Round and round the rooms she went, testing the windows and the door, turning and re-turning the keys in the security catches until she was exhausted.

At half past three in the morning she woke herself up, shouting and crying. She sat up and put the light on, shivering. It had been the same dream as the one after the miscarriage. A baby crying in a box. She could see it and hear it but she couldn't reach it.

Maggie spent the rest of the night awake, staring up at the ceiling, too frightened to close her eyes and sleep.

On her way in to the college the following morning, she thought she saw Jack standing in a doorway in Gower Street. Without stopping to think, she turned and ran in the opposite direction, eventually taking refuge in a coffee shop for more than an hour.

When she finally arrived at the college, she found that she had missed an important inter-departmental staff meeting.

A week later, she had another very severe panic attack in the toilet at college and was forced to cancel two lectures and take a cab home.

Rose telephoned her in the evening to say that the staff common room was buzzing with gossip and speculation. She begged Maggie to explain what was wrong.

'What on earth is the matter, Maggie? Are you ill? You can tell me, surely?'

'It's nothing, Rose. I haven't been sleeping well, that's all. So I missed a meeting and cancelled a couple of lectures, it's not exactly the end of the world is it? I don't understand what all the fuss is about. I've got to go; my pizza is burning. I'll call you tomorrow.'

She put the phone down with a heavy heart, knowing that Rose didn't believe her. Why would she? Nobody who knew her would believe it. She didn't believe it. She was trying to justify the kind of behaviour that she could never have imagined herself capable of.

Two days later, Maggie was summoned to a meeting with the new Head of Department, Professor Janet Robson, a dour Scottish woman. The pale blue eyes regarded Maggie dispassionately over the top of her spectacles when she sat down. A laptop computer and a blank A4 pad of lined paper with a black ballpoint pen lined up beside it were the only objects on the pristine surface of the large mahogany desk.

'Dr Savernake, good morning. How are you?' Janet Robson didn't wait for a reply. 'I've called this meeting because some of your colleagues have expressed concern about your… wellbeing,' she said briskly, ballpoint pen poised in her left hand.

Maggie forced a smile. 'Concerned about me? I'm not sure what you mean, Professor Robson. Who is concerned?'

'You missed an important staff meeting and cancelled a couple of lectures. That's very unusual for you, isn't it?'

Her tone was stern and disapproving.

Maggie gazed at a watercolour landscape of misty mountains on the wall behind Professor Robson's head. 'I've had a virus. You know what it's like, sometimes it takes a while to throw these things off,' she said.

Janet Robson's pale, thin lips were tight. 'A virus, you say? And someone said that you were mugged just before Christmas. Is that why you've been avoiding your colleagues?' She paused. 'Do you have a partner, Dr Savernake, because it occurred to me that you might be having some kind of domestic trouble?'

'No, I do not have a partner, nor do I have what you call domestic trouble,' Maggie said curtly, 'I've just told you. I had a virus. Surely I'm allowed to be ill once in fifteen years?'

Janet Robson sat back in her chair, and pushed her glasses up onto the bridge of her nose. Her eyes were cold and distant.

'I'm obliged to remind you that when a member of staff is not pulling their weight, for whatever reason, it puts an extra burden on the rest of the department. It's a good idea to get any problems sorted out as soon as possible. For the benefit of your colleagues. I expect you understand that, Dr Savernake?'

Janet Robson waited in vain for Maggie to say something. She sighed and put the pen down.

'Well then, I'm sure you've plenty to do today, as have I.'

She pressed a button on her laptop with her eyes fixed on the screen. Maggie stood up and went to the door. She didn't respond when she heard Janet Robson say, 'Talking to someone else often helps, Dr Savernake. It's no good bottling things up, you know.'

Maggie stood in the empty corridor, trembling with shock and humiliation. Hauled up in front of the Head of Department to be accused of not pulling my weight? That's another first. Is this what Jack Millfield has reduced me to? He said he wanted to wreck my career. It looks like he's getting his wish.

*

Dr John Sullivan couldn't hide his impatience when Maggie went to see him at the hastily arranged appointment the following evening. She had hardly sat down before she began speaking. Telling him how Jack was constantly harassing her, about her panic attacks, insomnia, compulsive behaviour and her increasing anxiety.

John Sullivan listened impassively until she stopped to draw breath.

'But I don't understand, Maggie. Why have you let this go on for so long? It's almost five months since the miscarriage, why didn't you say something before? You've lost a lot of weight.'

He pinched the skin on the back of her hand and watched it slide slowly back into position.

'Dehydrated too. We'll have to do some blood tests. But first, let's put a stop to this young fellow's antics. Do you have a solicitor or a legal adviser?'

'Only my father's solicitor, Andrew Bridgeman. But what can he do? I don't want him to know about any of this.'

She glanced anxiously at the closed door of the consulting room.

John Sullivan frowned. 'Why not? You haven't done anything to be ashamed of. I know Andrew. He acts for one of my other patients. I'll phone him now and tell him that you're being harassed by an abusive ex-boyfriend and that it's affecting your health. I won't say any more than that.'

He picked up the phone and patted her hand. 'Everything else is strictly confidential, between you and your medical adviser. Don't worry.'

After a brief discussion, Andrew Bridgeman agreed to

send a formal letter to Jack, warning him that legal action and a restraining order would follow if he persisted. He advised Maggie to keep a detailed record of everything that Jack said or did.

'Save everything, Maggie. Keep a diary. Make a note of anything and everything that might be relevant. We may need it if legal action is required later.'

After the phone call, John Sullivan gave her a quick medical examination and urged her to consider a short course of counselling.

Maggie was shocked. 'I've already told you that I don't need any pills and I definitely don't need any counselling,' she retorted. 'It's not complicated, John. I just want Jack Millfield to leave me alone. I can get over this on my own. I don't need any outside help either chemical or emotional. Let's face it, I went through a lot worse with my father.'

John Sullivan patted the back of her hand again.

'I know. I was there, remember? But if you don't mind my saying so, the hormonal changes that your body has been through during the past few months can sometimes result in a few emotional and physical difficulties. It's perfectly normal to feel depressed. Some of the symptoms you describe, like flashbacks, nightmares and panic attacks are very typical of post-traumatic stress disorder. Counselling can be very helpful. Especially if you're the type of person who finds it difficult to talk to people, friends and suchlike. As you clearly do.'

'I'm not depressed and I am not suffering with post-traumatic anything. I just want to be left alone to get on with my life and for everything to go back to where it was before. That's all,' she said. 'I thought that the termination...' she corrected herself, '... the miscarriage, would be the end of all of it.'

John Sullivan had seen the same look of hurt and betrayal on her face when she discovered her father dead at his desk with an empty bottle of pills beside him.

'Why didn't he call me? Why did he leave me without saying goodbye?' she had sobbed into his shoulder when he arrived at the terrible scene.

Having to cope with the challenges of life on her own from a relatively young age had made Maggie fiercely independent and stubborn. But when dealing with a life-changing experience like the one she had just been through, her steely self-control was proving to be a double-edged sword.

The old man's eyes softened as he took in her ashen cheeks, her chin held defiantly high and her back ramrod straight. Beneath that tough exterior was a young woman staggering under a heavy burden of self-reproach and a misplaced sense of guilt which she refused to acknowledge.

He knew it was pointless to insist on a counsellor. She would never agree.

'OK, Maggie, you win. As I've told you so many times before, please call me if you need anything. Even if it's only to talk. Don't forget.'

Maggie was already on her feet, knotting her scarf and buttoning her coat.

'Thank you, John. I'm fine, honestly. Now I know that Mr Bridgeman is going to send the letter, I feel better already. I'm sure that Jack will stop when he receives it. Legal action would damage his professional reputation. His father would come down on him like a ton of bricks.'

She threw him a tense smile. 'I'm sorry for bothering you with all this again. I don't know why I didn't call the lawyer myself. Perhaps it's me who's losing my grip, after all?'

John Sullivan crossed the room to lay a hand lightly on her shoulder.

'Don't forget what I've just said, call me if you're worried about anything.'

19

By the beginning of July, the warning from Andrew Bridgeman seemed to have had the desired effect, and although she had created a file marked 'JM', Jack had made no further attempts to contact her. Maggie was beginning to feel confident enough to remain in London for the summer. She had received a commission for a book, which would focus on the real women in Shakespeare's life and their possible inspiration for some of the fictitious women in his work.

In spite of the weather being uncomfortably warm and wet, she had been making her daily visits to the British Library on foot, in an attempt to improve her fitness levels, which John Sullivan was now monitoring regularly.

On her way home one evening, she caught a glimpse of her reflection striding energetically along the rain-soaked pavement. Rose won't recognise me when she gets back from Spain, she thought. Even I can see an improvement.

The single envelope and postcard in her pigeon hole was the first thing Maggie noticed when she opened the front door.

She hummed cheerfully as she ran up the stairs, examining the postcard. On one side it bore a reproduction of a sepia photograph of a pair of tango dancers dressed in the fashion of the 1930s. On the other side, a brief message, written in the familiar brown ink.

'Staying in B A with friends. Starting tango lessons! Hope you're well. Love David.'

Maggie looked at the photograph again, smiling fondly. Thank God he went away when he did. She put the postcard on her already crowded mantelpiece and frowned at the London University logo on the envelope. A letter from college? Don't tell me, we've all been given a pay rise, she thought with a grin as she ripped open the envelope.

'Due to a rationalisation of staff levels in the Department of Humanities, we regret to inform you that your annual contract with the University will not be renewed for the next academic year.'

Maggie stared in disbelief at the words. Not renewing my contract? Why? This must be a mistake. This can't be meant for me, can it?

The letter floated down to the floor unheeded as she threw her rucksack on a chair and kicked off her sandals. Not renewing my contract? But who will take over my course? My lectures? The exams? Who will supervise Yuki's thesis?

She bent to retrieve the letter, smoothing out the creases as she read it again. There was no mistake; it was addressed to her.

Maggie looked at her watch; it was only half past four. She dialled the university's administration office. Most of the teaching staff would still be away, but the office staff should be there.

Her request for Janet Robson's home number was met with silence. Maggie waited impatiently until the unfamiliar voice at the other end said, 'I'm afraid I can't divulge any personal details relating to a member of staff without the caller giving proof of their identity.'

'But that's ridiculous. I work with Professor Robson,' Maggie replied indignantly, 'I work in the English department. I've been a lecturer there for years. You ought to know that. Why don't you go and check the names on the staff list before you start asking me for proof of identity?'

There was another long silence before the woman spoke

again, 'I'm sorry, I need to have your full name, date of birth and your mother's maiden name.'

'My name is Dr Margaret Savernake, my date of birth is 21st January 1968, and my mother's maiden name is, was, Bouchard.'

'Can you spell that last one for me, please?'

Maggie recited the letters through gritted teeth.

'I like that, it sounds exotic. Where does it come from?'

Maggie didn't reply.

'Are you still there, Ms Savernake? Can I ask whether your enquiry is in connection with the university or is it a personal matter?'

'It's about a letter I've just received from Human Resources. Will you please give me Professor Robson's home phone number, or even better, her mobile number.'

'Do you have a reference there?' the woman asked, adding helpfully, 'It should be in the top left hand corner.'

Maggie read it out and heard the sound of typing, then a click followed by an incongruous burst of Vivaldi's Four Seasons. She resisted an overwhelming desire to slam the receiver down.

When the music eventually stopped and Maggie's legendary patience had been stretched to breaking point, a different, younger voice came on the line.

'I'm sorry about the delay, Dr Savernake. Professor Robson is in New York with her family. She's not due back until next week.'

Then, apparently emboldened by the absence of any superiors, she added in a conspiratorial whisper, 'Don't quote me on this, but I think I heard someone saying that they've appointed someone from Leeds, Dr Savernake. A part-timer'.

She paused, waiting for Maggie to speak before adding, 'I'm really, really sorry.'

Maggie put the phone down, momentarily distracted by the bizarre repetition of the adverb: then chided herself for noticing such a minor detail in the face of such devastating news.

What's the point of talking to Janet Robson if they've already made a decision? Have they sacked me because they think that I'm a liability? Or perhaps they think that I'm a manic depressive like my father?

She went to stand by the window, gazing down at the commuters hurrying along the street below. This is all about saving money. Part-timers are much cheaper. She wondered if this latest cost-cutting exercise would affect David's stay in South America.

She picked up the phone again.

'Rose? Where are you?'

'Sitting in a bar on the beach, darling. Where else would I be?'

'Are you enjoying your holiday?'

'What do you think?' Rose laughed. 'What about you, how's the research going?'

'I've been made redundant,' Maggie said.

'Redundant? What do you mean, you've been made redundant? But that's ridiculous.' Rose was shrieking hysterically.

Maggie cringed, imagining the attention she would be attracting in what sounded like a very crowded beach bar.

'I thought stuff was going on last term,' Rose said, more quietly. 'I heard rumours. But I never thought that you... How can they? Oh, Maggie, I'm so sorry. How long have you known?'

'I've just received the letter. Apparently I'm entitled to three months' salary. God knows how I'm going to manage. I'll have to find a job quickly, Rose.'

'Only three months? After how many years? They're bastards, all of them.' Rose was shouting again.

'If I don't find anything, I'll have to live off my savings. I'm worried about my flat. The lease is due for renewal in October. The other day one of my neighbours told me that the landlords are going to raise the rent. I definitely won't be able to manage.'

'You will find something. Of course you will. English

departments all over the country will be falling over themselves to have you,' Rose said.

'I doubt that somehow, Rose. But thanks for the vote of confidence.'

'I'll be back home at the end of the week. Try not to worry. I'll help you sort things out. See you in a bit. Love you.'

Rose ended the call with a loud 'Mwah, Mwah' and Maggie put the phone down.

20

David returned from Argentina at the end of August and after giving him a week to recover from his travels, Maggie suggested that they meet up for lunch.

She was surprised by the change she saw in him. He looked much older and somehow sadder. He listened sympathetically to her carefully edited version of the events after he'd left for Chile, but there was an unusual detachment and lack of interest in his manner which she found disturbing. He was almost dismissive about the news of her redundancy.

'Don't fret, Maggie. People with your qualifications and experience are very sought after. You'll find a placement in no time,' he said with a smile.

It was only at the end of the meal, after careful questioning from Maggie, that he told her, reluctantly, that he had been advised to have surgery on a damaged kneecap, which the surgeon suggested had been aggravated by his recent foray into tango dancing.

'So it looks like my travels are over after all, Maggie,' he said.

'You'll have time to write your memoirs, David.'

'Maybe. I'm going to stay with my sister in Shropshire after the op. Her husband died while I was in Chile, he'd been suffering from Alzheimer's for years. It's been a relief for her in many ways. But she's in need of a bit of company and I'll be grateful to have someone to make me the odd cup of tea.'

'Shropshire? That's a long way from London, isn't it?' Maggie looked anxiously at him.

'Don't worry, we'll keep in touch,' David said gently. 'Once you're settled in a new job, you can come and spend a few days with the ancient wrinklies.'

She struggled to hide her disappointment, and the meal ended awkwardly with David describing his trip while Maggie asked herself why she always expected life to stay the same.

*

By the beginning of September, it was clear that Rose's optimism had been misplaced. With the renewal of the lease on her flat imminent and no immediate solution in sight, it had become depressingly clear to Maggie that the search for a job was going to be much more prolonged than Rose had predicted, and she would have to make some important decisions.

After swallowing her pride and a large glass of red wine during supper with Rose and her two teenage children, she asked Rose if she would consider a short-term let of one of her rooms.

'Good heavens, of course we will. You don't even have to ask. I was thinking about it the other day,' Rose replied. 'We've got loads of room here and we'd love to have you, wouldn't we, guys?'

'Mm,' Seb, her eighteen-year-old son, mumbled through a mouthful of vegetable lasagne while his fifteen-year-old sister Phoebe stared silently at her mobile phone.

'You can have the room on the top floor,' Rose said excitedly as she leapt to her feet. 'Come on, let's go upstairs and have a look at it now.'

The decision was made very quickly and over the next couple of weeks Maggie put most of her possessions into long-term storage and settled herself into Rose's attic.

After the monastic silence of her own flat, it took her a while to get used to the pandemonium and chaos of living with a couple of rowdy teenagers and their battalions of friends.

Rose's house seemed to be an unofficial outbuilding for the three local high schools. At any hour of the day, and occasionally the night, a seemingly endless parade of noisy, sweaty youngsters came crashing through the front door, tossing their jackets and rucksacks in the direction of the coat stand and kicking their malodorous trainers onto an untidy heap on the floor. After which they would congregate in the huge basement kitchen, where they regularly emptied the fridge and store cupboards of everything that was even vaguely edible.

Rose herself seemed to be frequently absent, apparently preferring to spend most of her time at college or out socialising.

Maggie didn't complain. Within a few weeks, she had been pleasantly surprised to discover how much she enjoyed the company of Rose's children and their friends. She had been missing the stimulation of her students more than she cared to admit, and often found herself lingering at the long pine kitchen table, helping one or other of them with a particularly difficult piece of homework or simply listening to their noisy, good-natured banter and even joining in the heated discussions.

On such an occasion, Rose returned home from an evening drinks party and burst into the kitchen with her eyes sparkling and cheeks flushed.

'Oh my God, Maggie! You're not still listening to all their crap, are you? I don't know why you find them so entertaining,' she exclaimed as she flopped into the chair next to Maggie's and draped an arm affectionately around her shoulders.

'You'll never guess what I've just heard on the grapevine,' she whispered.

Maggie looked up from the textbook she was looking at with Seb.

'Professor Janet Robson has been made a Dame for sacking

all the staff in Humanities and reducing the national education budget,' she said drily.

Seb exploded with laughter. 'Nice one, Mags.'

'No. Jack Millfield's getting married!' announced Rose as though she was delivering an international news scoop.

Maggie's stomach clenched, and she kept her eyes fixed on the book in front of her. It was the first time she had heard his name for months.

'And you'll never guess who the girl is?' Rose continued happily as she removed her long pendant earrings and tossed them down on the table with a clatter. Her eyes flickered expectantly to Seb's girlfriend, Roisin, who was deeply engrossed in her mobile phone. Phoebe and her friend Tanya were sharing the remains of a pizza from a greasy cardboard box at the other end of the table.

'Penelope Cruz?' suggested Seb, after a long silence.

'Nicole Kidman?' chorused Phoebe and Tanya, giggling through a shower of pizza crumbs.

'Shut up, all of you,' yelled Rose irritably as she turned back to face Maggie. 'Jack Millfield is marrying Ana Valdéz.'

'Who is Ana Valdéz?' asked Maggie innocently.

'Ana Valdéz. The super model. She's nineteen years old, at least half Jack's age. And she's so thin that one of his shoes probably weighs more than she does. Can you imagine?'

Rose was almost incoherent with excitement.

'I've never heard of her,' said Maggie evenly, with her eyes back on the textbook and her mind racing, Jack's married. Thank God for that. It's over. I'm free at last.

'Maggie, you must have,' Phoebe and Tanya chorused.

'I must have what?' Maggie said, looking bewildered.

'You must have heard of Ana Valdéz. She's everywhere. Look.'

Phoebe grabbed a magazine from an untidy pile on the shelf behind her and flicked quickly through the pages.

'Look! Here she is! Hot or what?'

She held up a double-page spread of an advertisement showing an emaciated, dark-haired girl in minute shorts and very little else, pouting provocatively through a long, dark fringe and holding what appeared to be a giant perfume bottle close to her cheek.

Maggie shook her head. 'That's not helping. Sorry. I still don't know who she is,' she said, trying to imagine how such a young girl would cope with Jack.

'How was the party, Mum? Any good?' Seb asked.

Rose launched into a rambling description of a female guest who had apparently got very drunk and made a pass at the host. Phoebe and Tanya stood up and announced in unison that they were going upstairs to watch TV in bed.

'Tanya's sleeping over, OK?' Phoebe announced and closed the door before her mother could comment.

Rose shrugged and looked at Maggie. 'Did we behave like that when we were their age?'

Maggie laughed. 'Who? Me? I went to a very strict boarding school; I didn't get the opportunity. Not that I think it did me any favours. Your kids are much more balanced and normal than I was.'

Seb stood up, stretching. 'Thanks, Mags, I've never been called balanced and normal before. I'll make a cup of tea to celebrate. Anyone?'

He waved a mug in the air and Roisin, who was now reading Phoebe's discarded magazine, put her hand up. 'Me.'

Rose's yawn echoed her son's. 'I've got a headache coming on. By the way, any joy with that application you sent last week, Maggie?'

'Nothing. It's looking hopeless. I'll have to start thinking about changing my profession altogether if something doesn't turn up soon.'

Seb was pouring boiling water into two mugs. 'Would you seriously consider that? Doing something completely different, I mean?' he asked over his shoulder.

'It depends. Why? Have you got anything in mind?' asked Maggie, grinning.

'Tell her what your boss said this morning, Roisin,' Seb said.

'What? Oh yeah. I'm temping in an office just off Oxford Street,' Roisin took the steaming mug from Seb, 'and my boss asked me if I knew anyone who was looking for a job. Someone who might consider being a house sitter or a housekeeper or something. I can't remember exactly what she called it.'

'What's a house sitter?' asked Maggie.

'A house sitter is someone who looks after a house while the owner is away. Obviously. Like babysitting, only a lot easier. How long is it for, Roisin?' said Rose.

Roisin shrugged, her eyes glued to the magazine. 'What? No idea. Saz didn't say.'

'It's probably some multi-millionaire banker who wants someone to keep an eye on his Picassos while he suns himself in the Caymans,' said Rose.

'Do they actually employ people to do stuff like that?' Maggie asked. 'Where is the house, do you know?'

'No idea,' Roisin said, reluctantly tearing her eyes away from the magazine.

'It might be a luxury duplex in Kensington or even New York, if you're really lucky.' Rose dug her elbow into Maggie's ribs. 'Go on, Mags, give it a go. It'll be like having a holiday, only with pay. Have you got a number, Roisin?'

Seb handed Roisin a biro and tore a page out of his exercise book.

'My boss is called Sarah Jane Hodges, the office is just off Oxford Street, between Tottenham Court Road and Oxford Circus.' Roisin was scribbling quickly. 'This is the address and the phone number.' She handed the paper to Maggie.

'OK. I'll call her in the morning,' said Maggie. 'As Rose says, what have I got to lose?'

'I'll tell her that I've spoken to you as soon as I get in

tomorrow. She gave me the impression that it was pretty urgent.'
Roisin took a long gulp from her mug of tea.

'Make sure you say something nice about my friend.'

Rose wrapped her arm around Maggie's shoulders again and
squeezed hard. 'She needs a job. Badly.'

21

The journey on the Northern Line from Kentish Town took longer than Maggie had estimated, as her train came to a halt in the tunnel outside Camden Town station and stood there, hissing and groaning for seven long nail-biting minutes before it started to move again.

Travelling in the rush hour was a novel experience and the surreal atmosphere in the congested underground labyrinth only seemed to emphasise the unusual nature of her mission. Who could have predicted a year ago that she, Dr Maggie Savernake, specialist in sixteenth-century English literature, would one day be travelling to an interview for a job as a house sitter?

It sounds like the plot of a cheap novel, she thought as she made her way towards the escalators.

By the time she reached street level and emerged onto the packed pavement in Oxford Street, it was raining heavily. Maggie took shelter in a shop doorway to zip up her raincoat and pull the hood over her head. According to Roisin, her destination was fifteen minutes' walk away.

She put her head down and launched herself into the crowds of impatient commuters filling the pavements. Double-decker buses and black taxi cabs were nose to tail down the length of Oxford Street in both directions with their horns blaring non-stop. Maggie coughed. The air was reeking with the smell of diesel.

Twenty minutes later, with her rain-sodden trousers clinging uncomfortably to her calves, she found herself in a side turning off Wardour Street in front of a shabby, black-painted front door, very reminiscent of the one where she used to live.

Roisin had told her that the office she was looking for was on the second floor. Maggie searched the brass nameplates on the wall. Hodges and Green, Theatrical Agents, 2nd floor. This must be it, she thought, feeling mildly surprised that Roisin hadn't said anything about the firm being a theatrical agent.

She pressed the bell, and listened for the buzzer as the door swung open to reveal an uninviting, dimly lit, narrow hallway and a steeply rising staircase covered with a threadbare tobacco-coloured carpet.

The door closed with a dull thud behind her as she began her cautious ascent to the second floor, while trying to ignore the sinking feeling gnawing away inside her. The first impression wasn't exactly promising.

The building was eerily silent, apart from an elderly woman in a headscarf emptying waste paper bins into a large black plastic bag on the first-floor landing. She scowled unpleasantly at Maggie as she passed.

Behind a half-glazed door marked ENQUIRIES on the second floor, Maggie entered a featureless room, containing an unoccupied desk and chair and two large green metal filing cabinets. A stained polystyrene coffee cup sitting forlornly on top of an overflowing filing tray and a battered calendar with a photograph of a copse of leafless trees above the word 'October' were the only signs of any previous human occupation.

She glanced at her watch. She was twenty minutes late and it looked as though everybody had already left. She stood there, trying to decide whether she was disappointed or relieved. The only sound was the steady drip of the rainwater sliding off her raincoat onto the bare wooden floorboards.

Maggie nervously looked around at the bare walls; she was

keen to find a job, but was she really this desperate? As the seconds ticked away, she heard the sound of a vacuum cleaner being pushed around on the floor below; soon the old lady would be heaving all her equipment up the stairs and expecting her to move.

As Maggie turned to leave, a door was flung open by an attractive middle-aged woman in an immaculate black trouser suit. She held out her hand with a wide, friendly smile.

'Maggie Savernake? I hope you haven't been waiting long?'

'Yes. No. Not really. My train was held up outside Camden Town,' Maggie said.

'Ah, the dreaded Northern Line. I avoid it like the plague whenever possible. I'm Sarah Hodges, by the way. Call me Saz.'

Shrewd dark eyes swept over Maggie, from the dripping tendrils of auburn hair plastered to her cheeks to her squelching shoes.

'Don't tell me, it's raining again,' she said with a grin and beckoning Maggie to follow her into the inside office.

'Come in and take your raincoat off. I sometimes wonder if they'll ever run out of water up there.' She waved a finger at the ceiling.

Maggie removed her raincoat and glanced around.

The main office was a much larger room than the reception. There were posters advertising films and stage plays adorning two of the walls, and dozens of framed photographs, some of which had dedications and signatures scrawled across them, hanging in neat rows on the wall opposite the desk.

Maggie didn't recognise any of the faces; she sat down feeling increasingly anxious. Let's hope she doesn't ask me to identify anybody, she thought.

The large desk was barely visible beneath three telephones, an open laptop, and piles of files, newspapers and magazines. Some were spread open with sections of text highlighted with a bright green marker. Saz Hodges sat in front of a high window overlooking the street. Maggie watched the rain splattering against the panes as Saz made an unsuccessful attempt to clear a space on the desk with her arm.

'Sorry about the muddle,' she said apologetically. 'One of these days I'm going to be buried alive by all this stuff. I'm like one of those overworked pack animals you see in the charity ads on the inside back pages of the Sunday newspapers.'

As she spoke she rifled through the papers, apparently searching for something, and eventually held up a handwritten sheet of A4.

'Finally! Here it is.'

She put on a pair of heavy-rimmed spectacles and stared at the page.

'You're living with Rose Cooper and her family?'

The dark eyes stared expectantly over the top of the spectacles at Maggie.

'I'm renting a room in her house. Rose is an old university friend and colleague. Ex-colleague. It's only a temporary arrangement until...' Maggie didn't finish.

'Until you find a job?'

'Yes.'

Maggie wondered what Roisin had already told her boss.

'Do you drive?'

'Yes, but I don't own a car. I haven't driven for a few years. My flat was twenty minutes' walk from the university.'

'Lucky you. As we were saying earlier, public transport is a complete nightmare.'

The resounding notes of the William Tell Overture sounded from somewhere beneath the chaotic mountain of paperwork. Saz clicked her tongue and rummaged impatiently, sending papers and files tumbling onto the floor. Maggie bent to retrieve them, wondering how Saz ever found anything.

Saz grimaced at her mobile phone, pressed a button and shoved it back into its original hiding place.

'Bloody mobiles. Where were we? Oh yes. Roisin told me that she thinks that you're single and your age is somewhere between thirty and forty?' She peered over the spectacles again.

'I'm thirty-nine and single,' Maggie said, thinking, this is humiliating, what am I doing here? What possessed me? Why does this woman need to know how old I am?

Saz was scanning the sheet of paper again. 'And you're not married?'

'No.'

'Children?'

Maggie was unable to prevent the colour rising in her cheeks. 'No,' she said quietly as the stick from the pregnancy test with its two blue lines floated implausibly into her mind's eye. She blinked it away quickly.

'Are you pregnant?' Saz Hodges was watching her closely.

'No, I am not pregnant.' Maggie found it impossible to hide her indignation.

Saz bit her lower lip and began searching amongst her papers, clearing her throat noisily.

'Some of these questions are probably illegal,' she said at last. 'I apologise. I guess I should have warned you. But this interview is completely off the record. It was our solicitor who suggested that I get all this information and I'm hopeless at doing subtle.'

She gave a derisive snort. 'You've probably noticed. I'm pretty sure that it's against all the regulations to specify that we need someone with no ties and no children. But it's purely because of the nature of the job and the type of accommodation we have to offer.'

She glanced down at her handwritten sheet again. 'Do you have any experience of... running a home?'

'I've never been a professional housekeeper, if that's what you're asking,' said Maggie. 'My experience, if you can call it that, is restricted to normal, run-of-the-mill housekeeping in my own home and the home I shared with my father for a short while during his illness.'

Saz was scribbling notes in the margin of the handwritten sheet.

I'm not sure what I was expecting, thought Maggie as she watched, but this is definitely the most unusual interview I've ever attended.

Saz took off her spectacles with a loud sigh. 'This job is a bit unusual. We're not actually looking for a housekeeper, as such.'

Maggie looked up in surprise, wondering what was coming next.

'We are looking for someone with maturity, intelligence and discretion. Somebody who can be trusted to oversee the administration of two properties. There's a bit of driving involved, mostly between London and the property in East Anglia. I assume that won't be a problem?'

Maggie shook her head. Two properties? Roisin hadn't said anything about two properties.

Saz looked as though she had just solved a particularly difficult clue to a crossword puzzle.

'You'd be surprised how difficult it's been to find someone who felt right,' she said after a long pause. 'We want someone who is prepared to live in. There is self-contained accommodation provided in both properties.'

She lifted her blonde hair up and flicked it out over her shoulders with a well-practised gesture; it made Maggie think of her students.

'It's really weird,' Saz said, as though the thought had just occurred to her, 'Roisin has been temping here all summer covering for my permanent PA who's on what feels like an endless maternity leave.'

She rolled her eyes as though she couldn't think of anything less appealing.

'And I happened to mention how desperate I was to find

someone for this job. When she mentioned you, I thought she was joking. Your description ticked all the boxes on my list. I couldn't get you in here fast enough, to be honest.'

Maggie readjusted her back against the uncomfortable wooden chair, wondering if Saz Hodges would appreciate the irony she felt in being told that her current disastrous circumstances had made her the perfect candidate for a job as a housekeeper.

Saz stood up and moved around the desk to perch on the front edge with her knees close to Maggie's. She glanced across at the door before leaning forward, to whisper, 'This is definitely not a housekeeping job, Maggie. I wouldn't insult someone like you with such a ludicrous proposition. It's purely administrative. But it's more complicated than it sounds. I didn't tell Roisin the whole story the other day. It would probably be more accurate to describe it as a live-in executive PA. We have a contract with a company that deals with all the mundane stuff like cleaning, gardening and laundry. A major part of your responsibilities will be organising and administering.'

Saz folded her arms as she looked down into Maggie's incredulous face.

'The most important qualification as far as we are concerned is the capacity for undivided loyalty and total discretion. You'll be expected to sign a contract, incorporating a confidentiality agreement which will be applicable during the term of employment and for an extended period afterwards.'

'A confidentiality agreement? That sounds ominous?'

'It's difficult to be more explicit, without giving too much away, at this stage,' said Saz.

At this stage? Giving too much away? What does that mean? I'm beginning to feel like Alice after she fell down the rabbit hole, thought Maggie.

'My client is a very…' Saz hesitated, '… a very private person. As you probably already know, social media has made it almost impossible for some people to protect their privacy. I don't know whether you've had any experience of it, but if you have, you'll know what I'm talking about.'

Maggie thought about Jack's endless messages but said nothing.

'Mobile phones with cameras, Twitter, Facebook, YouTube and all the rest. They've made the lives of people in the public eye an absolute hell.'

Saz looked angry. 'Of course, some of my clients love it. In fact, they chase after it. Revel in it. But he's not one of those. He's only just come into the spotlight, so to speak. To say that he loathes publicity would be an understatement. The only way that I've been able to convince him to agree to this arrangement has been by promising that I would get a legal undertaking for total confidentiality. By the way, the rest of the team have also been asked to sign confidentiality agreements, including yours truly.'

The rest of the team? Who on earth is this person she's calling her client? Maggie thought.

'The person taking this job will not only be responsible for running two homes, he or she will also be living in them, often with my client in residence. So you see our problem? The legal requirement of a confidentiality clause is absolutely essential.'

Maggie's stunned expression spoke volumes and Saz's eyes narrowed.

'If you're having a problem with any of this, I would appreciate it if you said so now. Then we can finish the interview here and save ourselves a lot of valuable time.'

There was a distinct note of impatience in her hitherto friendly manner.

'No, of course it's not a problem,' Maggie said hastily. 'I understand. At least, I think I do. I misunderstood what Roisin said. I thought that this was just a job for a holiday cover. I thought that you were looking for a house sitter, someone to look after a home while the owner was away on holiday?'

'It's a bit more than that.'

'I've got a few questions,' said Maggie. 'For example, is your client a politician or a foreign diplomat? Because if he is, the job might be dangerous. And, how big are the properties? What kind of salary are you thinking of, and how long is the contract likely to last?'

Saz moved back behind the desk to sit down and make more notes on the sheet of paper.

'Fair enough, but first, tell me why you came to the interview. With all your qualifications and experience, it's difficult to understand, frankly. Or are things really that bad in education right now?'

Maggie hesitated; it was the question that she had been asking herself since she left Rose's house.

'Last year, the university conducted what they rather euphemistically described as a rationalisation in my department, Humanities. What that actually meant was a drastic cut in the staff levels, and I was one of the unlucky ones.' She paused. 'Apparently, it was due to a combination of factors: reductions in funding and fewer applications from new students. It seems sixteenth-century English literature is not as popular as I would like to think. They said it wasn't personal,' she added with a note of irony. 'Anyway, the sudden loss of my income meant that I was eventually forced to give up my flat. So, in a very short space of time, I was not only jobless but homeless too.'

The sympathetic expression on the other woman's face provoked an unexpected surge of emotion in Maggie.

'It's not all bad,' she said quickly. 'Rose Cooper has very generously let me rent a room in her house until I find a job. It's been a life saver. I've applied for lots of lecturing jobs during the past six months, with no success so far. Academic budgets have been slashed to the bone all over the country. They seem to be favouring part-timers now, for obvious reasons. But, unfortunately, I need a full-time salary to keep a roof over my head.'

She met Saz's eyes. 'I have to be honest, this job is something that I would never have considered under normal circumstances. But by some strange coincidence, it seems to be offering a lot of the things that I happen to need urgently at this particular moment.'

'I have no idea how you've managed to pick yourself up after all you've been through. I'm bloody sure that I would have struggled,' Saz said admiringly.

And you only know the half of it, thought Maggie. 'It wasn't easy,' she said. 'All I want to do now is make a new start.'

'I can understand that. A change is as good as a rest, they say.' Saz was searching through the papers on her desk. 'But I have to tell you that you could be our dream candidate.'

She smiled at Maggie's doubtful expression. 'Don't look so surprised. You tick every one of my boxes, Maggie. And, after what you've just told me, it sounds as though we might be right for you. Looks like everyone's a winner. My client is away a lot, which is why we need somebody living in. You'll get plenty of time to yourself. As to the salary, my client places a huge value on his downtime. That means there will be generous financial rewards for the person taking care of that side of his life.'

'I've spent my entire life in teaching, so big financial rewards have never been high on my list of priorities,' Maggie said with a hint of haughtiness.

'Lucky you, is all I can say to that,' Saz replied drily. 'Money certainly features at the very top of mine.'

She stood up, stretching and yawning expansively. 'I'm going to speak to the boss later on tonight. He's in Germany at the moment. I'll call you first thing tomorrow and we'll organise a visit to both properties. It will give us more time to talk and settle the rest of your concerns. What do you say?'

Maggie got to her feet. 'Yes, I'd like that. Thank you.'

22

The following Thursday dawned mild and cloudy. Maggie waited in the porch of the house in Kentish Town, watching the seemingly endless procession of commuters and school children with a pang of envy. There's nothing like being unemployed to make you appreciate the hidden advantages of having a job, she thought. The feeling that you have somewhere to go, that you're expected somewhere, that you're making a contribution. The last few months had been very hard.

The sudden, strident blare of a car horn and the loud screeching of brakes heralded the arrival of a small black car on the other side of the road.

'Morning!'

Saz was waving excitedly through the driver's window. Maggie crossed the road and got into the passenger seat. Saz was dressed in tight-fitting jeans, a long baggy beige sweater and a dark blue body warmer. Her blonde hair was held off her face by the large sunglasses resting on the top of her head.

'This is my wife-of-the-country-squire look. What do you think?' She tipped her head coquettishly. 'Don't say anything. I know. It's not really me. I'm just trying to blend in with the locals.'

Maggie smiled, wondering how many locals would be wearing anything as expensive as Saz's outfit. She pointed at her own well-worn corduroy skirt, leather boots and pale blue fleece jacket.

'As you can see, I've never been that interested in clothes or fashion.'

Saz put the car into gear and they nosed into the stream of traffic blocking the high street.

'Quite right too. The fashion hacks would have us changing our style every five minutes if they could. It's madness.'

As she spoke a black cab crossed lanes and slowed down in front of them. Saz swore and braked.

'Sorry Maggie. I don't normally use that language at this time of the morning. But just look at this traffic. We ought to have left earlier.'

It took them more than an hour to get on to the M25 and another to reach the A12. Neither woman spoke, apart from the numerous colourful expletives emanating from Saz, followed by hastily muttered apologies and guilty sideways glances at her passenger. Even those stopped as they left the built up areas and reached the open countryside, passing signs welcoming them first to the County of Essex and later Suffolk.

'Have you ever been to Suffolk before?' asked Saz, without taking her eyes off the road.

'No, I haven't spent much time in the countryside at all.' Maggie said, gazing at the seemingly endless expanse of ploughed fields speeding past the window.

'What do you think of it?'

'I'm astonished by the size of the sky.' Maggie said with a little laugh, 'It's huge. We hardly see the sky in London. You can understand why painters like Turner and Constable chose to live in East Anglia.'

Saz nodded, 'The land is very flat here, as you can see. I think that's what makes the sky looks so big. And the light is extraordinary because it's on the east side of the country. The dawns are spectacular.'

Maggie watched a herd of cows grazing in a field, moving slowly across the grass. They were all facing in the same direction. She thought they looked peaceful and contented. The scene was timeless; a million miles away from the chaos of life in the city they had left a couple of hours ago. A small sigh escaped her and she relaxed against the seat.

Saz had turned the car east, towards the coast, and soon they were negotiating down winding, narrow lanes. Maggie shrank instinctively as huge farm vehicles lumbered past: they looked like prehistoric monsters, forcing them against the hedges.

'Breathe in,' Saz laughed. 'Tractors and combine harvesters are a regular hazard here. You'll get used to them. It's never a problem, though. You'll find that the drivers here are much more considerate than the cabbies and white van men in London.'

A few minutes later, they were bumping down an unmade cart track.

'Old Farm Lane, at last,' Saz announced in a voice full of relief. She checked her watch. 'Just over two hours and twenty minutes. Not bad, considering all the traffic. It was heavy everywhere today, North Circular, M25 and even the A12 at first.'

They turned right between two wide field gates which were propped open with logs, down a long gravel driveway and came to a halt in front of an old white timber-framed house with an attractive red-tiled roof.

Evergreen climbers reached over a trellised archway framing the front door which was painted in a distinctive shade of blue denim. The house was neither as large nor as imposing as Maggie had imagined. It looked like a family home rather than the country residence of a celebrity.

Once they were out of the car, Saz turned to Maggie.

'Grade II listed, nineteenth-century converted farmhouse,' she said airily. 'First impressions?'

'Very nice,' said Maggie, staring up at the windows.

'Very nice? Only very nice? My God, you really are Mrs Understatement, aren't you?' Saz laughed, 'Come on, let's go inside.'

She unlocked the front door and switched off the alarm before ushering Maggie into a large square hall with a dark blue carpet that looked as though it had been there for years. She threw open one of the white-painted doors.

'Let's start the grand tour of this very nice house then, shall we?'

She led Maggie into the beamed lounge with windows on two sides offering long views over the garden and fields just visible beyond a distant perimeter fence.

The room was lined with crowded bookshelves, two large shabby sofas and three glass-fronted cabinets containing an assorted collection of ceramic ornaments and glassware. The wood-burning stove in the wide inglenook fireplace looked as though it hadn't been lit for a long time.

Maggie was surprised by the homely, understated atmosphere. It was not at all what she had envisaged as a home for the mysterious, reclusive celebrity Saz had talked about.

She followed Saz into a large well-fitted kitchen which had been extended into a Victorian-style conservatory, in the centre of which stood a large circular dining table covered with a blue and white spotted oilcloth. Saz was raising a couple of the blinds to show Maggie the views across the long garden.

Upstairs, there were three double bedrooms and a large study also lined with crammed bookshelves. Maggie noticed the names of many well-known classics and an impressive range of contemporary writers. Somebody likes reading as much as I do, she thought, with a flicker of pleasure.

'Come on, there's more to show you downstairs,' Saz called from the landing.

The house was built in an L shape with a single-storey self-contained annexe at the back which was accessed from the main house via a locked door in a utility room next to the kitchen.

'As you can see, this part of the house is completely self-contained. It was newly fitted and furnished a few months ago.

It's even got its own front door if you don't want to go through the main house.' Saz explained as she showed Maggie the double bedroom with a small en-suite bathroom, a cosy lounge with a study area leading off it and a small, fully equipped kitchen.

Saz turned to face Maggie. 'Well? What do you think now? Is it still just nice?' she said, half-jokingly.

'I don't know what to say,' Maggie said. 'It's lovely. Very quiet and peaceful.' She stared thoughtfully out of the window, 'It's very different.'

Saz unlocked the patio doors in the lounge and stepped out onto a small paved patio area.

'Come and see the gardens, Maggie. You've got full access to the main garden as well as this little private area, so you won't feel completely cut off.'

Saz waved at the view with a sweep of her arm.

'It's a great atmosphere for writing, isn't it?'

She searched Maggie's face anxiously.

Maggie nodded. She felt as though she was being carried along by a tidal wave of enthusiasm. There was so much to consider, to process.

'This garden is absolutely stunning in the summer. You're not seeing it at its best today. Everything is beginning to go over.' Saz said.

The two women stood side by side, enjoying the view, until the sound of Saz's mobile sliced through the silence. She walked away across the lawn, talking quietly.

Maggie went back into the lounge and sat on the sofa, trying to imagine how she would feel if she was living there alone.

Will I be able to cope with all this isolation and silence? What will it feel like at night? It must be pitch black here without street lights. Where are the neighbours? What about internet access?

Saz came bursting through the patio doors.

'There you are! Sorry about that. I think we're done, aren't we? Look, it's twelve o'clock and I don't know about you, but I'm absolutely gasping for a coffee. There's a lovely little pub in the village. It's about fifteen minutes' walk and a lot less in the car. Come on.'

While Saz reset the alarm and locked all the doors, Maggie looked up at the house, fixing the details in her memory. It would have been nice to take photographs; but out of the question, after all the dire warnings about guarding the privacy of Saz's mysterious client.

'Well, what's the verdict?' Saz asked with a touch of impatience as they drove towards the pub.

'It's a beautiful house. What's the other property like?' Maggie said after a small hesitation.

'Oh, that's very different. A first-floor apartment in St John's Wood.'

Saz was parking in front of a picturesque pink-washed public house with a sagging thatched roof.

'Have you been completely put off by what you've seen so far?' she asked as Maggie followed her towards the front door of the pub.

As soon as he caught sight of them, the face of the large shaven-headed man behind the bar was split by a wide grin, revealing a wide gap at the front where two teeth were missing.

'Hi Saz! How's *el jefe*? Is he here?'

'Hi Billy. He's fine and no, he's not here. He's working. What can I say? Is it too early for one of your delicious toasties? Maggie and I are hoping to get back to London before it gets too dark.'

'Never too early for you, Saz. Coffee? What's your fancy? Cheese, ham, tuna? I can even do you our new special: a fish finger sarnie with salad and mayo.' He said proudly.

'Ham with plenty of mustard for me. What about you, Maggie?' said Saz.

'Cheese would be lovely, thank you.'

After they had seated themselves at a table by the window, Saz laid a hand lightly on Maggie's arm. 'OK. Fire away. Put me out of my misery, tell me what's troubling you.'

'Well, first I'd like you to tell me a bit more about your client. Then I want to know how the confidentiality agreement will work. I'm wondering how will it impact on me and on my life. In other words, how much will I be allowed to tell my friends?'

Saz sighed. 'Look, Maggie, I think I may have given you the wrong impression. First, let me put your mind at rest. My client is thirty-eight, single and he lives alone. No wife, no partner and no children. Not even a dog. Or a cat for that matter.'

She chuckled. 'His excuse is that he's never in one place long enough to develop a proper relationship with anything or anybody. I tell him that he's just being too ruddy picky and antisocial. He doesn't smoke and he rarely drinks. In fact, he's one of those irritating keep-fit junkies who puts the rest of us to shame. He spends most of his downtime on his own. He calls it recharging his batteries'. She waggled two fingers on both hands to indicate speech marks. 'Which, I have to say, is a lot more common than you might think for people like him. I've had dealings with quite a few of them over the years. And to be fair, some of them really do need that isolation sometimes. Otherwise,' she clicked her fingers, 'they self-combust and go into meltdown. You've probably read about them in the papers. Anyway, I hope I haven't made him sound too disagreeable. He's not. But when he's not working, he wants to be as anonymous and quiet as possible.'

Saz touched Maggie's arm with a reassuring smile. 'Don't worry about the confidentiality agreement. It's nothing more than a legal mechanism to try and guarantee his privacy as far as is reasonably possible. Which is not very far. If you're in the public eye, you only have to tie up your shoe laces differently for someone to make a video of it on their mobile phone and put it up on YouTube for the rest of the world to make snide comments.'

She took an enthusiastic bite out of her sandwich.

'This is a new venture for us too. Over the past twelve months, I've been struggling to deal with all the domestic stuff myself. We've been friends since we were at college together. Totally platonic, I hasten to add. I've been married and divorced twice since then. The fact is that I have a business to run and I barely have time to organise my own private life, let alone his.'

She took another bite and a large gulp of her coffee.

'All the security is organised by professionals, either arranged by the company he happens to be working for at the time, or by us. You won't be expected to deal with anything even remotely dangerous, I promise. I'm not a complete lunatic, even if I look like one.'

Maggie flushed. 'Of course not. It's just that after our first meeting, I've been turning things over in my head and coming to some very wild conclusions.'

'There's nothing wild about my client, I can assure you. He is a very normal, down-to-earth kind of guy. By the way, he prefers to do his own cooking, so you won't have to do any of that either.' She paused, suddenly serious, 'Basically, your job is to field all the domestic crap. Order a bit of shopping, now and then. That sort of thing. There's an account already set up, so that's not complicated either. You can order all your own shopping at the same time.'

Saz was talking quickly. 'One of the team will let you know when and where he's going to be. And don't forget that he's often away for weeks on end, so you're going to have a lot of time to yourself. I hope you like your own company.'

'Oh, that's not a problem,' Maggie said.

'You won't have to stay put in London or Suffolk, either. If you decide to stay in London, you could just come up here occasionally to check everything's OK or vice versa. You'll have full use of the car, obviously. It's indispensable when you're here. Buses are an endangered species in this part of the world.'

Saz drained her coffee cup and got to her feet.

'Anyway, talking of London, I think we should be getting back, don't you? If we get a move on, we'll miss the worst of the school traffic.'

Maggie watched Saz go to the bar to speak to Billy. She picked up her bag and jacket. There must have been other applicants more suitable for this job than a redundant, middle-aged academic like me, surely? Why is she so keen on me?

Saz was in the car park talking on her mobile again. She held up the car keys and Maggie took them and went to open the car as she overheard Saz say,

'Yes, she does. Well, I think she does, it's hard to tell. No. OK. See you in a bit.'

As they drove back to London, Maggie was comparing the claustrophobic attic room waiting for her in Kentish Town with the house they had just left and the annexe she would have to herself. There was no contest.

On a sudden impulse, she turned to Saz, 'When would you expect me to start?'

Saz turned quickly, with a face wreathed in smiles.

'Straight away. We'll talk to the boss when we get to London.'

It was Maggie's turn to look startled. 'I thought you said he was out of the country?'

'He was. He's flown in from Munich for a couple of days for a publicity thing. I was talking to him, just now. It's the perfect opportunity for you two to meet, and, with a bit of luck, we might be able to tie this whole thing up.'

23

It was early evening when they drove into the almost deserted car park of a large apartment block in St John's Wood in North London.

The impressive building was set well back from the road, behind a wall of tall evergreen shrubs. Lime green conifers, lit from below with spotlights, pierced the shadows like glowing beacons.

Saz got out of the car to stretch with a loud yawn. 'Hallelujah. Home at last. Almost!'

Maggie tried to ignore the flutters of anxiety in the pit of her stomach. She took a deep breath as they reached the large glass doors and Saz shook her head in mock reproof, squeezing her hand. 'Courage, mon brave,' she said with a wink.

The white head of the porter was just visible behind the desk. He was engrossed in a newspaper, taking occasional sips from a large white mug emblazoned with the word Arsenal in large red letters.

Saz spoke into the intercom panel. 'Jim, it's me, Saz.'

He frowned suspiciously at the door, nodded and went back to his paper as the buzzer sounded.

Once inside the spacious entrance hall, Saz stretched again, flexing her spine with a groan. 'I'm getting old and creaky,' she said as she tapped the face of her watch. 'One hour, fifty-five minutes. Not bad eh? Considering all the congestion on the North Circular. Is that road ever empty?'

She linked an arm through Maggie's. 'Come on, let's get it over with!' she said as she led the way up the thickly carpeted staircase and along the corridor.

'Don't look so worried. You two are going to get on like a house on fire. Trust me.' She tapped the side of her nose. 'I have an instinct.'

Maggie's stomach lurched as she watched Saz press the doorbell to flat number three.

The door was opened by a very tall, dark-haired man dressed in shabby black jeans and a stained sweatshirt. His long pale feet were bare.

Saz stood on tip-toe as he leaned down to kiss her lightly on the cheek.

'Hi Rob, this is Maggie Savernake. Maggie, this is Rob Hunter,' she said.

Dark grey eyes regarded Maggie solemnly as he held out a large ink-stained hand. 'Hi.'

Maggie's hand disappeared. 'Hello,' she said, trying to hide her astonishment. Was this the mystery celebrity? He looked so normal, so ordinary, apart from his height. His voice was deep and resonant. Maggie wondered if he was a singer.

The apartment was located on the corner of the building, with the two exterior walls of the lounge glazed from floor to ceiling, which created a disconcerting impression of the room being open to the elements. Beyond the windows, Maggie saw a wrap-around balcony with some garden furniture and a couple of large, empty plant pots. A huge corner sofa upholstered in a light oatmeal fabric and two matching wing-backed chairs were grouped around a long glass coffee table, with newspapers and magazines heaped at one end.

The decor was immaculate but completely lacking in personality. Maggie thought that it must be what a luxury hotel might look like. Apart from the open rucksack, spilling its contents untidily across the sofa, it looked and felt as though no-one lived there. She stared at the pile of crumpled clothes and books as Rob Hunter sprang forward to gather up his belongings and disappear quickly through a door.

Saz threw her bag down on a chair and walked towards a tray of drinks and glasses on one of the shelves. She held up a glass to Maggie, 'Drink?'

'Nothing for me, thank you.'

Maggie perched on the edge of the seat of one of the chairs as she watched Saz take a bottle of wine out of a cupboard and open it.

Rob reappeared and folded himself into the corner of the sofa with the ankle of one long leg resting on the opposite knee. There was a shadow of dark stubble along his jaw. Maggie returned his friendly smile and looked away.

In spite of his unkempt appearance, there was a curious stillness about him, an aura of calm that was almost palpable.

She placed her bag on the floor and settled more comfortably into the chair.

'Well?' demanded Saz as she crossed the room, holding a glass of wine, 'Are you surprised, Maggie?'

She sat at the other end of the sofa and eased off her shoes with loud groans of relief.

'Surprised?' Maggie echoed, wondering what was coming next.

Rob frowned and shook his head warningly at Saz.

She ignored him. 'Are you surprised that the person we have been talking about is Rob Hunter?'

Maggie glanced at Rob with colour rising in her cheeks.

'Rob Hunter?' she said slowly.

'Yes. Rob Hunter,' Saz repeated, with her eyebrows raised.

'I'm sorry but I don't...'

Saz's mouth had formed into a disbelieving O.

'What? Are you saying, that you don't know who he is? You've got to be kidding,' she yelped.

There was an explosion of laughter from Rob as he threw back his head, revealing a set of flawless white teeth.

'For God's sake, Maggie. You must be the only person in the whole country who doesn't recognise Rob Hunter. Where on earth have you been? Don't you watch TV or go to the cinema?'

Saz sounded genuinely offended.

'I'm really sorry,' Maggie mumbled, 'I can't remember the last time I went to the cinema or the theatre for that matter. And I don't have a TV.'

'You don't have a TV?' Saz looked horrified.

'I'm sorry.' Maggie said.

'Stop apologising, Maggie,' Rob said, 'Saz is over-reacting as usual.'

Saz noticed the expression on his face as he spoke. For some reason he seemed to like Maggie's total lack of knowledge about him and his work.

'See what I mean? She's absolutely perfect,' she said.

'On the basis of what we've heard so far, she is,' he agreed. 'But are we perfect for her, that's the main question?'

He looked enquiringly at Maggie.

'I hear you're worried about the confidentiality agreement?'

Maggie ran a nervous hand through her hair and realised with horror that the last time she'd looked in a mirror was about twelve hours before. What on earth do I look like? What does he think of me? Not just an ignorant philistine, but a scarecrow as well.

She made a clumsy attempt to tidy her hair. She was finding it very difficult to reconcile the man sitting in front of her with her preconceived notions about celebrity, which were based on what she had gleaned from listening to the gossip of her students and Rose's children. This softly spoken, gentle man didn't seem to conform in any respect to the people they talked about.

'I suppose you don't need confidentiality clauses in academia?' he said.

'There are strict codes of conduct regarding behaviour towards students and suchlike,' she replied, 'but I've never heard of the type of gagging order that Saz mentioned. I'm probably being very naive, but I've always thought that it would be taken as read that an employee didn't discuss his or her employer with anybody.'

'In a perfect world that would be the case,' Rob said, 'but unfortunately for people like me, this is not a perfect world. There are many people and organisations who are only too willing to pay a lot of money for information about people in the public eye. You've probably read about some of the more sensational cases.'

'But surely personal integrity and a sense of loyalty and responsibility to your employer comes before monetary considerations?'

'You'd think so, but it doesn't,' Saz interjected. 'And we haven't mentioned the fans yet. Believe it or not, there are members of the public who seem to have an incomprehensible determination to confuse fiction with real life.'

'What do you mean?'

'They don't seem to be able to separate Rob from the fictional parts he plays. It results in some very weird behaviour from some of them. They can make life a bit hazardous, sometimes.' Saz said.

'Enough!' Rob held his hand up, looking anxiously at Maggie. 'We're frightening the poor girl off. We're making it sound much worse than it really is.'

Maggie's eyes flickered between them. They were describing a life that she knew absolutely nothing about and yet, what they were hinting at sounded a lot like the harassment she received from Jack Millfield. She wondered whether Rob had ever been followed in the street. Or even attacked? The memories of that terrible night were never far from her thoughts.

Rob was watching her intently.

'I understand why you're finding it difficult to get your head round all of this, Maggie. Especially since you've obviously had no contact with our crazy world.'

She wondered if he was making fun of her.

'I can promise you that I would never dream of talking about my employer to anyone. With or without a confidentiality clause,' she said primly.

The corners of Rob's mouth twitched. 'I'm sure you wouldn't. But if you invited a stranger to share your home with you, you'd ask for some kind of reference to safeguard your privacy, wouldn't you?'

'That's hardly likely at the moment. I haven't got a home.'

'Who knows what's round the corner for any of us? Things happen. Often when we least expect them.' Rob said, suddenly serious.

Maggie remembered her shock when she saw the hatred on Jack's face before he hit her.

'What did you think of Suffolk?' Rob asked after a pause.

'Do you mean your house or the county in general?'

'The house. I don't think you've had enough time to see the entire county today, have you?'

Maggie blushed, regretting her facetious response. 'The house is beautiful. It's very peaceful there.' she said.

Rob nodded as he glanced at his watch. 'Shit! Sorry,' he muttered apologetically. 'Is that the time? My appointment's at 7.30 and I still haven't showered. Can you show Maggie the other flat and give her the paperwork, Saz?'

He levered himself off the sofa, and held out his hand.

'My apologies. I've got to go. Thanks very much for coming.'

She watched him cross the lounge in long strides and close the door quietly behind him before turning to Saz.

'I hope that I didn't put my foot in it. I thought that it was better to be honest.'

Saz looked puzzled. 'What are you talking about?'

'When I said that I didn't recognise him. I hope I haven't offended him.'

Saz looked very amused, 'Rob loves not being recognised. I think you probably clinched it when you said that.'

She put her glass on a table. 'Come on, I'll show you the rest and we'll call it a day. We're all exhausted.'

Saz opened the door to the kitchen; the black granite worktops were immaculate and gleaming. It reminded Maggie of an exhibition in a showroom rather than a place where people actually prepared meals.

'There are two bedrooms in this apartment, both en-suite. Rob has one, and the other is for guests,' explained Saz as Maggie followed her into the hall where she unlocked a door which led into the neighbouring apartment.

'We've rented this other flat on a very long-term lease. This door has just been put in. The flat's a smaller version of Rob's. He uses one of the bedrooms as his study when he's in London, but the rest of it is yours.'

She opened a glass door leading onto a small balcony. 'Personally, I prefer this flat,' she said. 'It faces west, so you get the sun all the afternoon. What do you think?'

'The attic room where I am living at the moment is not much bigger than one of these cupboards,' Maggie replied ruefully.

'I am sure that's not true,' said Saz.

'The house in Suffolk has got a very different feel to it. It's homelier, somehow,' Maggie observed thoughtfully as they went back into Rob's apartment.

'Rob inherited that house from his grandmother. He spent a lot of time there when he was a kid. Anyway, you like the flat and you like the farmhouse. What do you think of Rob? Even if you don't know who he is.'

'He seems very normal and…'

'And?'

'Very tall.'

'Six feet four inches in his bare feet,' said Saz. 'He gets snow on the top of his head in the winter.'

She opened her briefcase and took out a large brown envelope. 'Rob's here until Tuesday. I'll phone you tomorrow and depending on what you decide, we could arrange one more meeting to sign the contracts before he goes back to Germany. If you've got any queries, call me on the mobile, my number is on here.'

She handed Maggie a business card. 'I'll be at home all evening.'

Rob reappeared dressed for the street in a battered brown leather bomber jacket with a very long black scarf wound untidily around his neck. Heavy walking boots made him look even taller. He stood in front of them with his solemn grey eyes trained on Maggie.

'How did it go? Has Saz told you that you can bring your own stuff with you, furniture and suchlike?'

'Thank you, Mr Hunter.'

'Rob.'

'Rob. Most of my things are in storage. I might bring a few pictures, a chair and my books. I do have quite a lot of books.'

'Maggie's going to take the paperwork home tonight and I'll phone her in the morning. I've suggested that if we're all prepared to go ahead, we could meet up one more time before you go back to Germany.'

Saz gazed up at Rob with her head tilted to one side. 'How's that for a plan?'

'Great,' said Rob frowning, as his mobile rang and he scanned the incoming message. 'Got to go. Ray is downstairs. We're due at the studio in half an hour.'

He gave them a mock salute and left.

Maggie put the brown envelope into her bag. 'I'd better be going too, Saz. I've got a lot to think about and not much time.'

'If you give me a minute, I'll give you a lift to the station. I'll just check that everything is switched off, and then I'll lock up. Rob's always forgetting, you'll need to bear that in mind.' Saz called over her shoulder as she went into the kitchen.

24

When Maggie got back to the house in Kentish Town, she put her head around the kitchen door to find Seb, Roisin and Phoebe sitting in a row on the sofa in the kitchen watching TV.

'It's me,' she said to the backs of their heads.

'Hi Maggie, Mum's out, I'm not sure where she's gone. How'd it go? There's a bit of leftover veggie lasagne in the oven, if you want it.'

Seb hadn't taken his eyes off the TV.

'Thanks, I'll be down in a couple of minutes,' Maggie replied as she closed the door quietly behind her.

Upstairs in her room, she opened the large brown envelope and took out the covering letter, a job specification and a copy of the contract. The confidentiality agreement was on a separate sheet.

There was nothing new. The paperwork simply confirmed everything that Saz and Rob had already told her. The duties were minimal, consisting of little more than those of a *de facto* house sitter. She smiled; it was exactly what Rose had said when Roisin first mentioned the job.

Maggie scanned the pages. She was entitled to a month's unpaid leave which had to be taken in two separate fortnights and a dedicated mobile phone which had an encrypted number.

The rather grandly named Team Hunter were listed in alphabetical order. Ray Brookes, Publicity; Felix Green, Agent; Sarah Jane Hodges, Manager; Kellie Wan, Personal Trainer.

Maggie imagined her name being added to the list. Dr Maggie Savernake, House Sitter? She grinned. That will be interesting on my CV.

*

She was still wide awake at 2am. The sickly yellow glow from the lights in the street below filtered through the small window above her head and filled the stuffy room with eerie shadows.

She tossed on the uncomfortable bed and thought about the immaculate, airy apartment in St John's Wood and the relief she would feel when she liberated her beloved books from their boxes.

Was she trying to escape from this tiny attic room and all the horrors that had led her to it? Was she being fair to Saz and Rob to accept the job for negative reasons? How would she cope with a solitary existence after the hectic buzz of teaching?

She knew that she had never found it easy to cope with change or any disruption to her life. But what alternative did she have at this moment?

Maggie stared up at the ceiling. Perhaps she ought to treat it like a challenge, an adventure, a character-building exercise? She thought of David, launching himself into unknown territories with the optimism of a man half his age. What would David tell her to do? She heard his reassuring voice in her head, 'Go on, give it a go, Maggie, it might be fun.'

The insistent ring of her mobile phone awoke her a few hours later. She squinted suspiciously at the unfamiliar mobile number flashing on the screen, then at the time. It was only ten minutes past eight.

She hesitated before pressing the green button, waiting for the voice at the other end, with her heart racing.

'Maggie?' Saz Hodge's unmistakable gravelly voice was as cheery as ever.

'Saz,' Maggie felt weak with relief.

'Have I called at a bad time?'

'No, no, not at all. I was in the bathroom.'

She struggled into a sitting position and rested her back uncomfortably against the cold wall.

'I'm calling to offer you the job,' Saz bubbled excitedly.

Maggie swung her legs over the side of the bed.

'Maggie? Are you still there?'

'Yes. It's just that I didn't expect to get the offer quite so quickly.'

'But I thought I told you that I would call this morning? You're absolutely perfect, Maggie. Exactly what we've been looking for, and this job's a perfect fit for you too. Isn't it?'

Maggie stood up, rubbing the small of her back. 'What did Mr Hunter say?'

'He was curious to know why someone with your qualifications would even consider a position like this. So I told him what you told me.'

Maggie's eyes were heavy with sleep.

'Well? What have you decided?' Saz demanded.

Maggie glanced around the shabby attic room. How much longer could she bear to live like this while she waited for a non-existent job to appear? How much longer before her savings began to run out?

'Maggie, are you still there? Is there a problem? Is it the contract? The confidentiality clause?'

'No, no, of course not. The paperwork is very straightforward. It's just that I don't know, I'm not sure if...'

'What? Whether the job is the right thing for you? Rob wondered if you would say that. I think we all agree that it's a massive change for all of us. Look, why don't we have a three-month probationary period, until the end of January? This is a new experience. We need to see how it's going to work.'

Maggie couldn't hold back her sigh of relief. The option of

having a potential exit made her feel better. The anxiety was ebbing away.

'Yes. I would prefer that. Thank you, Saz. Thank you very much.'

'Don't thank me. It was Rob's idea. He can be very sensitive, sometimes. For a man. God, I'm just relieved. I've been tearing my hair out. You can't imagine. We must get together again before Rob flies back to Germany. What about tomorrow, Saturday?'

'OK.'

'I'm going to call Rob now. He'll be delighted. I'll get back to you. He's probably gone for a run in Regent's Park.'

*

After showering and dressing, Maggie went downstairs to find that Rose and her children had already gone their separate ways, leaving the usual post breakfast chaos spread over the table and worktops.

She cleared everything away and loaded the dishwasher before going up to her room to get her laptop, which she took back downstairs to check her emails while she had breakfast.

The emails didn't take long. They were mostly junk, with a couple of the usual vague invitations from one of her friends or an ex-colleague.

'Must get together for a coffee or a meal one of these days.'

Lately, even those had begun to dry up. Which on reflection, Maggie thought as she buttered her slice of toast, is no bad thing under the present circumstances. It means there are fewer people to ask the questions that I won't be free to answer anymore. She bit into the toast and gazed at the seascape on her screensaver.

A new job, a new home, a salary and plenty of free time to write. What more could anyone ask for? Sounds like something out of a film. She laughed out loud. 'Talking of films, let's see what Mr Rob Hunter has done to turn him into such a superstar,' she said as she typed his name into the search engine.

'Robert Aiden Hunter, born on 1st November 1968, in a small village in Norfolk, the eldest of three children. His father still works as a plumber and his mother is a primary school assistant. He left school at sixteen to work with his father for two years, then won a scholarship to a London drama school.'

It looked as though Rob had had a moderately successful stage career before he was cast in a long-running TV series. Small parts in a couple of feature films had followed, before he had landed this latest leading role in a Hollywood thriller. There were a few clips from some of his performances and after watching for several minutes, Maggie realised that he was an accomplished and versatile actor.

She closed the laptop. Maintaining Rob's privacy would be a challenge. Perhaps even greater than Saz had suggested.

*

Maggie arrived at the apartment in St John's Wood at three o'clock the following afternoon, to find Saz waiting for her at the top of the main staircase.

There was no sign of Rob.

They spent nearly an hour going over the contract before Maggie signed it. Then Saz handed over what she described as a state-of-the-art mobile phone, explaining that it was already programmed with all the various contact numbers, including Rob's. This was followed with a bunch of keys and a sheet of paper with a series of codes for the burglar alarms. She asked Maggie if she would like to move in the following week and what she wanted to bring with her.

'I don't think I want to get much out of storage, apart from my books. The rest can stay where it is for the time being. By the way, I found Rob on the Web this morning.' Maggie lowered her voice to a whisper. 'I was shocked. He must think that I'm some kind of alien who has just landed from another planet.'

'I think it's us who are the creatures from another planet.'

Rob Hunter was standing in the open doorway in a shabby T-shirt and torn tracksuit bottoms. He was carrying his socks and trainers in one hand.

Maggie flushed. 'I hope you don't think that I was spying on you. I was trying to see whether I'd seen anything that you've been in.'

'And have you?'

She shook her head apologetically.

Rob grinned. 'Why am I not surprised? By the way, don't forget that ninety-nine point nine percent of what you read on the Web is either inaccurate speculation or malicious gossip. It has absolutely nothing to do with me or my life.'

He turned to Saz. 'The gym downstairs was empty, so I grabbed the opportunity, as you can see,' he tugged at his top. 'Have I missed anything?'

'I was telling Maggie that I'll get someone to go and pick up her stuff from Kentish Town and the storage depot and bring it all over here next week. Once we get all that organised, she could move in properly next weekend, when you're back in Germany. I've also given her a phone, a set of keys and a list.'

'Ah yes, the dreaded lists, where would we all be without the lists?' Rob said gravely.

'Ignore him, Maggie. It's the only way I stay sane. By the way,' Saz waved the contracts at Rob, 'you've got to sign these. Don't forget.'

'Can I have a glass of water first?'

'Let me get it, I ought to find out where everything is,' Maggie said.

'In that case, I'll have another black coffee, please. No sugar,' said Saz. 'The coffee pot is on the worktop.'

By the time Maggie returned, Rob had disappeared again

and Saz was tapping furiously on her laptop. She didn't look up as Maggie put the tray on the coffee table and went to stand by the window. It looked as though the meeting had come to an end while she was in the kitchen.

'If that's all, Saz, I think I'll go,' she said, picking up her coat and bag.

Saz looked up vaguely, 'Sorry? Oh yes, of course. Absolutely. We're done here anyway, aren't we? I'll leave a signed copy of the contract on the worktop in your flat when I leave. Rob still hasn't signed it.' She rolled her eyes in a show of exasperation. 'Did you give me your bank details?'

Maggie nodded.

'And I've given you a set of keys, and the list, haven't I? We'll deal with the Suffolk end once you're settled in here.'

Maggie followed Saz to the front door.

'I'll text you when I know which day the men can collect your bits. I hope that's everything? Anyhow, you've got the phone and all the numbers now, you can always call if there's a problem.'

Maggie turned at the top of the main staircase.

'Say thank you and goodbye to Rob for me, Saz. See you next week?'

Saz leaned forward and kissed her on both cheeks. 'I'm glad you've agreed to join us, Maggie. I'm really looking forward to working with you.'

Downstairs in the busy street, daylight was fading fast and there was a distinct chill in the air. Maggie walked quickly, preparing the speech she would give to Rose and the children.

When she'd asked Saz how she should tell her friends about the new job, Saz had laughed.

'You've got the job because Rob and I both think that an intelligent person like you is more than capable of dealing with everything. Obviously, you'll have to say something to friends and family, otherwise your life will become an impossible web of deception. You can say that you're working for Rob, just as long as you don't divulge any personal stuff. Focus on protecting his privacy. Not revealing his whereabouts, plans, or any personal information of any description. You'll soon learn to recognise the real lowlife, press, paparazzi and suchlike. Ray, the publicity guy, will give you a few tips. Don't worry! I've got a very good feeling about all this!'

Maggie walked towards the tube station, lost in her thoughts. *Whatever Saz says, it's not going to be easy.* She was still trying to imagine what Rose would say when she stopped at a small supermarket to buy a frozen pizza.

Following the sound of voices from the basement, Maggie was surprised to find Rose energetically kneading a large lump of dough on the kitchen table. Seb, Roisin and Phoebe were sitting in a row on the battered sofa at the other end of the room, seemingly engrossed in a very noisy talent show on TV.

There was a smudge of flour on Rose's nose when she looked up.

'Hi Mags, been shopping?'

'No.' Maggie put the plastic carrier bag down at the other end of the long table. 'I didn't expect to find you all at home. I've got some news,' she said as she took the pizza box out of the bag.

'Oh?' Rose went back to her pummelling.

'I've got a new job.'

Maggie took off her coat, folded it and laid it carefully over the back of a chair, acutely aware that four pairs of eyes were now watching her expectantly.

'Great! That is good news. Where?' asked Rose.

'I'll be leaving you all in peace, at last.' Maggie said as she began taking the pizza out of its box, removing the cellophane film and lifting it away from the polystyrene base.

'Leaving us? I don't understand.' Rose was rubbing her floury hands on the seat of her jeans.

'It's that job that Roisin mentioned.'

'What? The house sitter job?' Seb vaulted over the back of the sofa and came to stand in front of Maggie. 'Where's the house?'

'Well, it's a bit more than a house sitter. It's working for a high profile...' she paused, '... a celebrity, I suppose you could call him.'

Rose moved around the table and came to stand alongside her son. 'And?'

'His name is Rob Hunter,' said Maggie quickly, 'Can I put this pizza in the oven?'

'Rob Hunter! I don't believe you!'

Phoebe was standing on the seat of the sofa.

'Rob Hunter? Are you sure? But he's in that new film. Oh my god. Oh my god.' She was stabbing the buttons on her mobile phone while Maggie watched her in alarm.

'Phoebe, what are you doing? Who are you texting?'

'You're going to live with Rob Hunter? You little minx.'

Rose was squealing louder than her daughter.

Their reaction was much worse than Maggie had expected. 'Not with him! Of course I'm not going to live with him! I'll be working for him and living in. But not living with him, at least not in the way that you all seem to think!'

The sofa was groaning ominously. Phoebe was treating it like a trampoline, screaming, 'Oh my god, Oh my god, Rob Hunter! Oh my god. I don't believe it.'

Maggie slid the pizza back onto the polystyrene base, fearful of dropping it.

'This is ridiculous. What on earth has got into you all? I need to earn some money and this job comes with a decent salary and accommodation. I might even be able to save some money. Why don't you focus on that?'

'But have you met him? I mean have you actually spoken to him?' Rose's eyes were wide.

'Of course I've met him.'

'And is he as sexy in real life?' sighed Phoebe, wrapping her arm around Maggie's neck.

'I don't know.' Maggie bent to check the dial on the oven. 'Can I please put this pizza in the oven for ten minutes, Rose? I've got so much to do upstairs. I'm moving out next week.'

'Next week? Wow, that's quick! Where? Where are you going?'

'Oh not far,' Maggie said while she peered at the cooking instructions on the back of the pizza box.

'Where exactly?' Rose put her hand on Maggie's arm as though to emphasise the question.

'I can't remember the exact address.' Maggie bent to put the pizza into the oven, and moved to stand behind the now empty sofa. 'What were you all watching? Has it finished?'

25

By the time Jack Millfield and his new Spanish wife Ana arrived for the party, she was close to tears.

They were two hours late because Ana hadn't been able to decide what to wear and Jack had made the serious mistake of opening a bottle of wine while he waited for her; with the inevitable result that when she finally emerged, wearing the first outfit that she'd tried on, he was too drunk to drive. She had been obliged to take the wheel of his expensive sports car and negotiate the crowded streets across London for the first time in her life, with Jack barking angry, incoherent instructions beside her.

The informal drinks party was the idea of Dominic Goldman, who had also known Jack at university. The party was being held in a duplex apartment over an antique shop in the Fulham Road owned by Dominic's new partner, Saul Myerson, a graphic designer.

After his usual effusive welcome, Dominic led Jack and Ana into the lounge where he introduced them to a large crowd of already very animated guests. Jack struggled to contain his irritation when he noticed Dominic hauling Rose Cooper out of the crowd to introduce her to Ana.

'Ana, meet Rose Cooper, she's another old friend from our uni days. Rose, this is Jack's beautiful new wife, Ana.'

Rose held out her hand, with a cursory glance at the willowy figure towering over everybody, including her husband.

'Congratulations, Jack.'

'Rose?' Jack's eyes were on the crowded room behind her.

'Go and get yourselves something to drink before they finish it all. We've put the food and the wine in the kitchen,' yelled Dominic above the din, waving his glass in the direction of a doorway. 'They're like a pack of thirsty elephants at a watering hole. It must be the cold. We'll have to send out for reinforcements.'

Jack moved, glad to escape Rose's knowing, amused expression; she hadn't taken her eyes off them since they arrived.

When he returned to the lounge several minutes later, she was still deep in conversation with Ana. Jack's expression hardened. He knew that Rose worked with Maggie but he wasn't sure how close they were. How much does she know? Is she here to suss Ana out and report back? He drained his glass and sucked the wine through his teeth. Who gives a monkey's? That bitch has probably told her a pack of lies anyway.

He went back to the kitchen. The noise level seemed to be rising exponentially every time the doorbell sounded. He stood with his back to the room, glowering at a rack of herbs and spices.

Why did we accept this invitation in the first place? Who cares who Dominic has shacked up with? We're never going to socialise with them. So what's the fucking point?

He checked the array of drinks, finally selecting a half empty bottle of rosé, and filled his glass to the brim, watching without interest as the liquid splashed onto the floor. He walked through the puddle of wine he had caused and went back to the lounge where Dominic was standing on a chair and holding his glass above his head.

'Quiet, everybody! Let's drink a toast to Jack and his beautiful new wife.'

Ana was standing next to Saul looking at a large painting propped up against the wall. A loud chorus of 'Jack and Ana' prompted Jack to go and stand next to her.

Dominic jumped off the chair and came towards them. 'Jack, has Rose told you the latest news?'

'What news?' Jack drawled, aware that several heads had turned in their direction.

'Maggie Savernake's going to work for Rob Hunter.'

'What? *The* Rob Hunter?' said an amazed female voice.

Dominic nodded.

Jack was finding it increasingly difficult to focus. 'Don't know what you expect me to say to that Dom. Except, who the fuck is Rob Hunter?'

He slurred his words with a crooked smile.

'Rob Hunter. Rob Hunter, the actor. He's been on TV and he's in that new film. You must have heard of him.' Dominic said.

Jack picked an olive out of a dish and placed it in his mouth with exaggerated care, trying to organise his muddled thoughts. Why had Maggie left her job at the university? Why was she working with an actor?

'Jack?'

Ana slipped a hand into the back pocket of his jeans and squeezed his buttock rhythmically with her long bony fingers.

'It's nothing, sweetie,' he slurred the words as he hooked an arm round her waist.

'Bit of a come down, isn't it? University lecturer to house sitter, or whatever Rose said, even if it is with the dishy Mr Hunter,' said a woman standing nearby, as she put a forkful of potato salad into her mouth.

'It just goes to show what a parlous state education is in these days. Someone said she's had some kind of nervous breakdown.' She lowered her voice, as though she expected Maggie to appear. Jack looked around nervously.

'Apparently, she's lost everything, job, flat, everything.' The woman went on as she helped herself to another forkful of potato salad. 'It's frightening how life can change suddenly, just like that, isn't it?'

Jack stared at the specs of mayonnaise around her mouth and spat the olive stone into his hand, before tossing it into a nearby plant pot.

'I heard that, Karen. Don't be so spiteful,' Rose said as she joined them.

Jack steadied himself against a cupboard, causing the crockery inside to rattle alarmingly.

'I've been telling Maggie for weeks that she needed a change. It's a new start. You ought to be pleased for her.' Rose glared at the red-faced woman and then at her watch. 'God, it's almost midnight. I'm off, before I morph into a pumpkin, or something.'

She smiled at Ana's confused face.

'It'll take too long to explain, Ana. Ask Jack about the Cinderella and Prince Charming story.'

Rose held out her hand and Ana took it with a languid yawn.

'Looks like your wife's ready for bed,' Rose commented.

'Yes. Take her home, Jack. You've exhausted the poor girl, by the looks of things. Or is that the other way round?' Dominic stood in the doorway, winking at Rose.

'Mind your own fucking business, Dom. What do you know?' Jack said as he stepped away from the cupboard, swaying dangerously on his feet.

Dominic raised an eyebrow at Rose. 'Come on guys, let's find your coats.'

Jack held onto Ana's arm, 'Come on, we're leaving. Apparently your selfish husband has exhausted you.'

'Shellfish?'

Ana's kohl-rimmed eyes were huge.

'SELFISH! You dim… oh never mind, I'll explain later.'

Jack pushed his wife unceremoniously out onto the landing, and Dominic led them down the stairs, through the darkened shop on the ground floor and out into the street.

*

As soon as they arrived home, Jack told Ana to go to bed, muttering that he was going to check his emails in the study next door.

An hour later he was slumped in front of the blank screen with the anger still simmering inside him. *Maggie's having a new start, is she? That bitch doesn't fucking deserve a new start. Not after what she's done to me. How dare she think she can just walk away as though nothing's happened.*

He heaved himself up and went to fill a glass from an open bottle of wine perched in a gap on one of the bookshelves.

Ana will be asleep by now. I'll have to wake her up. He smirked at the prospect. *Mustn't complain, though. You're the envy of every man in London, judging by all the tongues hanging out at that party tonight.* He frowned. *Why did Dominic have to go and spoil it? Why did he have to mention Maggie? I was enjoying it until he opened his stupid mouth.*

'Whoops,' he sniggered as he narrowly missed the chair and another thought occurred to him. *I wonder if Dominic knows what happened? I wonder if he knows what that bitch Maggie actually did to me?*

The smiling face of the baby in Hyde Park loomed, as it did every time he thought of Maggie now. Somehow, that baby had become the other baby. His baby. The one that Maggie got rid of. The one that she killed.

He swilled the remains of the wine through his teeth as his eyes filled with the easy, superficial tears of a drunk. His lower jaw trembled like a small child who is about to cry.

'I'll never forgive you, Maggie fucking Savernake. So prim and proper, so bloody perfect. You've wrecked my fucking life, that's what you've done. You've destroyed my chance of a decent future.'

He tipped the chair back, balancing it at a dangerous angle on one of the wheels, then let it fall forward again with a satisfying crash. He ran his tongue around his lips. He could feel acid burning the back of his throat.

That last glass doesn't want to stay down, better go to bed, he thought as he gripped the edge of the desk to haul himself upright once more.

'Making a new life for yourself, Maggie? I don't think so. Not on my watch.' He let go of the desk and made a hopeless attempt to stand up straight.

'Darling, you are not well? What time it is?'

Ana stood in the doorway and Jack struggled to focus on the wraithlike figure.

'No. You're alright,' he muttered as he staggered behind her into the bedroom.

One eye was already closed as he tried to discern the details of her naked body, outlined beneath the delicate fabric.

He ran his hand along her spine as she crawled across the wide bed in front of him and all thoughts of Maggie evaporated as he stumbled forward and collapsed, unconscious, on top of his wife.

*

When dawn broke the following morning, Jack was already awake, still fully dressed, with his head pounding and the nauseating taste of stale alcohol in his mouth.

Ana lay curled up beside him, sleeping peacefully like a child with her cheek cradled in her palm. He rolled away from her with a scowl. She even smiles in her fucking sleep. How can she be so happy all the time? Eighteen years between us and it's already beginning to feel like thirty.

He perched on the edge of the bed, his elbows on his knees and stared miserably at the floor. What a mess. It's all my mother's fault. It was her that got me into this.

Ana's parents owned a holiday apartment near Lucinda's on the South West coast of Spain. It was Lucinda who had suggested that Jack might be able to find Ana a modelling job in London.

She was right about that bit, Jack thought bitterly. Ana had been signed up by a leading cosmetic company the same week that she arrived and she hadn't stopped working since.

Jack rubbed his eyes. And here we are, four months later and fucking well married. What was I thinking of?

The sky was getting lighter and his stomach was complaining loudly. Memories of the previous evening were gradually surfacing. Somebody had mentioned Maggie; they had said something about her house keeping for an actor, or something like that.

'They said she's making a new start,' he said aloud, 'Yeah, that was it. A new start.'

He struggled off the bed, making no attempt to contain the noxious gases emitting from every orifice as he wove his way unsteadily towards the bathroom.

26

After the initial excitement of moving in, unpacking and reorganising her books and possessions, it had been a pleasant surprise and the source of much relief to Maggie when she discovered that the solitary nature of her new employment seemed to suit her very well indeed.

Rob Hunter had flown straight to Los Angeles from Munich when he'd finished filming in Germany, and apart from the occasional visit in person when she'd dropped in for a coffee or a glass of wine, most of her contact with Saz had been by email or text.

Maggie had seized the opportunity afforded by so much free time and had made very good progress with the research for her new book. With her days spent in the British Library and fortnightly weekend trips to check on the house in Suffolk, the time seemed to pass very quickly.

It was something of a surprise when the unfamiliar ringtone of the 'Team Hunter' mobile broke the silence at 7.30 on a cold and sunny Monday morning in late January. Maggie was eating a slice of toast and trying to decide whether to go to the British Library again or buckle down and make a start on her writing.

'Hi Maggie, how's things?' Typically, Saz didn't wait for a reply. 'This is just a quick one. Rob called yesterday. He's arriving at Heathrow at around 3pm this afternoon. Terminal 5.' There was a short pause and then she added breezily, 'So, would you mind driving to Heathrow to pick him up?'

Maggie swallowed; Saz didn't seem to realise that this was the first time she'd mentioned that she might have to drive Rob Hunter anywhere.

'I'll email you all the details now. Flight numbers and so on. I'm assuming that you've driven to Heathrow before? In any case, Heathrow is signposted all over London. I reckon that it takes about fifty minutes from St John's Wood. But I'd leave plenty of time and get there early. The traffic is always an absolute nightmare on the North Circular, and Rob gets a bit grumpy if he's left hanging around in Arrivals.'

Maggie was silent. There didn't seem to be anything to say.

'I know, going to pick him up in the car doesn't make much ecological sense. Carbon footprints and all that. But Rob prefers it, he thinks there's less chance of him being recognised or harassed by the photographers.'

'I suppose that's true,' agreed Maggie. 'What about getting food in for him? Milk, bread, that kind of thing?'

'It's all done! It was such short notice that I organised his usual delivery last night. It will be with you by ten o'clock this morning. I've told them to knock on your door, although, frankly, food's not really a priority for Rob. He's more likely to spend next week asleep. Anyway, I've got a million meetings today. Tell him I'll try to phone him tomorrow. Have a nice day.'

Maggie threw her half-eaten slice of cold toast into the bin and did a quick tour around Rob Hunter's apartment to check if there was anything she needed to alert the cleaners about. She raised the blinds and opened the patio doors a fraction to banish the stale atmosphere. The bleached wooden floors dazzled in the sudden burst of winter sunlight.

*

The drive to Heathrow Airport took Maggie considerably longer than fifty minutes, thanks to getting lost several times in the enormous parking areas. Fortunately, she'd taken Saz's advice and left early so that by the time she was approaching the Terminal 5 Arrivals lounge, it was still only 2pm.

The Arrivals board announced that Rob's flight was on schedule and due to land just after three o'clock, which left her plenty of time to get herself a drink and take up her position at the gate.

As she stirred the steaming cup of hot chocolate, she had a brief moment of panic, wondering whether she would recognise him, or whether he would recognise her.

She toyed with the idea of holding up a placard with his name displayed in large black capital letters, like some of the other drivers she'd noticed walking around, then imagined his appalled expression when he emerged to find that his anonymity had been destroyed. My job would be finished, she thought. We'd probably get buried under an avalanche of screaming female fans.

It was close to four o'clock by the time the crowd of weary passengers finally emerged through the exit doors. She needn't have worried; the tall, slim figure dressed in an old black anorak and jeans, with a well-worn baseball cap shadowing his face, was head and shoulders above the other passengers. He was wearing spectacles and glancing warily at the faces of the people behind the barrier.

She pushed quickly through the crowd until she was level with him. 'Mr Hunter?' He acknowledged her with an imperceptible nod and Maggie struggled to keep up with his long strides as they walked quickly towards the exit doors and the car park.

It was not until they were actually driving out of the airport that Rob removed his baseball cap and spectacles. Maggie had forgotten how pale his face was; the lack of colour was accentuated now by heavy shadows beneath his eyes. He looked as though he hadn't shaved or slept for days.

'Thanks for coming to pick me up,' he said without looking at her.

Maggie nodded but didn't take her eyes off the road. The interior of the car seemed to have shrunk with his large frame wedged into the passenger seat beside her. Each time he shifted his position, she caught a faint waft of cologne combined with a pungent scent of male body odour.

They completed the rest of the journey in silence. Rob was apparently lost in his own thoughts and Maggie was concentrating on the return route, which was more complicated now that it was getting darker and the traffic was much heavier.

When she finally brought the car to a halt outside their apartment block, she couldn't stifle her exhausted sigh of relief.

Rob turned to lift his rucksack off the back seat and left the car without saying a word. She stared after him, lips parted in surprise. Why didn't he say anything? Surely a small thank you wasn't too much to expect?

She locked the car and walked slowly towards the building. As far as he's concerned, I'm just another employee. She saw a light go on in one of the windows on the first floor. He was already upstairs.

There was no sound behind the communicating door when she passed it on her way to the kitchen to pour herself a large glass of water. She leaned her back against the sink to drink it, straining her ears to listen. It was as quiet as it had been before he arrived, but now that she knew that Rob Hunter was on the other side of the wall, it felt very different. She wasn't sure if it was an improvement or not.

She could see the adjoining door from where she was standing in the kitchen. Presumably Rob would expect it to remain unlocked now, so that he could have free access to his study?

She tiptoed over to the door and tried the handle. It turned and the door swung open. Rob had unlocked it already.

She crept back to her desk in the lounge and flicked on her CD player, taking care to lower the volume. If he was in bed, he definitely wouldn't appreciate being disturbed, even if it was by Mozart.

An hour later, she was back in the kitchen, half way through a plate of microwaved lasagne when she heard a door close in the hall. The unfamiliar noise made her jump. She wrenched open her kitchen door to see Rob Hunter standing in the hall, barefoot and still wearing the same clothes that he had worn earlier, including the anorak.

'Mr Hunter?' she said uncertainly. How long had he been in the study? Why hadn't he said something, knocked on the door, told her he was there?

He looked equally surprised to see her but said nothing before disappearing through the communicating door and shutting it firmly behind him.

Maggie flushed. He wasn't as approachable as she'd thought the first time she'd met him. She contemplated the congealing remains of her meal, feeling very uncomfortable. Is he annoyed that I'm here after all? Perhaps he's changed his mind about this arrangement?

She scraped what was left of her second meal of the day into the waste bin, resolving to call Saz.

The following morning, Maggie woke very early, still troubled. It's too early to call Saz yet, I might as well go and get some of the exercise John keeps nagging me about. She pulled on her tracksuit and trainers.

When she'd told John Sullivan about the new job, his reply had been unequivocally enthusiastic.

'That sounds like a very good interim solution, to me. It's been nearly a year since the miscarriage. It's time to move on. A change might be just what you need. Why don't you work on those fitness levels a bit? Sounds like you'll have plenty of free time. Take it gently, though. Mind and body, Maggie. Mind and body.'

Outside in the sharp January morning air, Maggie grinned as she remembered John's kind face. She did a few preliminary stretches outside the front entrance before jogging slowly towards Regent's Park.

As she passed the boating lake she saw two joggers approaching, one much taller than the other. They were both dressed in matching black tracksuits with black beanie hats and scarves, and the ubiquitous sunglasses. Sunglasses seem to be an essential component of the North London jogging uniform, whatever the weather, Maggie thought, then did a double take and a 180-degree turn as the two joggers passed her. She was almost certain that one of them was Rob Hunter. Long strands of black hair were escaping from under the hat of the shorter figure and they were deep in a very animated conversation.

If that was Rob, why did he ignore me again? She touched the hastily tied knot of auburn hair on top of her head. Perhaps he didn't recognise me? Or have I already reached the age when I've become invisible?

When she arrived home half an hour later, the door between the two apartments was wide open and wedged with a couple of books. She could hear Rob laughing behind the closed door of his study.

Maggie went into her bedroom and closed the door, locking it carefully before stripping off her running clothes.

If Rob has decided that this arrangement won't work, I need to know now. Saz said that he wasn't keen when she suggested it in the first place.

She showered and dressed quickly and dialled Saz's number.

'Hi Maggie, how's it going?' Saz sounded as ebullient as ever.

'Fine. Sort of.'

'What do you mean, sort of? What's the matter?'

'I want to know if Rob is unhappy about me being here. I think that he might have changed his mind about the whole arrangement.' Maggie whispered.

'What on earth are you talking about? Of course he hasn't changed his mind. And why are you whispering? Where are you?'

'I'm in my bedroom. Rob's in the study next door. He hasn't spoken since he got off the plane yesterday. This morning, he jogged right past me in Regent's Park.'

Peals of laughter rippled down the phone line. 'Is that all? Don't be idiotic. Of course he wants you there. I want you there. We all want you there. Was Rob with Kellie? She's about two feet shorter than he is. We call her our little pocket rocket.'

Maggie said nothing.

'Listen to me, Maggie. Just ignore him. The last few months have been very hard work. He's finding the publicity stuff very challenging. He needs a bit of time to refuel. I told you the other day, he's a man of very few words. Once you get to know him, you'll understand. Just carry on as though he wasn't there. Honestly. Don't take any notice of him. Look, I've got to go. I'll call you in a couple of days.'

Maggie sighed and unlocked the bedroom door. The study door was closed and Rob was still talking on the other side. On a sudden impulse, she went back to the bedroom to collect her coat.

I'll go to the British Library; I can work there until it closes. Let's face it, it'll be a lot more comfortable than tip-toeing around the fragile ego of a superstar until bedtime.

27

The following morning, after a much more peaceful night's sleep, Maggie had just returned from her run when she heard her personal mobile ringing. But by the time she had located the phone in a pocket of the coat she had worn the day before, the ringing had stopped. The screen showed a mobile number she didn't recognise. She shrugged; it was obviously a wrong number.

The rest of the morning passed quickly while she transferred the notes she'd made in the library the previous day to the computer. She heard Rob Hunter's front door slam at around lunchtime: it was difficult to know whether he was coming in or leaving.

After a light lunch she was back at her desk when her personal mobile rang again for about ten seconds. The same number appeared on the screen. Whoever is making these calls obviously hasn't managed to work out that they've got the wrong number yet, she thought as she pressed the delete button and went back to her computer.

An hour later, it rang again and this time Maggie answered it.

'Hello?'

There was no sound at the other end.

'I think you have the wrong number,' she said.

Silence.

Why don't people realise how upsetting it is when they don't speak? She thought as she put the mobile down on the desk.

She was making a cup of coffee when the mobile rang for the third time. She checked the time on her watch; it was exactly one hour after the previous call.

Maggie tried to ignore the palpitations in her chest as she sat down.

Another hour passed and right on cue, the phone rang again and stopped. Maggie's throat felt dry. Jack's face seemed to be floating in front of her. It couldn't be, could it? He wouldn't dare, would he?

She sat there for several minutes before she summoned enough courage to dial Rose's mobile.

'Rose? It's Maggie.'

'Mags! It's lovely to hear from you. How's it going? Oh, it's so lovely to hear your voice again. We miss you so much, Maggie. All of us. Even the cats!' Rose sounded tearful.

'Rose, listen, I want your advice.'

'My advice? Are you sure? What's the problem? Do you need a plumber or something?'

'No. It's nothing like that. It's my mobile.'

'Your mobile? I can't help you with mobiles, sweetie. Seb could, but he's gone up to Edinburgh with Roisin to stay with friends. Why don't you take it back to the shop where you bought it? Or try switching it off and then back on again. That's what they tell you to do with computers, isn't it?' Rose sounded amused.

'There's nothing wrong with the phone, Rose.' Maggie snapped, 'It's just that since last night, it's been ringing and when I answer it, nobody speaks.'

'Is that all? It's probably kids. Teenagers. They've dialled your number by mistake and now they're having a laugh. Ignore them. Turn it off. They'll get bored eventually and pick on someone else. Or perhaps it's one of Rob Hunter's female fans. How is that gorgeous creature, by the way?'

'Why would they call my mobile? In any case, nobody knows I'm working for Rob Hunter, apart from you and the kids. The phone's been ringing every hour, on the dot. It's more than a coincidence Rose, and it's beginning to worry me.'

She could hear Rose breathing.

'You haven't told anybody that I'm working for Rob Hunter, have you, Rose?'

After a very long silence, Rose said, 'Dom and Saul had a party just after Christmas. Jack and Ana were there. I might have mentioned...'

'What? You told Jack Millfield? I don't believe you're saying that. How could you? Why? Why did you tell Jack Millfield?' Maggie was screaming hysterically.

'It was Dom who told Jack,' Rose said. 'I'm sorry Maggie, I had no idea that you felt so strongly.'

'But how did Dominic know?' Maggie was still shouting.

'I told him. I think.'

'But I don't want Jack Millfield to know anything about me.'

'I'm really, really sorry, Mags. You know what Dom's like when he's had a couple.' Rose laughed nervously.

'Jack Millfield is the very last person.' Maggie stopped suddenly.

Why am I shouting at Rose? She doesn't know about any of it. The pregnancy, the attack, the miscarriage or the restriction order. All I'm doing now is arousing her suspicions. I'm making it a thousand times worse. She'll probably tell everybody.

'I'm really, really sorry, Maggie. Honestly. I had no idea you felt like that. Dom will be absolutely mortified as well. I'll ask him to call you, now. Shall I?'

Rose was crying.

'What good will that do? It's too late, he knows. It must be Jack. It's got to be him.'

She took several deep breaths, exhaling slowly.

'You think Jack Millfield is harassing you? But why on earth would he do that? He just got married.' Rose said after another painful silence.

Maggie cringed. She knew that Rose's imagination would be going into overdrive. She must limit the damage quickly.

'No. No. Of course. You're absolutely right, Rose. I'm really sorry. Don't take any notice of me. I'm tired. I've been working on my book. Yes, you're right, it must be kids. I'm overreacting, as usual. Sorry I bothered you. You must think I'm paranoid. Pretend you didn't get this call.'

'Don't apologise, Mags. It's not a bother. Of course it's not. It's lovely to talk to you. Just ignore it. Turn the bloody phone off. Whoever it is will soon get bored and go and look for someone else to bother.'

'Thanks, Rose, I'm sorry I shouted.'

'Don't worry! Maggie, before you go, have you seen you know who yet?' Rose's voice had dropped to a loud whisper.

'Who? Rob? Yes. Of course I've seen him,' said Maggie, surprised by the sudden change of subject.

'And…?' Rose coaxed.

'And, nothing. Look, I'm really sorry for making such a fuss, Rose. Kiss the kids for me, will you? I'll call you later, I've got to go.'

Maggie put the phone down and sat with her head in her hands.

It's Jack. It must be. The restriction order must have elapsed weeks ago. She scrolled through the call log until she located the unknown number and typed Jack's name beside it.

He won't catch me out again, she thought. Then remembering the last words of advice from her solicitor after John Sullivan contacted him, she went to the computer and opened the JM file, and made a list of the date and time of each phone call as well as a summary of her conversation with Rose.

28

The following day, Maggie decided to go back to the library; she was putting on her coat and preparing to leave when the door between the two apartments was flung open by Rob Hunter, dressed in his usual sweat-stained running gear.

'Oh. You're on your way out?' he said looking mildly surprised.

'I'm going to the British Library. Do you want something?'

'I was thinking about going up to Suffolk this weekend,' he said, leaning against the door frame with a warm smile.

Maggie zipped up her coat.

'I visited the house a couple of weeks ago. Everything looked fine then,' she said curtly.

There was a flicker at the corners of Rob's mouth. He looked as though he was laughing at her.

'I was wondering whether you would...?'

'What? Drive you to Suffolk?' she said, unable keep the annoyance out of her voice.

Rob looked taken aback. 'Is that alright?'

'How long are you planning to stay? Shall I order some food for you?'

'No. We can deal with all that when we get there. There's the small shop in the village and the pub. It'll only be for a couple of days.'

He turned, then stopped as though struck by a sudden

thought. 'Are you enjoying it? Working here, I mean?'

Maggie flushed, realising that Saz had told him about her phone call.

'Yes. I think so.'

'Only think so? I'm not sure how to take that.'

Maggie said nothing.

'I thought we could leave about half past seven tomorrow morning? If that's alright,' he said.

'Fine. I'll be ready.'

Maggie watched him close the adjoining door. Spending a weekend in Suffolk with someone who prefers to be left alone all the time will be worse than being there alone, she thought as she picked up her rucksack again.

29

Friday morning dawned bright and sunny. By the time Maggie had showered and packed a small overnight bag, there was no time for breakfast. Rob was already downstairs waiting for her, dressed in torn jeans and an old anorak. The stubble on his chin was almost a beard. Maggie thought that he looked as though he had just fallen out of bed.

I wonder what your female fans would think of you if they could see you now, she thought.

'Off we go,' she said brightly, ignoring the curious stare of the porter as they passed. Rob held the heavy glass door open for her and Maggie felt the old man's eyes following them as they walked towards the car.

Rob opened the passenger door, threw his rucksack onto the back seat and sat down. Maggie put her own rucksack beside his and made a mental note to ask Saz whether he knew how to drive. She was tempted to ask him, but the reappearance of his solemn expression wasn't encouraging.

As she drove Maggie let her thoughts return to the angry exchange with Rose. She had been so incensed that she couldn't remember exactly what she had said while she was screaming into the telephone. She completely forgot that Rob was only a few metres away in the flat next door and it was very likely that he had overheard most of it.

She glanced sideways. His earphones were still firmly

plugged in and his eyes were closed. He's probably forgotten by now, and there's not much I can do about it, anyway.

They were passing a sign advertising an upcoming service station. Maggie slowed the car down and tapped Rob's arm. His eyes snapped open and she noticed that the grey irises had a surprisingly blue tinge. Reminds me a bit of the North Sea on a clear day she thought abstractedly, then cringed inwardly at her impropriety.

'We'll be passing a service station in a couple of minutes. Would you like to stop for a coffee?' Her voice was strained.

'Take-out, black, no sugar. Thanks.'

'Two coffees, black, no sugar and a chocolate biscuit bar,' she announced, when she returned to resume her seat behind the wheel.

Rob took out his earphones and watched her break the biscuit bar into two before offering him a section. He took it and they finished the coffee, elbows touching occasionally and both staring silently at the overflowing waste bin in front of the car.

'You can't beat a quick chocolate fix.' Maggie said as she held her hand out for Rob's polystyrene cup.

When he didn't reply, she turned to see that the earphones were firmly back in place and his eyes were closed again. She lifted the cup out of his hand and got out of the car, without seeing his grin when he opened one eye.

She steered the car back onto the busy A12. He doesn't seem to have many social skills. God knows how he's managed to accumulate so many fans, she thought. He might be a good actor, but he's not exactly the ideal travelling companion.

Maggie was very relieved when she finally turned into the familiar gravelled driveway. Rob got out, flexing his back and knees with a grimace before taking a few clearly painful steps. Maggie guessed that the joints in his long legs were protesting after being confined in the small space.

They walked towards the front door and Maggie waited for

Rob to produce a key, assuming that he would prefer to open it himself. He patted his pockets and shook his head.

'Sorry, I don't carry the keys to the house around with me. I thought that you...'

Stung by the implied criticism, Maggie scrabbled in the bottom of her bag and produced her set and opened the door without a word.

Rob walked past her and straight into the lounge, where he stood staring out at the garden while Maggie watched him from the hall.

He seems to be miles away, lost in another world. Perhaps he's got some kind of romantic problem. If he has a girlfriend, she's got my sympathy. Only a saint could put up with those moods.

Maggie picked up her rucksack and went through to the annexe feeling depressed. This weekend is going to be a trial of my patience and understanding, if he continues to behave like this.

The rooms in the annexe felt very cold and she was grateful when she heard the radiators clicking and gurgling as the hot water rushed through them. At least he knows how to put the heating on, she thought as she rolled her painful shoulders.

She warmed herself next to the radiator and stared out at the garden. Many of the shrubs and trees in the garden were still bare of leaves, but there were snowdrops and daffodils popping up all over the flowerbeds; some were already in bloom. Every time I come here, there are so many changes.

She watched a blackbird tugging a worm out of the lawn; he was determined and focussed. Life and nature, it's all going on around us all the time, she thought. Always changing and yet constant, it's reassuring.

Maggie glanced across at the main house. I ought to offer to go and buy something for breakfast.

She found Rob reading a book. He looked up with a smile.

'I thought I'd drive over to the village and get something for breakfast. Any special requests?' she said.

'Whatever you choose will be fine.'

'What do you normally have for breakfast?'

'That depends where I am. It varies. A lot.'

'I imagine it does. But when you are here, in Suffolk, what do you eat at this time of the day?'

'A black coffee and then another black coffee and then another...'

Maggie went to the door 'Fine. I'll buy coffee then.'

Rob grinned and went back to his book.

30

Maggie parked the car in her usual place, next to the duck pond on the edge of the village green which was surrounded by pretty pastel-coloured thatched cottages.

The shop was next to an ancient timber-framed public house with a blackboard propped up against the front wall proudly proclaiming that it dated back to the middle of the sixteenth century and was 'the oldest public house in the area'.

I wonder how many oldest pubs in the area there are in Suffolk? she thought as she pushed the shop door open and set the bell tinkling above her head.

'Morning. Anybody at home? Peter?' she called as she picked up a wire basket from the pile next to the door.

An elderly man appeared from behind a plastic curtain at the back of the shop; he wiped his hands on his apron.

'Morning Maggie, haven't seen you for a while. I was making a coffee; do you want one?'

He came out from behind the counter to take her hand.

'Not today, Peter. I just need a couple of things,' she said, with her eyes on the shelves and unsure whether she should tell him that Rob was in the house.

In spite of the cramped space, the little shop was packed with a surprisingly wide range of goods: everything from fresh milk to screws and shoe laces. They had locally produced dairy products in a refrigerated display cabinet, as well as a shelf piled high with freshly baked bread, rolls and cakes.

Maggie selected milk, butter, a small loaf, a bag of croissants, a few pieces of fruit, ground coffee and a packet of the same brand of chocolate biscuits that she had bought in the petrol station.

If Rob decides that he wants something else, he's got plenty of time to come here and get it himself, she thought as she lifted the basket up onto the counter.

'Glad to see that you've come down with an appetite this time.' Peter commented as he began transferring the goods into a plastic carrier bag and ringing up the prices on the till.

Maggie grinned, handed over the money and said nothing. Either he's guessed that Rob's here or he thinks I've developed some sort of eating disorder, she thought as she walked back to the car.

Rob was still deeply engrossed in the book, now minus his boots and his socks, which were strewn across the carpet in front of him. His rucksack had disappeared.

He put the book down and got to his feet to take the shopping bag out of her hand, groaning loudly as he carried it to the kitchen.

'Feels like you've bought half the shop,' he joked.

'What we don't eat we can take back to London. And if you decide that you want something else, the shop is open till eight every night except Sundays, when it closes at six,' Maggie said shortly.

Rob looked bewildered by her abrupt reply as he unpacked the bag and spread the contents out on the worktop.

Maggie hung her fleece jacket on the back of a chair, 'I could make some toast or warm the croissants,' she said, 'or do you want to do it yourself?'

'Are you going to eat something?'

'Of course I am. I haven't had any breakfast.' She retorted impatiently.

Rob raised his hands in a show of mock protection.

'I'm sorry. That's my fault. I thought it would be less of a hassle if we left early. Fridays on the A12 can be hell.'

'I was joking. Toast or croissants?' she said, realising that she had been unfair.

'A croissant would be great.'

Rob began laying the large table in the conservatory for two, glancing up from time to time, as though he was seeking her approval.

'Don't lay a place for me, Rob. Saz said that you prefer to be left alone, I'll take mine through to the annexe.'

She removed the plate of croissants from the microwave.

'That's crazy. I don't know why Saz said that. I think we both need a bit of company this weekend, don't we?'

Rob filled the coffee percolator with boiling water and Maggie bent to search in the cupboards for a butter dish, in a vain effort to hide her mortification. It was obvious that Rob had overheard the row with Rose.

Once they were seated, Rob pushed the plate of croissants towards her. 'Come on, I thought you said you were starving?'

He was finishing his second croissant by the time Maggie had summoned up enough courage to speak again.

'Which do you prefer, London or Suffolk?' she said, regretting the absurdity of the question before it was out of her mouth.

Rob gazed thoughtfully through the window. 'I used to prefer London, but now it's Suffolk.'

'You don't mind the isolation, then?'

He smiled. 'Not at all. I love it. I love the silence. Just the sound of the birds and the trees. It's magic,' he said.

I suppose he sees this house as a sanctuary now, Maggie thought, no wonder he's making such a big deal about keeping it secret.

'Do you come down here often?' she asked.

'When I'm in the UK, which doesn't seem to happen very

often anymore. What about you? Which do you prefer? Saz said you hadn't visited the countryside before you started working with us.'

'I'm afraid not. I'm London born and bred,' she admitted, 'although I did go to university in York and stayed on to teach there for a few years afterwards. But even then I didn't stray far from the campus. I find the seclusion a bit…unsettling. Anywhere north of Watford and all that…' she said, with a self-conscious laugh.

'Uncivilised?' Rob suggested,

'No, not at all,' Maggie protested quickly. 'In fact, just now I was thinking that being closer to nature is kind of reassuring. It makes you feel better. It's the isolation that takes some getting used to. I think it's because I live alone. I feel a lot more comfortable when I know I can open the front door and find myself in the middle of a crowd. Which is exactly what you want to avoid, I suppose.'

'When I'm not working I like to live as far under the radar as I can get. We had one or two unpleasant incidents with the press in Germany. Some of the journalists can be very persistent and intimidating. It's been a very steep learning curve for me. It's not that long since I could go anywhere without being recognised.'

Maggie felt a rush of sympathy.

'I know what you're thinking. Here we go, another whining celebrity complaining about the press.' Rob held his hands in front of his face, in a parody of a celebrity shunning the photographers.

'No, I'm not thinking that at all. It must be very difficult.' Maggie said.

'The fans are my bread and butter and I know that I owe them,' Rob said through a mouthful of croissant. 'And ninety-nine per cent of them are absolutely fantastic. But there's a small minority who sometimes step over the line. They can be challenging, even for a big bloke like me.'

He dipped the remainder of the croissant into his coffee and stuffed the soggy pastry into his mouth, wiping the drips and crumbs escaping down his chin. Maggie found his total lack of guile and sophistication appealing. He had an integrity about him that she hadn't noticed before.

'They don't seem to understand that it's all make believe.' Rob looked serious as he drained his coffee.

'That's presumably because you're very good at what you do?'

Rob stared into his empty cup in silence.

'I knew absolutely nothing about you or your world before I came to work for you,' she said as she refilled their coffee cups.

Rob's s eyes crinkled with amusement. 'I don't think I will ever forget that moment when Saz asked you…your baffled expression.'

Maggie blushed. 'I've been living and working in the world of academia all my adult life. It's a kind of artificial bubble, a bit like you in the world of acting. Miles away from reality.' She paused, looking straight at him, 'When you think about it, there's a kind of symmetry between my world of theory and yours of fiction.'

Their eyes held for a long moment.

'Interesting,' Rob said finally, 'looks like we've got something in common after all.'

He pointed at the clock on the wall. 'It's almost midday. I'm going for a run. Are you coming? Although I better warn you that it's not exactly Regent's Park here. I go across the fields, there's plenty of wildlife. Deer, rabbits, pheasants and even the odd insomniac badger, if I'm really lucky.'

'Do any of them recognise you or ask for your autograph?' she said mischievously.

Rob stood up, 'Not so far. Coming?'

She looked up at him, 'No. Thank you. I think I'll go and do some work.'

She stood up to begin clearing the table.

'Sorry! I should do that.' Rob exclaimed as he picked up his cup and saucer, 'You've done the driving and the shopping. I'm such a slob.'

'Leave it. Go and enjoy your run. This will only take a couple of minutes.'

He hesitated, as though he was reluctant to leave. 'Saz said that you're writing a book. I'm full of admiration. What's it about?'

'Oh, something I started a while ago,' she said with her back to him as she put the milk jug into the fridge.

'Novel or textbook? Fact or fiction?' he asked, head cocked to one side.

Maggie wiped the table, 'You'll think it's boring. Gender in fifteenth-century literature. I'm not sure whether that comes under fact or fiction.'

'Sounds like a bit of both to me. I'd like to have a look at it sometime. I did a lot Shakespeare when I was at drama school, and in Rep. Not much since, though. I'd like to see it.'

Maggie threw the piece of kitchen towel into the bin, smiling enigmatically.

Rob hovered uncertainly a moment longer, 'Right, I'm off, then. Thanks for breakfast'. He patted his midriff. 'Better go and lose some of those calories, or the next part I'll be offered will be Falstaff.'

31

Maggie finished tidying the kitchen and returned to the annexe, humming to herself as she switched on her laptop and double clicked on the email icon.

There were thirty-seven emails in her Hotmail inbox, all from Jack Millfield.

The tune died on Maggie's lips. How did he get hold of my Hotmail address? Not from Rose, surely?

The only other person she could think of who had had any contact with Jack recently was Dominic.

She stared at the list. What was the point of trying to find out how Jack had got the address? He had got hold of it somehow and now he would never stop.

'Don't give up, mate. Keep at it. Drip, drip, drip. Like water on a stone. Sooner or later they all buckle under the pressure.' Jack's portentous words from the time when they were students and she had inadvertently overheard him talking to one of his friends, echoed in Maggie's ears.

Jack was tenacious, even then, she thought. He's always hated being out-manoeuvred by anybody or anything.

She watched the dark clouds rolling across the sky above the main house, trying to decide which one of her friends had given him her Hotmail address. It took several minutes before she remembered that Jack had asked her for all her contact details on their first date after the Reunion. She had handed over her mobile phone and let him copy her email addresses and phone numbers into his phone.

'Now we'll never lose each other again,' he'd whispered.

Maggie shuddered. How could I have been that stupid, that gullible? I was setting a trap for myself. Nobody else is to blame for this, I brought this entire nightmare on myself.

*

She was still watching the rain bouncing off the terrace when Rob came jogging around the corner of the house. He shook himself like a wet dog outside the patio doors, before removing his mud-soaked trainers and socks and disappearing inside.

He doesn't like wearing shoes, I wonder why, she thought absently.

Maggie's eyes lingered on the discarded footwear. There's too much at stake. There are other people to consider. Innocent people like Rob and Saz. They've been so kind to me. I must stop Jack before it's too late and somebody else gets hurt.

She transferred all the unopened emails into the JM file, blocked Jack's email address, then copied all the texts and calls he had made onto the memory card in her mobile phone before blocking his mobile number as well.

She knew that it wouldn't stop him for long; he could always use another mobile phone or another email address. But at least it would give her time to call the solicitor, Andrew Bridgeman, and ask him to threaten legal action again. It worked before, so why not now, she told herself as she disconnected the computer.

She dialled the solicitor's number and listened to the recorded message.

'The office is closed until Monday morning. Please leave your name and a contact number and we'll get back to you.'

Maggie had completely forgotten that it was Saturday.

32

Jack Millfield had slept very badly for the third night in a row.

'The only time I ever sleep well is when I'm completely off my bloody head', he muttered as he dragged himself reluctantly out of bed.

Unfortunately, that particular solution had been completely out of the question since he married Ana and she had decided to put the overhaul and management of his lifestyle at the very top of her list of conjugal duties.

In the three months since they'd been married, he'd lost nearly three kilos in weight, thanks to agreeing to go with her to the gym three times a week. She was even attempting to reduce his alcohol intake to a paltry couple of glasses with meals at the weekends. He'd managed to outwit her on that front, but it hadn't been easy.

She's too bloody used to getting her own way, just like the rest of her sex, he thought, coughing loudly and taking a large gulp of strong black coffee as he sat in front of the computer.

It took him less than ten seconds to discover that Maggie had blocked all his phone and internet access. That didn't take her long, he thought. What's the matter with the stuck up bitch? All I want to do is talk to her. A friendly chat. A little catch up. What's wrong with that?

He swivelled his chair around to survey the rolling greensward of Hampstead Heath, with the endless parade of early morning joggers and dog walkers. Who am I kidding?

he thought, that's not the reason. Maggie's got to be made to understand that I haven't forgotten.

He picked up a ballpoint pen, rolling it slowly backwards and forwards between his fingers for several minutes before throwing it high into the air and catching it with a whoop of delight.

Simple! Why didn't I think of it? The block only applies to my mobile. All I need to do is get another mobile with a different SIM card and register another email address under a different name.

He tossed the pen into the waste bin and picked up a new one.

'You're a frigging genius, Jack,' he said as he hammered out an email to his new PA, nineteen-year-old Catherine Boyce-Jones, Val's unlikely successor.

'Get me 2 new BlackBerrys and 2 new SIM cards, ASAP. J x'

He punched the SEND button with the flourish of a concert pianist at the end of a performance. The new phones would be sitting on his desk when he arrived at the office on Monday morning. Catherine was always so delightfully willing. Jack grinned to himself.

During her interview she'd explained that her father was a senior civil servant. Jack had forgotten the precise details; all he'd registered was that the man had contacts which could be useful. Ever the pragmatist, he believed that there was no point in having either colleagues or friends if they didn't have a potential use to him.

Later in the shower, images of Catherine's endless golden legs filled his thoughts. He imagined her striding down Knightsbridge on her way to the mobile phone shop, with her glossy mane swinging out behind her. She's a thoroughbred. He made a mental note to reward her with a drink after work. It's the least I can do. A humble token of my appreciation.

Jack's day dream was abruptly disturbed by the sound of the bathroom door opening. Ana stood there naked, peering through barely open eyes in a face that was pale and drawn.

'You're up very early, cariño. Can't you sleep?' she whispered.

'I'm fine, go back to bed. I'll be out in a minute.'

'I feel little sick,' she whined plaintively.

Jack's jaw tightened; her habit of speaking like a small child was becoming tiresome.

He turned off the shower and watched her walk unsteadily towards the toilet, where she retched unproductively for several agonising minutes.

At last she straightened up, wiping her mouth; her dark eyes were hollow and terrified.

Jack struggled to overcome his revulsion as he led her slowly back to the bedroom.

'Oh Jack, I am sick,' she wailed.

He helped her into bed, and drew the cover across her, staring down and scratching his head.

'What did we eat last night? Takeaway, yes. That must be it. Food poisoning.'

Ana's eyes were closed.

Thank God, she's gone back to sleep, he thought, as he slid open the wardrobe door.

'I think I might be pregnant, Jack.' Ana had raised herself up on one elbow, smiling weakly.

Jack froze. 'Pregnant? No. That's not possible, sweetie. Not yet, surely?' he said slowly.

'My last period, it didn't come,' she whimpered as she sank back against the pillows.

Jack turned away, making a show of searching the shelves for underwear and socks. Pregnant already? How the fuck? She's made a mistake, the dozy cow. She must have.

Ana's eyes were closed again and she was breathing evenly. He shook his head in exasperation. She attributed her ability to relax to her daily yoga practice every time he mentioned what he called her lazy Latin genes.

It's just a stomach upset, she'll sleep it off, he told himself as he pulled on the expensive new tracksuit and trainers she had purchased for him.

He let himself quietly out of the apartment, ran down the stairs and after a few half-hearted stretches, was soon jogging slowly along the path next to the ponds and trying to ignore the doubts that were beginning to nag him. *If Ana is pregnant, why has she allowed it to happen so quickly? Why do women always ruin everything?*

He stopped; he could feel his hamstrings protesting and knew from previous experience that humiliating cramp was not far behind. He slapped the backs of his thighs and stretched, supporting himself against a tree trunk.

'Bloody women!' he yelled into the bare branches above his head.

'Too right, mate!' agreed a passing jogger, slapping Jack hard between the shoulder blades.

Jack staggered, watching the man glance back grinning, as he disappeared into the distance.

'Twat. You don't know the half of it,' he muttered.

An hour later, he was back at home, still simmering and now high on adrenaline.

Ana was fast asleep. He stood over her inert form, curled up in the middle of the king sized bed. She seemed to sleep a lot lately, often until lunchtime on the days when she wasn't working. Jack took it personally.

How can she sleep like that after what she's just dropped on me, he thought as he showered and changed, deliberately crashing the doors and drawers like a resentful adolescent. Ana mumbled something in Spanish and rolled over.

Jack slammed the bedroom door and went back to his desk with a large mug of black coffee. *Missing a period is hardly a confirmation of pregnancy,* he thought, *the stupid bitch has probably made a mistake with the dates. Let's face it, she's not exactly the sharpest tool in the box.*

33

Ana eventually appeared around two o'clock in the afternoon, gliding quietly into his study, now dressed in tight-fitting jeans and a cashmere sweater. She was still very pale, greeting him with her usual affectionate embrace, rubbing her cheek softly against his.

Jack didn't look up. 'Feeling better?' he said.

'Still little bit sick. I think I buy pregnancy test. You want to come?'

Jack was astonished. 'Pregnancy test? You don't think that it's really a possibility, surely?'

'I miss periods. What else can be?'

'It could be anything. I often feel off colour after a night out.' He gave a dry, humourless laugh. 'If I didn't know you better I'd say it sounds as though you're hoping that you're pregnant.'

'You not want baby, Jack?'

Ana's enormous brown eyes reminded him of Merlin, his father's black Labrador, when he used to tease him with a biscuit in the school holidays.

Jack stood up and pulled her roughly against him.

'Don't cry, sweetie. Of course I do. Just not yet. I was hoping we could have a bit of time to ourselves first. A bit of fun before we start the screaming kids bit.'

He buried his face in her long dark hair, his hands gripping her slim buttocks. Ana winced as she wriggled out of his grasp and moved away.

'Coming?' she asked, head tipped to one side and lips pouting seductively.

'Nah, I'm going to watch the rugby,' he lied. 'Don't forget to buy something for dinner. I'll cook.'

She'll spend the rest of the afternoon trawling the boutiques and spending a small fortune, he told himself as he double clicked the email icon.

Fifteen minutes later, he heard the lock on the front door, followed by a piercing scream, and rushed into the hallway to see Ana's bag and its contents strewn across the floor.

The bathroom door was wide open and Ana was crouched on the toilet. Her bloodstained jeans were lying in a crumpled heap on the floor around her feet and there was blood everywhere.

'Call doctor,' she whispered.

*

Inside the ambulance, Jack sat next to the paramedic facing Ana who was lying on the stretcher opposite.

'Four months pregnant? But that's impossible,' Jack said, 'my wife has only just missed a period. She was on her way to buy a pregnancy test when this happened. She was sick for the first time this morning. She can't possibly be four months pregnant.'

The man in the green uniform looked sympathetic. 'I'm sorry, sir, but I think I know what I'm talking about. Your wife was about four or maybe four and a half months pregnant. I'm sorry.'

Jack's face was almost as white as Ana's.

'Four months? That means that she was already pregnant when we got married. Why didn't she say anything?'

The paramedic looked sympathetic but said nothing.

*

As soon as they arrived at the hospital, Jack was advised to take a seat in reception from where he watched with increasing alarm as doctors and nurses rushed in and out of the cubicle where they had taken Ana. He could hear her moaning softly behind the swinging curtains.

At last one of the doctors came across to him.

'Mr Millfield? I believe that you've already been told that your wife has had a miscarriage. Unfortunately, she's lost a lot of blood. We're going to give her a transfusion and keep her in overnight, to keep an eye on her. She's asked to be moved to a private room, I'm assuming that's alright with you?'

Jack nodded. 'Are you able to say how far into the pregnancy she was?' he asked.

The young doctor frowned.

'It's difficult to be precise. But we think about sixteen weeks, which is why we are keeping her in.'

He patted Jack's shoulder. 'I'm sorry.'

'I don't understand,' said Jack, 'she told me this morning that she was going to buy a pregnancy test. She said something about having missed a period. Is it possible to be pregnant and still have periods?'

The doctor removed his spectacles and wearily massaged his eyes with a thumb and forefinger.

'No, it is not possible to menstruate during a pregnancy, Mr Millfield. Menstrual bleeding stops automatically when women are pregnant. Some women can have what we call 'light vaginal bleeding', which they might confuse with a period. But that is usually a symptom of an impending miscarriage or a more serious condition. I'm afraid that your wife is not capable of answering any questions about her periods at the moment. She's extremely distressed. My advice to you is go home and try to get some sleep. We should have more news by tomorrow. I won't be here, but one of my colleagues will have all the notes.'

'Can I see my wife before I leave?' Jack asked as he stood up.

'Of course. They're going to take her up to a private room on the first floor. You can follow them. And try not to worry.'

The doctor gave him a formal smile and disappeared into another cubicle, where Jack caught a glimpse of what appeared to be two parents bending over their child with her arm swathed in a towel.

Upstairs in the private room, Ana's long dark hair was spread across the pillow and her eyelids were fluttering. Jack watched as a tear made its way slowly down her cheek. The only sounds in the room were coming from the monitors and various drips surrounding her bed. He averted his eyes quickly.

God, I hate hospitals. Even the smell of them makes me want to throw up.

He glanced back at the motionless figure in the bed. She bore no resemblance whatsoever to the vivacious, glamorous young woman he'd been sharing his life with for the past few months.

A nurse put her head around the door. 'Better leave your wife to sleep now, Mr Millfield. She's had a rough time. You can phone us whenever you like.'

*

Back at the flat, Jack opened a bottle of wine and sat on the sofa to wait for a pizza delivery.

'And another Millfield heir bites the dust,' he said aloud. 'Looks like there's a pattern forming here. Perhaps someone is trying to tell me something?'

He refilled his glass from the bottle at his feet. The only difference is that Maggie killed the first one, he thought. In fact, come to think of it, if she hadn't had the termination in the first place, we'd still be together and none of this would have happened to me. Which means, surprise, surprise, that she's responsible for everything.

The sound of the doorbell heralded the arrival of his pizza.

He ran down the stairs to the Hall and pushed three £10 notes into the hand of the astonished delivery boy.

'Keep the change,' he muttered as the porter watched from behind his desk.

The dark eyes beneath the raised visor of the motorcycle helmet widened when they saw the exorbitant tip.

'Wow, thanks, mate.' The boy said as he stuffed the notes into his pocket.

Jack ran back up the stairs, tearing the box open and stuffing a section of the pizza into his mouth. Despite the burnt cheese topping, the dough was almost raw in the centre. He didn't care, after twenty-four hours without food, his stomach cramps were crippling.

Hardly stopping to chew, Jack gulped the food down greedily.

He drained the wine bottle into his glass. Not the best pizza I've ever tasted, but so what, it's doing the job, he thought as he wiped his mouth and chin with a handkerchief.

He glanced at his watch. No point in calling the hospital now, Ana's probably still out cold.

He took the remains of the pizza and the wine into the study, and sat spinning the chair restlessly from side to side, tapping a syncopated rhythm on the desk with a biro. He felt twitchy and irritable; life was getting far too complicated.

He stared at the screen of the laptop and let his thoughts return to Maggie.

Why don't I step things up a gear? Increase the pressure on her. Might as well set up a new email address. He gazed up at the ceiling, drumming the biro against his teeth.

Something with a Shakespearean ring? That ought to get her attention.

34

It was about six o'clock in the evening, when Maggie looked up and saw the familiar figure walking purposefully across the lawn.

Rob raised his hand to wave and she went to open the patio door. As he brushed past, she caught a faint whiff of aftershave and noticed that he had changed into clean jeans and a sweater.

'Why didn't you come through the communicating door?' she asked.

'Oh, I don't think that's appropriate. This is your home after all and I think I should get permission to come aboard.'

His eyes were twinkling mischievously.

He glanced around. 'You've made this look very cosy. Did you do these?' He bent to peer at two small watercolours depicting different views of the church in the nearby village.

Maggie laughed dismissively, 'No. I bought them at a local art show in the village church hall. Would you like a cup of tea or a coffee?'

'No, I don't want to interrupt you. I only came to ask you what time you want to eat. I thought we could go down to the pub tonight?'

'Oh, I don't...'

'You don't what? Have dinner? Why not? What do you do when you're here by yourself?'

He cast a critical eye over her slim frame. 'Always assuming that you eat dinner, of course.'

'I microwave one of those instant meals. I bring them down with me in a cold box.'

'Not the healthiest option,' Rob observed with his eyes on the book shelves.

'Full-scale cooking's not really practical on these short visits. It's too much hassle. I think the microwave option is the best solution. In any case, I've never felt comfortable going into strange pubs on my own,' she admitted a little shamefacedly.

Rob smiled. 'Not exactly a twenty-first-century woman, are you, Maggie?'

She flushed deeply. Now he thinks I'm some sort of throwback to the 1950s. Why on earth did I tell him that?

Rob went to the patio door and turned, 'After dragging you down here, the least I can do is to buy you a decent meal. And don't worry, I'll protect you from all those pillaging Vikings lurking about in the shadows. Is 7.30 OK for you?'

She nodded.

'See you later.' Another grin and he was gone.

Maggie closed the patio door and went back to her desk. She could see Jack Millfield's mocking face leering at her through the blank computer screen.

'I've called a cab, so we can both have a pint. How's that for forward thinking?' Rob announced proudly an hour later when he led her across the lawn and around the side of the house to where the cab was waiting.

Maggie sat in the back, watching the dark shadows speed past while Rob and the driver chatted about the unseasonably cold weather and the driver's new baby son.

This must be one of the rare occasions when Rob gets the opportunity to behave like everyone else, she thought.

Outside the pub, Rob handed the driver a £5 note before getting out to open the back door for Maggie.

'Give me a ring when you're ready, Robbie,' the driver called. Rob gave him a thumbs-up sign and Maggie was struck by the affectionate ease of the exchange. They seemed to know each other very well.

'Do you come down here a lot?' she asked curiously as they entered the crowded bar.

'The farmhouse belonged to my Gran. I used to play with Tom when I stayed with her in the holidays. I was born in Norfolk, where my parents still live. In the same house, as it happens. We're not a very adventurous lot. Hunter is a misleading name,' Rob said.

Billy stretched across the bar to shake his hand enthusiastically and wink at Maggie.

Rob raised his eyebrows, 'Do you two know each other?'

'Saz brought Maggie in here for lunch the first time she came down here,' Billy explained, 'and I bump into her in the shop sometimes. She never comes in here, though, do you?' He wagged an admonitory finger at her.

'You probably scare her off,' Rob said as Billy led them to a table in the corner, near the fire.

Maggie noticed a few heads turning as they passed and looked anxiously at Rob as they sat down.

'Don't worry, they're looking at you,' he said.

'Me? Why?'

He grinned at her horrified expression. 'We don't see many strange faces in here, do we Billy?'

'None as cute as this one, that's for sure,' said Billy, 'I recommend the beef and ale stew,' he added as he handed each of them a menu. 'We've also got some very nice cod, fresh in from Lowestoft, and the veggie option for today is mushroom risotto.'

'What's it to be?' Rob looked enquiringly at Maggie.

'Cod and chips, please.'

'OK, I'll have the beef, with a pint of the usual, Billy. What do you want to drink, Maggie?'

'A glass of cider would be lovely,' she replied as she wriggled out of her coat.

Rob leaned over to help with a muttered apology. 'Sorry...
I'm sorry.'

Maggie gave him a smile of reassurance. She found his lack
of social skills very appealing and she wasn't sure why.

Billy returned with the drinks and Rob waited until he had
gone back to the bar before he clinked his bottle of beer against
Maggie's glass.

'Cheers. Thanks for driving me down and listening to my
whinge. I don't suppose Saz told you that listening to my whinge
is an essential part of the job?'

'She did say that there would be some driving, but she didn't
mention whingeing.' Maggie said before swallowing a mouthful
of the delicious cider.

Rob wiped his mouth with the back of his hand.

'I thought that you might prefer a change of atmosphere for
a couple of days. Like me.'

Maggie hesitated before she said, 'I suppose you heard me
shouting yesterday, I'm sorry.'

'Don't apologise. I was worried. You sounded very upset.'

She took another sip, trying to decide if she should give him
an explanation. 'I don't know what Saz has already told you.'

'Not much.'

'I had a few health problems last year. Then I was made
redundant and I had to give up my flat. It was... a bit
complicated.' She looked up at him, hoping that would be
enough.

'And something has resurfaced?' he prompted gently.

She looked away, unsure whether he was genuinely
concerned or simply curious.

'It's nothing I can't deal with,' she said quickly, trying to
recall the details of her argument with Rose. The prospect of
Rob and Saz knowing about Jack Millfield and the whole sordid
story was unbearable. They would think she was a fraud, a cheat;
and probably ask her to leave.

'Do you mind if we don't talk about it, Rob? Don't let's spoil the meal,' she said.

He took a long drink from the bottle and set it down on the table.

'Absolutely right. This weekend was meant to give us a change of scenery and an opportunity to get to know one another better, now that we're sharing a roof, so to speak.' He gave her another impish smile. 'I want to be absolutely sure that you're comfortable with the idea of taking us – well, me and my crazy world – on.'

Maggie stared unseeingly at the table. The idea of feeling totally at ease and relaxed was an impossible dream at the moment.

'Of course I am. Although I have to admit that it's not a job that I would have thought of applying for two years ago.' she said.

'I'm sure it isn't. But Saz and I are very pleased that you have agreed to join us. We consider ourselves very lucky.'

'It's me who's been lucky. This job has been the perfect solution for me. In fact, it's almost too good to be true.'

Maggie clinked her glass against Rob's bottle of beer and they both drank. This time their eyes met.

'Here we are, one beef pie and one cod.' Billy placed the two steaming plates of food in front of them, his shrewd eyes darting between them. 'What are we celebrating tonight?'

'Maggie joining the team,' said Rob quickly.

'I'd say she's going to be quite an asset.' Billy said as he winked at Maggie.

'I agree.' Rob tucked the flimsy paper serviette into the neck of his sweater and they ate in silence until Rob said, 'I always forget how good Billy's beef and ale pie is. How's the fish?'

He took a couple of chips from her plate and stuffed them into his mouth.

'Delicious. It's a real treat to eat fresh food,' said Maggie with a little thrill of pleasure at the familiarity of his gesture.

'Do you cook when you're at home?' Rob asked through another mouthful of her chips.

'No. As I said before, I always think that it's too much bother.'

'I'm the same. When I'm in London, it's oven ready meals and when I'm in Suffolk, it's here.' He nodded at their surroundings.

'What do you do for food when you're working?' she asked.

'When I'm filming, it's either in the canteen on the set, or a sandwich in the trailer while I learn my lines. Home cooking is restricted to my visits to see my family. Mum's cooking is the best.'

'Lucky you,' she said. 'I've never known what Mum's cooking tastes like. My mother died just after I was born.'

Rob's face was full of sympathy. 'I'm really sorry. That's tough. But don't you remember any of the food you ate when you were a child? Birthday cakes or Christmas dinners? Those memories never leave anyone.'

Maggie shook her head sadly. 'No. After my mother died, my dad employed an elderly Scottish housekeeper until I was sent away to school. I've tried very hard to forget the disgusting porridge and stews she made for us; the food at boarding school wasn't much better either. I think it's probably when I stopped eating meat.'

'I'm sorry.' He looked genuinely moved.

Maggie shrugged. 'Don't be. As far as I was concerned, it was the norm.'

Billy had returned to check on their progress. 'Everything OK, folks? What can I get you now? Coffee?'

Maggie nodded.

'Make that two, Billy. And will you call Tom and ask him to collect us in about fifteen minutes?' said Rob.

As soon as they had drunk the coffee and Rob had settled

the bill, they went outside, past a group of smokers who were huddled around an outdoor heater and an overflowing ashtray.

'Doesn't look particularly enjoyable, does it? I don't know why they bother,' Rob whispered.

As he opened the rear door of the car for her, Maggie turned to look up at him. 'Thank you for the meal, Rob. I really enjoyed it.'

She slid across the back seat and to her surprise he climbed in beside her.

'Me too,' he said as the car pulled away. 'The food's good quality and always cooked to perfection by Billy's wife, Brenda. No fuss, no frills. Just the way I like it. And they leave me alone to enjoy it in peace. What more could I ask for, eh Tom?'

Tom smiled in the rear view mirror. 'Suffolk pubs are the best in the world,' he said firmly.

'And the oldest,' said Maggie.

Fifteen minutes later they were back in the house. Rob took off his jacket and walked into the lounge. 'Will you join me for a nightcap?'

'It's very tempting... but it's getting late. Thank you,' she said.

'No. Thank *you*. It's been a long time since I had such an enjoyable evening,' Rob said.

Maggie pushed the kitchen door open, 'Now that we've locked the front door, I might as well go through here to the annexe, if that's OK?'

'You don't need to ask, Maggie. Sleep well.'

35

Jack Millfield was woken at five o'clock in the morning by a persistent pounding in the right side of his head and neck. He sat up and rubbed his face, wincing when his fingers touched the place where it had been pressed against the keyboard of his laptop. It took several minutes to locate his spectacles which were on the floor, perilously close to the wheels of his chair.

In the bathroom, he was horrified to find that the patches of dried blood, which he had made drunken attempts to remove the night before, were still there. He steadied himself against the wall as a wave of nausea washed over him and the memories returned. Ana's in hospital. She had a miscarriage. She was four months pregnant.

It took nearly fifteen minutes of standing under an alternating cascade of hot and cold water before Jack felt even vaguely capable of speaking to anybody, let alone making a phone call to the hospital.

He dressed slowly and went back to his office, where the stench of alcohol and stale pizza which filled his nostrils made him heave.

The empty wine bottle and his glass, together with the pizza box and the remainder of its contents lay strewn across the floor. Jack heaved again as he placed his coffee mug down on the desk with exaggerated care before kneeling to pick up the mess with his temples throbbing painfully.

Finally sitting in his chair, and breathing heavily, he watched the screen on the laptop light up before searching impatiently for the draft of the email from Beatrice Benedick which he had started to compose before he passed out the previous evening.

He typed quickly.

Your crime will be punished.

Beatrice Benedick? Bloody genius. No need to send more than one at a time. Let's play it a bit clever this time, he thought as he pressed SEND.

He swallowed a mouthful of the strong black coffee, listening to his stomach protesting loudly.

Why do I drink this stuff? He took another large gulp.

When he rang the hospital an hour later, a staff nurse told him that Ana was making a good physical recovery but she was still very emotional and upset.

'Don't worry, Mr Millfield, it's quite normal after a miscarriage. She'll be fine in a few days. We'll have more news after the doctors have done their rounds. Perhaps you could phone again at lunchtime?'

The nurse's voice sounded as though it was coming from a long way off. Jack put the phone down. 'Bloody women.'

Two minutes later the phone rang and Jack grabbed it.

'Hi Jack, got your message. I'll get the phones on my way in tomorrow morning. Got to dash, my dad's just arrived to take me out to lunch.' The breathless voice of Catherine made the hairs on the back of his neck tingle.

'Thanks, honey.'

He put the phone down, picturing her soft pink mouth as he ran his tongue around his parched lips and realising that he'd forgotten to tell her that he wouldn't be in on Monday.

After drinking the contents of a two-litre bottle of mineral water and eating an overripe banana to settle his stomach, Jack was feeling slightly better when he rang the hospital for the second time.

A staff nurse told him that after examining Ana, the consultant had decided that she was well enough to go home. She added that the consultant had referred Ana to one of his colleagues in the psychiatric department as an outpatient and she would be given her first appointment early the following week.

'Psychiatric department? Is that really necessary?' Jack tried to keep the irritation out of his voice. 'You do realise that I have a business to run?'

There was a heavy silence and the nurse said, 'I am sure you do, Mr Millfield. But we can't keep your wife here indefinitely. She's made a good recovery physically. It's her emotional state that needs some attention. We think that being back in her own home will help. Perhaps you could arrange to get a friend or a relative to stay with her while you're working?'

'Is that medical speak for suicidal?' Jack asked sarcastically.

'Certainly not. We wouldn't discharge her if she was suicidal. Your wife simply needs plenty of TLC, lots of peace and quiet and she'll soon be back to normal. I really do have to go now. Mrs Millfield will be ready to leave at four o'clock this afternoon.'

Jack put the phone down; he felt as though he had just been punched very hard in his already painful gut.

What the fuck is going on? How has Ana been turned into a basket case in the space of three days? Is this what happens to women when they have miscarriages? Why are they sending her home if she hasn't recovered? Who the hell is going to look after her? How long is this going to take?

He sat back in his chair and closed his eyes, until a cautious tap on the door jerked him awake. He grabbed a ballpoint pen. 'Yes?'

The head of Senka, the pretty Serbian cleaner, appeared around the door.

'Good morning, Mr Millfield, shall I make coffee?' she asked with her customary smile.

'Thank you, black, no sugar.'

Senka closed the door and Jack remembered the blood stains on the bathroom floor. 'Senka, SENKA!' he yelled.

The girl's face reappeared expectantly. 'Mr?'

'There's been an accident. My wife is in hospital. There's blood in the bathroom. I'm sorry,' he finished quietly.

Senka's blue eyes were wide. 'Accident? Mrs hurt?'

'She had a miscarriage,' Jack said.

Senka looked puzzled.

'She was pregnant.'

Jack stood up and outlined the shape of a pregnancy bump on his stomach with his hand. 'Finished. *Finis. Terminado!*' he said brushing his hands against each other for extra emphasis.

'Oh?' Senka's uncomprehending frown deepened. She shook her head.

Jack waved her away. 'Never mind. Forget it.'

The girl closed the door and Jack held his breath.

There was a brief moment of silence and then a piercing, horrified scream. Jack buried his face in his arms. Fuck. Fuck. Fuck. Why didn't I clean it up properly last night? Now she'll go and tell the agency that Ana has tried to kill herself. Or even worse, that I tried to kill Ana.

He stood up with a heavy sigh and went to reassure Senka, who was now screaming hysterically outside his study door.

By the time Jack arrived at the hospital in the afternoon, he had managed to convince himself that the medical staff had been exaggerating about Ana's mental state. A bit like politicians and weather forecasters, he thought.

He ran up the stairs, whistling tunelessly under his breath and carrying a bunch of wilting pink roses from the florist's shop on the ground floor.

She's going to be fine. Of course she is. I'd put money on it. I'll take her out to dinner tonight, somewhere expensive and then on to a club. She loves dancing.

He walked jauntily down the corridor and pushed open the door to her private room, where the sight that greeted him brought him to a sudden halt.

Ana was huddled in a wheelchair, wrapped in a blanket. Her long dark hair hung limply around her pale face and there was no recognition in her eyes when he bent to kiss her cold cheek. She murmured something in Spanish and began to whimper like a small child.

Jack crouched down beside her. 'Don't cry, sweetie. I've come to take you home.'

She turned her head to look at him, lips trembling. There was a trickle of saliva running down her chin.

'Quiero ver a mi Mamá,' she whispered.

Jack stood up biting his lip anxiously as the door was opened by a young nurse who walked briskly towards them.

'My wife wants to see her mother,' he said, almost as though he expected the nurse to produce Ana's mother.

'Yes. She's been asking for her since last night. Your wife doesn't speak any English. Luckily, one of the night staff speaks Spanish, so she was able to interpret for us.' The nurse's tone was matter of fact.

'Of course she speaks English.'

Jack put his hand on Ana's shoulder.

'Does her mother live in London?'

The nurse was holding the clipboard with Ana's notes on it and Jack realised with a shock that the bed had been stripped. They obviously expected Ana to go home.

'No. Her parents live in Spain. Ana's father is Spanish. He's a consultant in a clinic in Madrid.'

'Do they know what has happened?'

The nurse was fixing a blood pressure monitor around Ana's arm as she spoke.

'No. I didn't call them because I didn't want to worry them,' Jack said, avoiding the young woman's critical expression.

'I thought it was better to wait. I didn't realise that it was going to...'

The nurse patted Ana's arm. 'I think Ana would feel better if her mother was here. Perhaps you could call her? Is she able to travel?'

'Yes,' said Jack. 'Yes. I'll call her now.'

He moved towards the door, grateful for an excuse to leave and wondering why he hadn't thought of it before. It's the perfect solution. Ana will be much happier with them, he thought as he ran down the stairs to join the raggle-taggle group of smokers gathered outside the main entrance of the hospital.

Surprisingly, some of them were dressed in hospital gowns and still attached to their intravenous drips. An emaciated woman in a wheelchair was chain smoking. Jack watched them in amazement as they chatted to each other, oblivious to the bizarre tableau they presented to the endless flow of visitors and passers-by.

Ana's mother's frantic reaction was deafening when Jack delivered the news, which she insisted on relaying to Ana's father, who was apparently with her.

Within minutes, they had decided to get on the first available plane out of Madrid, assuring Jack that they would be arriving in London the following morning at the latest.

Elated, he took the stairs back up to the first floor two at a time, where he found that Ana hadn't moved and the nurse had disappeared. He crouched next to the wheelchair so that his face was level with his wife's.

'Ana, can you hear me? It's Jack. I've phoned your parents; they'll be here tomorrow morning.'

She didn't react.

Jack glanced at his watch; it was half past three, an hour later in Spain. 'They might even arrive tonight, if we're lucky,' he muttered as he stood up, opened the holdall and began to spread the contents on the bed. 'I'm going to take you home, Ana. I've brought you some clean clothes.'

'Mamá?' She whimpered.

'Yes. She's coming. We'll go home and wait for her.'

Jack lifted the pink silk dress he had grabbed out of her wardrobe and held it out. 'Look, this is your favourite.'

'No. No. NO.'

She pushed the dress away with unexpected force and a nurse rushed in, one hand over the watch clipped to her breast pocket. 'Everything alright?'

'No, everything is not alright,' Jack said loudly. 'My wife is very upset; she refuses to get dressed. She's very... look, can I have a word, outside please?'

The nurse followed him out into the corridor where they stood facing each other.

'I don't think she's well enough to leave the hospital. I don't understand what's happened. Frankly, she's unrecognisable.'

Jack rubbed his hand nervously through his hair. 'I'm finding this very difficult, actually. Can I speak to a consultant or somebody in authority?'

The young nurse glanced up and down the empty corridor. 'I'll go and find a staff nurse. Wait here please.'

A few minutes later, she reappeared with a male nurse dressed in a different coloured uniform.

'Mr Millfield? Nurse tells me you are worried about your wife,' he said with a polite smile.

'My wife had a miscarriage on Saturday morning. Since then her mental state seems to have deteriorated very quickly. I was told by one of your colleagues that she's ready to go home. But I can tell you that she isn't. I've telephoned her parents and they'll be here either later today or first thing tomorrow morning. I think that Ana should remain here until they arrive.'

The man listened impassively.

'The consultant has already decided that your wife is ready to go home, Mr Millfield, I can't countermand that decision. I agree that Mrs Millfield is a bit depressed, which is perfectly normal after a miscarriage. To be fair, she does seem to have taken it particularly badly. But she will get over it, and you'll be surprised how quickly. It's very early days yet, you must be patient.'

Jack could feel the anger building up inside him; his neck muscles were very tight and his head was throbbing.

'You don't seem to understand what I am saying to you,' he said, 'Ana is in an appalling state. She's a different person. I don't know what went on in this hospital on Saturday after I left, but something clearly did and I intend to get to the bottom of it. I want to speak to the consultant. Now.'

'As I've just said, Mr Millfield, your wife has made a good recovery after a completely straightforward procedure. There have been no complications. Her emotional distress is only to be expected under the circumstances. I am not clear why you are finding all this so difficult to understand? I don't know what else I can add. If you insist on speaking to a consultant, I'm afraid I will have to ask you to wait; the doctors are doing their afternoon rounds. I'll take you to a waiting room, if you like?'

'Yes, thank you,' Jack said.

The waiting room was painted in a very unattractive shade of green. A very overweight man in a shabby khaki camouflage anorak and a girl who might have been his daughter sat in one corner. Jack acknowledged them with a nod and sat down. They stared at him without interest.

The posters adorning the walls depicted the effects of smoking and alcohol on various organs of the body in lurid colour. Jack swallowed nervously and averted his gaze. A clock on the wall showed that it was almost four o'clock.

How much longer before Ana's parents call to say they are on their way? he wondered as the door was opened by a young doctor dressed in shirt and jeans, with a stethoscope slung casually around his neck. Jack recognised the brand of the very expensive trainers he was wearing.

'Mr Millfield?'

'Yes.' Jack stood up.

'I understand that you have some concerns about your wife?'

'That's an understatement.'

'Shall we go and have a chat with her?'

'A chat? Why not? Let's do that,' Jack drawled as he cast a meaningful glance at the overweight man and his daughter, who were now listening with great interest.

As they made their way down the echoing corridor to Ana's room, the doctor was flicking through several buff folders he was carrying.

Poor bugger, thought Jack, he's probably been on duty for seventy-two hours already. This is probably the last thing he needs.

Ana hadn't moved. The young doctor laid a hand gently on her shoulder. 'Ana?'

He moved around to stand in front of her and squatted down on his haunches to look directly into her face. 'Ana? How are you feeling?'

Ana's eyes were blank and lifeless. The doctor checked her pulse while he carefully studied her expression. He passed a forefinger backwards and forwards in front of her face. She didn't move.

Jack leant against the wall, with his arms folded tightly across his chest. So tightly that he could feel his heart pounding against his forearms.

The silence in the room was broken by the vibrating buzz of Jack's mobile. He mouthed an apology at the doctor, before reading the message.

'Arr. Luton tonight 9pm.'

The message was followed by a flight number.

A deep sigh of relief escaped through Jack's lips. 'Her parents are due to arrive at nine o'clock tonight,' he announced triumphantly, adding under his breath, 'thank God'.

The doctor stood up without looking at Jack. 'I'm going to have a word with one of my colleagues.'

Once they were alone, Jack touched Ana's arm warily.

'Your mamá and papá will be here tonight, Ana. They've just sent me a text. Flying into Luton at nine, so they should be in London by ten. That's good news, isn't it?'

Ana didn't react and Jack resumed his position near the door, leaning his back against the wall.

The unappetising smell of boiled vegetables was seeping into the room. God, if that doctor doesn't come back soon I'm going to throw up, he thought as he checked his watch. It was only fifteen minutes to six. He could hear voices in the corridor, the sound of a trolley and plates rattling. Jack shifted his weight from one foot to the other and folded his arms.

Another thirty minutes passed before the doctor returned accompanied by an older man, also in shirtsleeves and with the ubiquitous stethoscope dangling around his neck. Jack wondered vaguely whether doctors were advised about stethoscope etiquette in medical school.

The older man spoke first. 'Mr Millfield?'

Jack unfolded his arms and stepped forward.

'I'm Jim Pearson, Psychiatric Consultant. I've been looking at your wife's notes. I understand that you're concerned about her mental state.' He paused, looking directly into Jack's eyes, 'I expect that you are aware that losing a baby can be a very traumatic experience for a woman. Some women deal with it better than others.'

The doctor patted Ana on the shoulder.

Tell me about it, thought Jack as Maggie's face floated into his head.

'Your wife is clearly finding it very difficult. I understand that this was her first pregnancy?' continued the consultant.

Jack lowered his gaze. Are they all missing the point deliberately? Why do they keep saying that Ana is finding this difficult? We can all see that. Why can't they understand that the real problem here is that I can't fucking deal with it, any of it?

The consultant was outlining the importance of patience and giving Ana time. He suggested taking her away for a holiday, 'perhaps somewhere warm?' he said with a superficial smile.

Jack's anger and frustration erupted.

'I've heard the same story several times already this afternoon, Mr Pearson. I don't need to be reminded that my wife had a miscarriage, I was there. OK? I also know that she is finding it difficult.' His eyes were blazing and his voice shook. 'I think you need to realise that I am also finding it difficult. Very difficult. OK? I just want you to tell me whether she can remain in the hospital for another night. Her parents are arriving from Spain in a few hours. Once they're settled in their hotel, we'll make a plan about Ana's convalescence. Her father is a consultant surgeon in a clinic in Madrid. He is much more capable of dealing with this,' Jack waved a hand at Ana, 'than I am. I have an advertising agency to run.'

The two doctors exchanged glances and Jim Pearson said quietly, 'If you are quite sure about that, Mr Millfield, we can arrange for your wife to be transferred to another private room on a different floor.'

'Oh don't worry, I'm very sure. Very sure.' Jack was almost crying with relief. 'And I can assure you that money is absolutely no object. Give her the best room in the house, whatever the cost.'

The doctors looked at each other again, and the younger man went to the door.

'I'll go and get that organised immediately then,' he said. 'I'm afraid I have to go, there are several other patients waiting.'

Jim Pearson was bending to look into Ana's face, his hand on her wrist. 'We're going to move you to another room, Mrs Millfield.'

Jack watched as Ana nodded and the doctor straightened up.

'I'm sure she'll recover very quickly, Mr Millfield. In a year from now, she'll be in our maternity wing delivering a beautiful baby for you.'

Jack bent to kiss his wife's cold cheek, with tightly closed lips.

36

It was raining when Maggie got up on Sunday morning. The sky looked dark and threatening with thick clouds hanging low above the fields. She glanced across at the main house and frowned when she saw that all the curtains were open. Had Rob gone to bed without closing them?

She leaned her forehead against the cold glass, remembering their meal together in the pub. He had surprised her. His boyish grin when he stole the chips from her plate and the way he wiped his mouth with the back of his hand. The sympathy he'd shown when she talked about her childhood had felt genuine and sincere. Despite his size, he was sensitive and gentle; she realised with a small shock that she hadn't felt threatened or intimidated by him, quite the reverse.

Rob is what they mean when they say someone's a gentle giant, she thought with a smile. I'm beginning to understand why Rose and Phoebe were making such a fuss when I told them I was going to work for him.

Then other memories intruded and Maggie's smile faded.

I need to check my emails.

She searched the list quickly. There was nothing from Jack. Maggie switched off the computer with a growing sense of unease. After the conversation with Rose, she was certain that the calls to her mobile had been from Jack. He didn't need to speak. It was a signal. He was telling her that he knew where she was.

She went into the kitchen, picked up a dishcloth and began polishing the gleaming stainless steel draining board. What if he tries to jeopardise this new job or contact Rob? She threw the dishcloth down. No that's impossible. There's too much security.

Back in the little office, she stared at the main house, which still looked dark and deserted. Maggie frowned, wondering why Rob hadn't mentioned that he was going to be out on Sunday.

Perhaps he's just gone for another run? A long run. She gazed at the flat surfaces of the puddles on the lawn. It's stopped raining at last. Why am I standing here? A walk will clear my head.

During her previous trips to the house, she'd worked out several different routes. The one she liked to call 'the six-kilometre option' would get her back to the house in a couple of hours. That will give Rob plenty of time to reappear, she thought as she walked down the muddy lane outside the house.

At the end of the lane, she turned right through a gap in the hedge and onto an uneven path which skirted around the edge of the fields in the direction of the river.

After half an hour, the clouds had begun to move west, away from the coast, and soon she felt the sun warming the top of her head. Her raincoat was becoming uncomfortably heavy and her feet were swelling inside the heavy walking boots. Undeterred, Maggie unbuttoned her coat and tramped steadily along the bumpy pathway with her spirits lifting with each step.

She had been humming quietly to herself for several minutes when a small rabbit suddenly darted out from under a nearby hedge and froze, staring at her with big frightened eyes and its nose and whiskers twitching.

Maggie was spellbound, hardly daring to breathe as the little creature sprang sideways and disappeared back the same way it had come.

'Sorry I scared you, rabbit,' she said, 'Not sure what came over me then. It's a long time since I felt like singing.'

It was nearly three o'clock when she arrived back at the house, only to find the front door was still firmly locked.

She unlocked the door and went inside, calling Rob's name and trying to ignore a small flutter of anxiety. There was no response. After leaving her coat and shoes in the hall, she made a quick tour of the rooms on the ground floor trying to think of a possible explanation for his absence. Perhaps he has been called back to London, unexpectedly? But surely Saz would have told me, wouldn't she?

Upstairs, Maggie discovered that Rob's bed had been made. She stared at the cushions arranged in a neat line against the headboard. It was difficult to decide whether he had slept there or not. Would he really be that meticulous about the cushions?

She ran back downstairs, where a brief check confirmed that the car had also disappeared. Well, wherever he is, it's further than walking distance, she thought, perhaps he's gone sightseeing. She grinned at the unlikely prospect; sightseeing was out of the question. The last place Rob would want to be was amongst a crowd of tourists in a local beauty spot.

She relocked the front door from the inside and went through to the annexe, wondering why she was getting so anxious. There was no reason why Rob should explain himself to anybody, least of all to her. Just because we had a meal together last night, doesn't give me the right to know everything about him or his life.

'I'm not his personal private secretary after all.' she said aloud as she made a cheese sandwich and a mug of coffee, 'Don't get ideas above your station, Savernake.'

After disconnecting the internet, she switched on the laptop. It was time to start editing the first three chapters of her book. It was a task that required a great deal of concentration and would be the perfect antidote to her nagging apprehension about Jack, and now the mysterious disappearance of Rob.

It was almost eight o'clock in the evening when the distinctive ringtone of her Team Hunter mobile broke the silence in the sitting room, where Maggie was curled up on the sofa, half asleep. She went to retrieve the phone from the pocket of her coat. If this was Saz demanding to know Rob's whereabouts, what was she going to say?

To her immense relief, Rob's name was flashing on the screen.

'Rob!' She exclaimed.

'Sorry, Maggie. I suppose you've been wondering where I'd got to?'

He sounded guilty.

'At first, I thought that you had gone back to London. Then I realised that you or Saz would have said something. Once I realised that the car had gone as well, I decided that you were with friends. Let's face it, there's not much else you could be doing in this part of the world on a Sunday.'

'I would never go back to London and leave you stranded here, what kind of a fiend do you think I am?' Rob replied, then, 'Don't answer that! Actually I went to spend the day with my parents, so you weren't far off the mark.'

'To enjoy some of your mother's fabulous cooking, I imagine?' Maggie said, wondering how his parents were coping with their son's new celebrity status.

'Yes I did. And it was even better than I remembered. In fact, it was so good that I brought some of it home with me.' He paused, 'I was wondering whether you would like to come over for a drink? Mum's made a massive fruit cake and I thought that you might like to try some?'

A drink with a piece of fruit cake, at this time of night? That will be... interesting. Maggie grinned to herself.

'Thanks, I'd like that. Give me a couple of minutes.'

She pulled the curtain back and saw that all the lights were on and Rob's outline was framed in the glass patio doors in the lounge.

Maggie switched off the computer and grabbed her jacket before tip-toeing gingerly across the saturated lawn. Rob slid the patio doors open for her.

'If you come through the house, you don't need a jacket and you wouldn't get your shoes wet,' he said as he hung her jacket carefully over the back of a chair.

Maggie slipped off her shoes and left them by the patio door. 'I know, but like you, I think that it is a bit presumptuous to just barge in when you are in residence.'

'Don't say that, you make me sound like the Lord of the Manor. In any case, I can't imagine you barging in anywhere.' Rob said.

'Beer, cider, or wine?' he indicated the array of bottles on the old oak sideboard. 'Mum's stocked me up with a selection, as you see.'

She noticed a half full bottle of white wine. 'A small glass of the white wine would be lovely,' she said.

Rob had put his bottle of beer on the coffee table, next to a big, square fruit cake and a large hunk of cheese.

Maggie sat on the sofa while Rob poured her wine.

'I always come back from my parents loaded up with stuff,' he said. 'Will you have a piece of cake? We always eat it with cheese in our family. It's an old Yorkshire custom.'

Maggie nodded. 'Why not?'

She settled herself against the cushions, watching the logs crackling in the stove. The room felt warm and homely.

'You're supposed to eat them at the same time, to properly appreciate the contrast in flavours,' Rob said as he handed her a plate loaded with a slice of cake and a piece of the cheese. He cut more for himself before taking his place at the other end of the sofa.

They watched each other surreptitiously as they each took a bite of the cake and then the cheese and chewed solemnly, both struggling not to laugh.

'Well?' said Rob finally. 'What's the verdict?'

'Delicious. What a great combination. I love it.' Maggie said enthusiastically.

'Result!' Rob looked delighted. 'On the other hand, what else could you say, after I told you that my mum made it?'

'Not at all. It really is a match made in heaven and your mum is a great cook. I can't remember the last time I had a piece of homemade cake.'

'I'll tell her that the next time I speak to her. Now, I want to hear what have you've been doing with yourself all day.'

'I went for one of my walks across the fields on the other side of the lane and down towards the river this morning. I think it's about six kilometres. I saw a rabbit.'

Rob smiled. 'I didn't know you like walking.'

'I find it very therapeutic. I think that it's something to do with the rhythm. A bit like jogging. Exercise is good for the mind as well as the body, according to my GP. Talking of the body, can I help myself to another slice of your mother's delicious cake? I haven't had anything to eat since breakfast apart from a sandwich,' she said.

'Really?' Rob cut another slice, balancing it on the knife to slide it unceremoniously onto her plate.

'Sure that's enough, or shall we go to the pub? I'm sure Billy could rustle something up for you. Or I could make you a sandwich. Have I got any bread?'

Maggie giggled. 'I've no idea. Have you eaten the loaf I bought yesterday already?'

Rob looked perplexed and she laughed again. 'Don't worry, this lovely cake is more than enough.'

He filled her glass and opened another bottle of beer.

'I bet your parents were delighted to see you, weren't they?'

Rob's face softened. 'Yes. I haven't been home for months. They usually travel to wherever I happen to be filming. I make sure they stay in decent hotels and they treat it like a holiday. But

I prefer going home to see them. You know, with Mum doing the Sunday lunch and Dad bringing vegetables from his allotment. All the usual stuff.'

'Wish I did,' Maggie said quietly, 'sounds idyllic.'

'God, that was thoughtless. I'm so sorry. I forgot.'

'Don't be. You're very lucky.'

'I can't imagine what it must have been like for you to grow up without a family.'

'As I said last night, if you've never had one, you don't miss it. Have you got any siblings?'

'Yes. A brother and a sister. I'm the youngest. They're both married with five kids between them. They divert Mum's attention away from my tardiness in the grandchildren stakes.'

He took a long swallow from his bottle of beer. 'Do you have a boyfriend, partner or whatever?'

'No. Do you?'

'I don't stay anywhere long enough.' Rob leaned back on the cushions to stare up at the ceiling.

'Have you ever had one, a partner I mean?' Maggie ventured.

Rob's smile disappeared.

'That's classified.'

Maggie flushed, realising that she had unwittingly stepped over an invisible barrier. Rob's reaction was clear. This far and no further.

'I'm sorry.' she said as she put her glass down.

'I never discuss my personal life,' Rob said more gently.

'I'm really sorry.' She stood up. 'I ought to go.'

'But it's early. Don't go yet,' he said, 'I don't know why I said that. It's like a conditioned reflex. Don't go, Maggie, please.'

He patted the seat cushion beside him and Maggie sat down again.

'There's been a lot of gossip in the media recently,' Rob said. 'All totally fictitious, of course. The press just invent stuff because we've put a strict embargo on questions about my private life. As far as I'm concerned, it's not a subject for vicarious entertainment. Obviously, that doesn't apply to you, Maggie,' he said. The familiar warm smile had returned, 'So, to answer your question, yes I have had two relationships and both were a disaster. The last one ended about a year ago. They were both actresses. I won't name them. Although I wouldn't name them even if they weren't,' he added.

As Maggie listened, she realised with a sudden feeling of panic that Rob's revelation gave him a certain right to ask her about her own experiences. She put her glass down carefully.

'I'm sorry, Rob. I was out of line. I won't make the same mistake again. I really ought to go to bed now. What time do you want to leave tomorrow?'

Sensing her sudden withdrawal, he stretched his arm along the back of the sofa and touched her gently on the shoulder.

'Forget it Maggie. It's my fault. I'm an idiot.'

'Of course you're not.' She stood up. 'What time tomorrow, Rob?'

He gathered up the remains of the fruit cake on his plate and stuffed them into his mouth.

'Saz phoned last night. She was annoyed because I kidnapped you on Friday morning without telling her. She announced that I've got appointments for the rest of this month and half of the next, starting on Tuesday. It's the start of the six-week publicity jamboree for the film. Press showings, press conferences, premieres all over the place and interviews on TV and radio. You name it, we do it. It's endless, boring and more exhausting than making the film, so they tell me. Unfortunately, it's an important part of the job, bums on seats and all that. So it has to be done. I'm going to hate it.'

'Does that mean that you'll be staying in London for a while?'

Maggie lifted her jacket off the chair and Rob scrambled to his feet to help her. She looked up to thank him, realising that he was even taller when she didn't have her shoes on.

'We'll be in London for some of the time,' Rob said. 'Then Europe, the States and Australia.'

He saw her look of astonishment. 'I know. It's mad. So, to answer your question, we ought to go back to London tomorrow. I'm thinking before lunch, but if you want to leave later, I don't mind.'

'I'll go with whatever you decide.'

Maggie pointed at the coffee table. 'And don't worry about all that, I'll get up early and do it. But make sure that you wrap the cake in foil or something.'

'Mum gave it to me in a tin. I'll put it back in there.' He followed her into the hall. 'So you're going back through our secret door?'

'I'm ashamed to admit that I'm a bit nervous of the little furry creatures I hear walking about on the lawn in the middle of the night,' Maggie looked embarrassed.

'You can take the girl out of the city but you can't take the city out of the girl,' he said.

'Something like that. Thank you for the cake, Rob.' She held out her hand awkwardly and Rob took it, bending over her to brush her cheek very softly with his lips.

'Thank *you*. I've enjoyed this weekend very much.'

Maggie closed the door quietly behind her and stood for a moment, touching her cheek with tears in her eyes. Rob's kiss had felt warm and undemanding.

Rob went back to the lounge, staring thoughtfully across the lawn at the curtained windows in the annexe and watching the lights going on and off as Maggie moved from room to room.

She had a mysterious, indefinable quality that he had never encountered before; an intriguing natural beauty with none of the cosmetic artifice and self-awareness of other women he'd known, and yet, in spite of her incredible smile, he'd seen a hint of sadness deep in her eyes that troubled him.

It was well past midnight when all the lights in the main house and the annexe had finally been extinguished and the peaceful silence enveloping the garden was broken by the eerie call of a barn owl. It was signalling as it quartered the fields in search of prey in the undergrowth far below.

37

Maggie yawned and stretched. Seven o'clock. It was the first time that she'd slept through the night without waking up for many months. Suffolk seems to be doing me good after all, she thought as she got out of bed to open the window.

The sun was rising and the birds were already competing in their morning chorus. Dew sparkled on the surface of the lawn and little rivers of condensation were running down the windows of the summer house. Maggie touched the cold window pane: the temperature had dropped during the night. On a spontaneous impulse, she grabbed her dressing gown, put on her slippers and stepped outside into the crisp morning air.

She made her way under the old pergola, covered in a tangle of gnarled, leafless branches of jasmine and honeysuckle, towards a rickety wooden bench and a small pond, wrapping her arms tight around her ribs against the chill as she walked to the perimeter fence. It was the first time she had ventured this far in the four months she had been working for Rob and Saz.

She wasn't sure how long she'd been standing there when she heard the sound of footsteps padding behind her. Turning with her heart racing, she was relieved to see Rob, dressed in baggy jogging pants and a faded T shirt, his hands thrust deep in his pockets.

'When the sun shines, you know it's Monday!' he said cheerfully. 'Did the birds wake you too?'

Maggie nodded, pulling the collar of her dressing gown up around her neck as she stared across the fields beyond the fence.

'I can't believe how far you can see from here, it must be miles,' she said, desperate to distract Rob's attention from her dishevelled hair and a face devoid of makeup.

'I'm not sure how far it is to the river. My nan did tell me. A long time ago.' He squinted at the horizon, 'A couple of miles?'

'I've never been right down to the end of the garden before. I thought it was too good to miss on this beautiful morning.' Maggie turned to look up at him and noticed the stubble along his jaw: it was almost a beard. His tousled hair made him look vulnerable. She looked away quickly.

'When the weather starts to improve I often think about moving down here permanently,' Rob said as he picked a stray dead flower from a rose bush and pressed his nose into it before tossing it into a flowerbed.

Their eyes met again and Maggie took an involuntary step backwards.

'I'd better go and finish my packing.'

Rob followed, carefully maintaining a discreet distance between them as they walked towards the annexe.

'What time do you want to leave?' she asked, noticing that he had slipped on the muddy trainers he'd left on the patio after his run.

'I don't want to leave at all, on a day like today,' Rob said after a pause. 'It takes about two hours. Shall we say ten o'clock?'

*

After she'd dressed and finished her packing, Maggie went to find Rob. He was in the kitchen, filling a mug with coffee and holding a half-eaten banana in the other hand.

'Hi.' He indicated the coffee percolator, 'Want one?'

Maggie shook her head. 'No thanks. Have you finished upstairs?'

'Yes. I've even stripped my bed and put the sheets into the laundry basket. How's that for efficiency?' he said proudly.

Maggie was transferring the contents of the fridge to the table. 'I'll take all this back to London. It will be out of date before our next visit.'

Rob lounged against the worktop watching her, chewing the banana and taking large, appreciative slurps of coffee.

Maggie carried the freezer bag into the hall and put it down next to his rucksack which was already propped against the wall by the front door.

When she returned to the kitchen, Rob was standing with his back to her, in front of the open doors of the conservatory.

'Right. I'll go and get my bag and start locking up,' she said briskly.

'I'll dream about the garden and how it looked this morning when we're back in London. Will you?' Rob glanced over his shoulder.

'Mm,' Maggie couldn't look at him. 'It's still only quarter past nine, I've got time to check my emails before we leave,' she said.

Rob turned back to his contemplation of the garden.

*

Maggie scanned the list unfolding down the screen in front of her. Most of it appeared to be junk and there was nothing from Jack Millfield. With a growing feeling of relief, she moved the cursor quickly until her attention was caught by an oddly familiar name.

Beatrice Benedick. She frowned. Beatrice? Benedick? Is that real? It can't be, can it? She double clicked on the message and her stomach contracted.

'your crime will be punished'

Beatrice and Benedick, the names of two of the characters in Shakespeare's famous comedy, *Much Ado About Nothing*, followed by that horrific threat. There was only one person who could have sent it and he had sent it to her Hotmail account.

'Now I'll never lose you again.' Jack's words rang in Maggie's ears. Once flirtatious and now mocking and ominous.

She was trembling, suddenly cold. Why did I open it? Andrew Bridgeman warned me not to open anything if I didn't know who had sent it or where it had come from.

She looked across the garden. The house was dappled in thin spring sunshine. The bare branches of the apple tree threw shadows across the grass. Rob would be waiting for her, probably wondering what she was doing.

She closed the email and dragged it quickly into the file marked JM, and closed the laptop. Locking the chilling message out of her sight.

I'm never going to be free of him.

She covered her face with her hands. I mustn't cry. I don't want Rob to see me like this.

An urgent rap on the window made her look up; Rob was standing outside his face full of consternation.

'Alright?' he mouthed.

Maggie nodded and forced a smile, wondering how long he had been there. She stood up and steadied herself against the desk as Rob let himself in. He was at her side in two strides, towering over her. He put a hand on her arm. 'Are you sure? You're very pale.'

She struggled with an overwhelming urge to bury her head against his chest and tell him everything.

'I'm fine. It's just a bit of a headache, probably got up too early.' She began gathering up the papers on her desk, shuffling them needlessly.

Rob hesitated, watching her carefully before he picked up her overnight bag and leaned across for the laptop.

'Are these ready to go to the car?'

Maggie put her hand on the laptop. 'I'll take that.'

Rob was startled, then grinned uncertainly, 'Why? Scared I might drop it?'

'No, of course not. You've got more than enough with the case,' she said, realising too late that she sounded ridiculous. The 'case' was a very small rucksack. She watched him cross the lawn, swinging the rucksack in one hand, with his head down.

'I didn't mean it like that. It's not your fault,' she whispered.

Maggie's throat ached with the effort of not weeping as she walked slowly from room to room, checking that all the doors and windows were locked, first in the annexe and then the main house. She was struggling to find the composure she would need in order to drive Rob back to London. Finally setting the alarm and double locking the front door, she was surprised to find him sitting in the driving seat tapping a message into his mobile phone.

'All locked up?' he asked.

She nodded as she took her place beside him, stowing her laptop on the floor at her feet.

'What about some music?' Rob eyed her over the top of his sunglasses and placed one of his large hands over the tightly clenched fists in her lap.

'Come on, Maggie. Give us a smile. You were so happy in the garden this morning. What's happened to upset you? Surely not the laptop thing?'

'What do you mean, the laptop thing?' she snapped.

Rob started the engine and checked the mirrors, 'When you got annoyed because I wanted to carry it to the car,' he said evenly.

'Of course not. I don't know why I reacted like that.'

'Who's upset you, Maggie?' He turned to look at her.

'Nobody.'

Rob revved the engine. He was certain that she was lying

and it seemed to be connected with the laptop. Her hands were cold and rigid with tension when he touched them.

Maggie searched in her handbag as Rob drove through the gates. Out of the corner of his eye he could see her dabbing at her face.

They had been driving for more than an hour in silence when he turned into a small service station on the A12. He raised his sunglasses a fraction to peer at her from beneath them. 'Coffee?'

With the sunglasses now resting comically half way up his forehead, Maggie couldn't prevent a smile from lifting the corners of her mouth.

'I'll go,' she said quietly. 'You stay in the car.'

'No. It's my turn.'

A few minutes later, he was back, proudly brandishing a small brown paper carrier bag. 'See? I even remembered the chocolate biscuits you bought for us on Friday.'

He handed her a paper cup. 'Black, with no sugar, right?'

'Thank you.'

'Don't say thank you. I owe you. I was very presumptuous when I asked you to work this weekend. Saz is furious.'

'She has no reason to be. In any case, you can hardly call it work. I really enjoyed it. Your house is a sanctuary.' Her voice shook on the last word.

Rob put his hand over the clenched fist in her lap.

'Sure there's nothing I can do to help?'

Maggie swallowed. The tears were burning the backs of her eyes.

'No, Rob. This is something that I have to deal with myself. And I will, just as soon as we get back to London.'

She held out her hand for his empty cup, 'Here, give that to me, I'll go and put it in the rubbish bin.'

38

Jack was woken from a dreamless sleep by his mobile phone. His mother-in-law's unmistakable, strident tones pierced his eardrum.

'Jack? Is that you?'

He winced. 'Hi Maude, where are you?'

He scratched his chest with his eyes still closed.

'We're on our way to the hospital. José wants you to meet us there.'

'On your way to the hospital already?' He peered at the alarm clock. 'That's a bit early, I don't think they'll let you in.' he said.

'We've already spoken to them. They said we can go in at any time.'

Jack swung his legs off the bed, forcing his eyes open with difficulty.

'And you want me to be there?' he mumbled, still scratching his chest.

'Yes, Jack,' she said. 'We're going to take Ana home.'

'Take her home? What, back to Spain? Why?'

'José has decided. It's just for a while, Jack,' she added when she heard his intake of breath. 'He thinks she'll get better treatment in Spain. He has a friend who's a senior consultant in psychiatric medicine at the clinic. We need you at the hospital Jack, to countersign the paperwork. I think they called them discharge papers. Anyway I have to go, we're outside the hospital now. The parking looks impossible.'

Jack went to the shower, scowling. Ana's parents had been against their daughter's marriage from the start. Her father hadn't made any attempt to hide his disapproval of the match. As far as he was concerned, Jack had taken shameful advantage of his 'princesa' from the moment she arrived in England. Jack grinned; he was probably right.

He didn't hurry his walk across the heath; a desperate attempt to delay the inevitable frosty reception he knew he would receive. He dreaded what Ana's parents would say when they saw their beloved daughter. All José's suspicions would be vindicated.

By the time he arrived at the main entrance, Jack had decided that the best course of action would be to collaborate with Ana's parents and do everything possible to expedite her return to Spain with them.

Better for her, better for them, and much better for me, he thought.

The woman sitting behind the main desk in Reception told him that Ana had been moved. 'According to my records,' she said officiously, as she tapped the computer screen, 'Mrs Millfield is in a private room in the Psychiatric Unit.'

Jack tried to ignore the nightmare images of straightjackets and barred windows floating into his head as he made his way through the endless labyrinth of hospital corridors.

Ana's mother was sitting on the bed, cradling her daughter in her arms; they were both weeping. Her father was nowhere to be seen.

Jack closed the door quietly and laid a tentative hand on Maude's shoulder. She looked up with Ana's head resting against her chest like a small child.

'Ana? It's me, Jack,' said Jack, leaning down to touch his wife's face. She opened her eyes briefly and closed them.

'José has gone to speak to the head of the department. I think they're going to talk to the people in Spain.'

Maude was stroking her daughter's hair as she spoke.

'Is she fit enough to travel?' Jack tried not to sound too hopeful as he stared at the limp figure in Maude's arms.

'They said she's OK to travel, as long as she's with us. The doctor thinks she's got a serious case of depression, but they're hopeful that she can be treated. Do you mind if we take her, Jack?'

Jack looked straight at her. Maude was only ten years older than him and still a very attractive woman. A mature version of Ana, with the same dark eyes and slim, elegant figure. Don't they always tell you to look at the mother if you want to know what your wife will look like when she's old, he thought as he smiled back at her.

'Mind, Maude? Of course I don't mind. I want Ana to get better more than anything else in the world, and if you and José think that she will recover faster in Spain, then of course I won't object to her going. Why would I?'

He squeezed Maude's shoulder and she tipped her head to lay her cheek against his hand.

In fact, the more I think about it, the more I can see that it's a perfect solution for everybody, Jack thought as the door opened and Ana's father came in, followed by two doctors. Maude settled Ana gently back against the pillows and stood up.

José Valdéz' dark brown eyes were hard to read when he greeted Jack with a formal handshake and a slight inclination of his head before introducing the two doctors.

'This is my wife and this is Jack Millfield, my son-in-law,' he said.

The English public school and Cambridge University education was only too evident in his clipped accent and impeccable command of the language.

'We've had a long discussion with my colleagues in Madrid

and we all agree that Ana is well enough to travel. I've already booked seats for us on a flight back to Spain at seven o'clock this evening. Club Class of course, so she will at least be comfortable. She will sleep at home tonight and tomorrow we will take her to the clinic. It's all arranged.' José smiled affectionately at his daughter.

Jack leaned over to stroke Ana's forehead.

'Do you understand what your father said darling? You're going back to Spain,' he whispered.

Ana didn't react and Jack felt a twinge of uneasiness.

'Does she understand what's going on? She looks as though she's lost the plot completely,' he asked as he glanced up at the faces of his father-in-law and the two doctors.

'Of course she understands. She has not 'lost the plot' as you so charmingly put it. She has lost a child, and she is very, very sad. I think it is you who doesn't understand, Jack.' José Valdez said coldly.

Maude watched the interchange between the two men and held her daughter close.

One of the hospital doctors stepped forward.

'We agree with Dr Valdéz, Mr Millfield. Your wife will recover more quickly in Spain with her family. It has been a terrible shock for both of you, but Ana is in urgent need of specialist care now. Her father has been talking to his colleagues in Madrid and we are very confident that she will receive the appropriate treatment when she arrives. And I must stress that Ana herself seems to be eager to go. It is the only thing that she's been saying since she was admitted. We wouldn't let her travel if we weren't convinced that she's able to make the journey. As you've heard, she'll be travelling in great comfort with both her parents, one of whom is a highly qualified doctor. You couldn't ask for a better assurance of her safety.'

Ana's hollow eyes were focused unwaveringly on her parents. It was obvious that she wanted to be with them.

If she wants to go back, why would I try to stop her? I can't cope with her in that condition and I don't even want to try, Jack thought as he watched José talking quietly to his daughter in Spanish, holding both her hands in his and eliciting a weak smile. She will be much happier in Spain, cosseted and pampered by her parents in ways that I couldn't begin to understand.

Maude stood up. 'Jack, why don't we go downstairs to get a coffee, while they prepare Ana?' she said. 'Then we could go straight to your apartment from here to pack her clothes and anything else she wants to bring home with her.'

Jack shrugged, 'Whatever you say, Maude. I'll do whatever I can to help,' he said, 'I just need to make a couple of phone calls to my office first. If you want a coffee, go ahead. I'll have one later.'

He saw Maude's face relax. She's almost as relieved as I am at the prospect of not having to drink coffee together, he thought.

'Shall we wait for you here or downstairs?' Maude asked.

'I'll see you at the main entrance in twenty minutes,' Jack replied as he blew a kiss in Ana's direction and left the room. He was desperate to have a few minutes to himself before the Valdéz family invaded his apartment.

He ran down the stairs and walked quickly away from the main entrance with his mobile phone already clamped to his ear. Catherine Boyce-Jones answered immediately.

'Mr Millfield's phone?'

'Hi Cat, it's me.'

'Hi Jack.' The delight in her voice brought a smirk of anticipation to Jack's face.

'Look, sweetie, I've got caught up in a meeting with a new client, looks like it's going to last all day. If you've got any problems, you can always buzz me on the mobile. 'Hasta la vista Babee,' he growled, in a poor imitation of Arnold Schwarzenegger's famous line.

Catherine giggled and Jack was still smiling as he walked towards the hospital entrance to wait for his wife and her parents.

*

By early afternoon there were two very large monogrammed trunks and six matching suitcases piled up in the reception of Jack's apartment building. José had organised a specialised transport company to take the luggage to the airport separately.

Jack had watched Ana's possessions being systematically removed from each room while she lay, tearfully watching, from the sofa. He'd felt a brief pang of regret when he noticed that Maude had helped Ana to put on the outfit that she'd worn to travel to Mauritius for their honeymoon. The exquisite cream silk trouser suit was loose on her emaciated frame.

Nice touch, Maude, he thought bitterly, very subtle.

Ana didn't appear to notice him. He couldn't decide whether it was because she hadn't realised that he was there or whether she was deliberately ignoring him. Jack wondered if she was blaming him for the miscarriage. Someone ought to tell her, make her understand that I had absolutely nothing to do with it. I didn't even know that she was pregnant, until she told me on the day she went out to buy the pregnancy test, he thought.

He toyed with the idea of explaining it to her parents, to ensure that they knew his side of the story and then dismissed it. What's the point? The cab is due at any minute and I'll be left with half of it untold.

Jack went out onto the balcony to gaze across the heath. His spirits lifted momentarily when he noticed distinct traces of green sprouting on the tops of the trees. An early promise of the dense foliage that would follow.

He could hear the staccato sound of Ana's parents talking in Spanish in the room behind him. He was glad that he understood very little of what they were saying. His eyes hardened. What do I care? Soon they'll all be gone, he thought. He mused on how quickly his life had changed during the past four days. There were still so many unanswered questions. Will Ana want to come back when she's recovered? Do I actually want her back? Why did I marry her in the first place? Was it to score points off Maggie, or just to have sex with a very beautiful young woman whenever I felt like it?

Jack fought the desire to laugh out loud. Does it really matter now? It was fun while it lasted, that's what counts.

His mobile vibrated in his pocket, signalling the arrival of a text from his PA.

'2 new BlackBerrys on your desk. C x'

Jack's reply was concise.

'X'

He put the phone back in his pockets and clicked the joints of his fingers one by one, with his eyes back on the skyline. Some important, unfinished business was still waiting for attention.

39

Andrew Bridgeman telephoned Maggie at nine o'clock on Tuesday morning. He told her that after receiving her frantic messages from Suffolk, he had looked at all the evidence with two of his colleagues. They agreed that in view of Jack's previous history and the seriously threatening nature of the most recent email, the most effective approach would be to send Jack a formal warning that he would face a civil action if he persisted.

The solicitor advised Maggie to contact the police as soon as possible so that she could give them what he called a 'Victim's Personal Statement'. He explained that this would mean that the police would then be able to apply for a restraining order which would prevent Jack from approaching her or trying to contact her.

Maggie readily agreed, with the proviso that all the details of her present address and employment must not be disclosed or revealed to anybody. She explained that she had signed a confidentiality agreement which her job and accommodation depended upon.

She was reassured when Andrew suggested that everything could be done through his office, including any meetings with the police. He reminded her again that she should continue to keep records of everything she received from Jack until the restraining order was in place and afterwards, if Jack decided to ignore it.

'We'll take advice from the police as soon as I can organise the meeting, probably sometime next week. This is now a damage limitation exercise, Maggie. Carry on with your life as usual until we get this restraining order in place. It might be a good idea to stop using your personal mobile and your landline altogether.'

'I've got a work mobile, but it's strictly for work.' Maggie said.

'In that case, I suggest you go and buy yourself another mobile phone with a new SIM card and tell people that you've lost your old mobile. It's all about reducing the stress levels, Maggie.' Andrew Bridgeman's tone was slightly impatient, when he heard her intake of breath. 'I'll let you know as soon as I've sorted out the meeting with the police and I'll get the letter off to Millfield straight away. Don't worry. This time, we'll get it sorted out, once and for all.'

Maggie put the phone down. While she had been talking to him, Andrew Bridgeman's confident manner had given her a momentary feeling of relief, but as she stared at the busy road beyond the car park, her anxieties started to resurface again. All these legal measures would take time, meanwhile Jack might be down there, hiding somewhere behind the shrubs in the forecourt, waiting for her.

She shivered and lowered the blind so that her face couldn't be seen from the road. She stood in the darkened room for several minutes before raising it and moving away from the window.

I am being ridiculous. I can't hide from Jack for the rest of my life. In any case, he won't be out there now, he's got a business to run and a wife to look after. I've got to go to Andrew's office to hand over the Victim's Personal Statement next week and I've got to go out now and buy another mobile phone.

But by the time she was ready to leave for the mobile phone shop, Maggie's fragile courage had failed her. She called for a cab and told herself that it was more sensible to be cautious until Jack had received the letter from Andrew Bridgeman.

Just over an hour later, when she was standing outside the

mobile phone shop, waiting for another cab to take her back to the flat in St John's Wood, her Team Hunter mobile signalled the arrival of a text.

'Keep smiling R x'

Maggie's eyes filled with tears.

*

Rob had sent the message from a large private room in the flagship store of a leading menswear designer in Bond Street. He was with Saz and the personal stylist she had engaged to select his outfits for the press and media events they were due to attend.

Most of the day had been spent patiently enduring the attentions of a makeup artist, a hair stylist and two photographers, while various permutations of suits, shirts, sweaters, scarves, shoes, hats and even sunglasses were tried on, rejected or accepted and photographed for Saz's complicated records of what Rob would wear, when and where.

Saz had positioned herself on a sofa, alternately shouting into her mobile or yelling instructions at the various people fussing around Rob.

Rob gazed over their heads, lost in thought.

Maggie's spontaneous smile while they were having dinner in the pub had been haunting him. He'd been given a tantalising glimpse of another Maggie. A happier, more relaxed Maggie. He was sure that it was the real Maggie and he wanted to find her again.

'This way, Mr Hunter, please. Over your shoulder, that's right! Eyes down! Great! Now look straight at the camera. Give me a glower, Mr Hunter. Oh … yes!'

The young female photographer circled around him, kneeling on the floor and standing on the furniture, whispering her instructions.

Rob sighed as he watched Saz chatting to the stylist and the makeup artist and handing over a credit card to a shop assistant for what he suspected would be an astronomical figure.

Saz believed implicitly that physical appearance and presentation were indispensable on the road to success. You either accepted it, or rejected it and paid the price. The current forensic attention he was receiving from both the media and the public had forced him to accept her advice together with the disappearance of a sizeable chunk of his income. He was being dragged inexorably into the dreaded commodification web of celebrity.

He thought of Maggie again, trying to imagine what she would say if she was there to witness what was happening to him at that moment.

He pictured her solemn expression, her green eyes widening with amazement and his expression softened. She's like me, he thought, she wouldn't be impressed.

'OK guys, that's it. We're done. You can wear that one now, Rob. The rest can be delivered later today, please.' Saz glared at the shop assistant.

Rob felt himself relax. Saz's raucous instructions had never been more welcome. She was signalling to him that they were leaving as she tapped her watch.

'Come on, Rob. We're late. We've got to be at the TV studios in half an hour. We'll have to get a cup of their bloody awful coffee when we arrive.'

They climbed into the back of the hire car and Saz handed him three sheets of A4, closely typed with colour coded, scripted questions and answers.

Rob gave them a cursory glance. Although he was meticulous about doing his research before every role, and was always prepared to give an accurate and informed reply to any question about his work, they both knew that it would be an endless battle to ensure that certain journalists stuck to the script.

Press releases had been sent out before the visits to radio and TV studios, warning them that any subjects that were not connected to the production would not be permitted. Unfortunately, it wouldn't prevent some of the more intrepid journalists from going *off piste*. Saz had told him to smile diplomatically and say nothing if that happened.

She had reassured him that the international press tour would be much less stressful, apart from the travelling and the time involved; mainly because the director and other members of the cast would be with him which meant there would be much less attention on him.

Rob wriggled his feet inside the new shoes, which were pinching painfully around his toes.

'What size are these shoes?' he groaned.

'How the hell should I know? Yours, I hope. Why would they get it wrong? In any case, you're only going to wear them for a few hours. You can trash them once we've finished the TV stuff. It won't matter what you've got on your feet for the radio interview.'

Saz was typing furiously on her laptop and clearly irritated by the interruption.

'Where are my Doc Martens?' Rob ventured cautiously after a pause.

'Your what?' Saz frowned, 'No idea. Where did you leave them? They're probably in your wardrobe, where else would they be? Do you want me to call Maggie and ask her to check? I'll ask her to bring them down to the studios now, if you want.'

'No! Don't do that. It's not important,' Rob protested, cringing at what Maggie might think if she was asked to bring a favourite pair of boots to a studio on the other side of London, simply because he didn't like the new £700 designer pair he was wearing. It would validate all her notions about pampered, self-obsessed celebrities.

Mercifully, the first interview was straightforward. Rob

already knew both the presenter and the critic and there were no surprises or tricks. The director told Saz that they were hoping that the film would be mentioned in a programme to be shown on TV that evening.

The second interview was less relaxed. It was held in a hotel suite, booked at very short notice, because the main studios were outside London and the interviewer and her camera crew had arrived late, apparently due to a signal failure on the trains. Rob had never met the interviewer before and Saz managed to crank up the tension when she announced, 'Mr Hunter is on a very tight schedule. This will have to be quick,' as soon as they arrived.

In spite of the questions being aggressive and intrusive, somehow Rob managed to remain calm; his answers were polite, non-committal and delivered with a friendly smile.

Back in the car, on their way to a local radio station, Saz touched his sleeve.

'My God, how the hell do you do it?' she asked admiringly.

Rob looked confused by the question.

'How do you manage to be so bloody nice to everybody? Some of these hacks are little shits.' Saz said.

'I'm supposed to be an actor, aren't I?'

Saz laughed and Rob yawned and looked at his watch. 'How many more?'

'Just this next one. We've got several tomorrow. All one-to-ones with journalists and interpreters, from Japan, France, Germany and two with American TV stations. We'll do those in an hotel I went to last year with another client. I've booked one of the rooms.'

Saz was typing as she spoke. Rob peered over her shoulder; it was another press release. He bent down to untie his shoe laces while her attention was diverted.

'Don't!' she shrieked without taking her eyes off the screen. 'You'll never get them back on again!'

Rob sighed and leaned back against the seat, flexing his feet inside the shoes. He closed his eyes for a second, then opened one to squint sideways at her.

'I thought you said it didn't matter what I wore on my feet to do radio interviews?'

'That was only if you changed into the boots we were going to ask Maggie to bring to you. I draw the line at no shoes. At least, not with a £2,000 suit.'

'I don't see why not. I could start a trend.'

'I wouldn't recommend it, at least not yet,' Saz said dryly, 'We've only just started on the one you've got!'

She closed her computer as the car came to a halt outside the hotel, where, to Rob's dismay, a small group of photographers were gathered. 'Smile, Mr Hunter,' she said.

40

Jack left the office early, telling Catherine that he was going to meet a prospective client for a drink after work. She pouted with mock disappointment and he realised that she was hoping to be invited.

He leaned across her desk to put his lips close to her ear, whispering, 'Not tonight, sweetie. I thought we could go out for dinner tomorrow? You deserve a very big thank you.'

Catherine's clear, blue eyes gazed up at him; she looked nervous and excited. Jack liked that. He held up the large brown envelope containing the two new BlackBerry mobile phones, shaking it like a child with a new toy.

'You choose where, honey. Money's absolutely no object,' he called, winking over his shoulder as the lift doors closed.

*

Back in his apartment, Jack hurried towards his study.

The email from Beatrice Benedick had not been returned.

'Excellent. That means that you're still using your Hotmail address,' he said aloud. His mouth twisted into a cruel caricature of a smile.

'You've read it and you're scared shitless. I know you, Maggie Savernake. All women are gullible and you're no exception. You've already proved that, my darling. You might be an expert on English literature and William fucking Shakespeare, but you're a pathetic, unsophisticated muppet where a man like me is concerned.'

Jack tore open the envelope and took out the two new mobiles, relieved to see that Catherine had charged them.

'Didn't think the little sweetie had that much intelligence,' he said as he lifted his newly purchased copy of the *Complete Works of William Shakespeare* off the shelf behind his chair.

'Now let's find our little Beatrice Benedick a couple of mates.'

He opened a page at random.

'Here we are, *Love's Labour's Lost*.'

He stabbed randomly with his ball point pen, then wrote Armado and Moth on his blotter, and flicked through the pages until he stopped at *Pericles, Prince of Tyre*.

He stabbed again: Marina and Boult.

'OK. That'll do for now. You're on a roll, Millfield. Firing on all cylinders, my man. No one can stop you now.'

Jack slammed the book shut and tossed it onto the floor with a crash.

'Thanks, Will. That's all I need for the time being.'

He typed identical messages into each of the phones.

'An eye for an eye.'

One from Armado Moth and the second from Marina Boult.

Then, holding a mobile in each hand and yelling 'Pow! Pow!' like a schoolboy with a toy pistol, he resent the message again and again, until seventy-two messages were winging their way through the ether to Maggie's inbox.

Then, breathless from his exertions, Jack took an indelible marker and scrawled the names on the backs of the phones.

'This one has got legs,' he muttered breathlessly, 'I can make it run for months and months.'

He lifted a bottle of wine out of the rack and filled a glass.

'This is a cause for celebration.'

He picked up the remote control, aimed it at the TV and pressed it as he threw himself onto the sofa.

A couple of hours later, the wine bottle was almost empty, Jack was half asleep and the TV was still on.

Two men were perched on stools, discussing a new film. One of them was describing an interview he had done with an actor called Rob Hunter. He thumbed at a large studio portrait of the actor projected onto a screen behind them.

Jack peered at the screen and heaved himself into a sitting position as the portrait was replaced by a poster, depicting a tall, shadowy figure running down a dark street and brandishing a revolver.

'Rob Hunter? That's the guy Maggie's working for, isn't it?' he said as he forced himself to focus on what the two men were saying. Apparently they had both been to see the film and were in complete agreement. The film was excellent and Rob Hunter's performance was outstanding.

'This one's definitely a must-see,' said one of the men, with a cheeky grin at the camera. 'Don't miss it.'

Jack punched the Off button on the remote control and emptied the wine bottle into his glass as the phone rang.

He snatched up the receiver and could hardly believe his luck when he heard the voice of Saul Myerson, Dominic Goldman's partner.

'Hi Jack, apologies for calling at such a late hour.'

Saul explained that he wanted to confirm the timetable for the design job he was doing for Millfield Advertising and Jack replied in curt monosyllables, impatient to put his own question.

At last Saul seemed to have reach the end, 'Oh, and before I put the phone down Jack, how's Ana?'

'Ana? Oh, she had a miscarriage.' Jack's casual manner shocked Saul.

'Oh my God! I'm so sorry to hear that. Poor darling. How shocking, how awful.'

'Her parents took her home at the beginning of the week.' Jack said coldly.

'Ana's had a miscarriage. She's gone back to Spain with her parents.'

Jack closed his eyes as he listened to Saul relaying the news to Dominic, followed by incomprehensible, muffled whispering before Saul said, 'Send her our love, Jack.'

'Thanks,' Jack replied, 'By the way Saul, remember the actor that Dominic mentioned, the one Maggie is working for? Is his name Rob Hunter? Only they were talking about a new film on TV just now and his name came up.'

There was an imperceptible hesitation before Saul said, 'I'm not sure, Jack. We didn't see the programme, did we Dom? Maggie's not taking calls from anybody now. Not even Rose.'

'Probably too busy massaging Rob Hunter's ego or whatever he pays her to do for him,' Jack sniggered.

Saul was silent.

'OK Saul, thanks. I'll see you with the layouts next week.' Jack put the phone down. 'You're a bad liar, Saul. That silence said it all. If Rob Hunter's in that film, he will be very easy to find. And... wherever he is, Maggie will be.'

Jack's cackle of hysterical laughter echoed around the apartment.

41

There was no sun streaming through the bedroom windows to wake Jack the following morning, which meant that when Senka, the cleaner, arrived at 10am, he was still fast asleep.

Through the open door of the bedroom, she could see him, spread-eagled across the bed, and still fully dressed. The acrid smell of stale alcohol pervaded the air; she wrinkled her nose with disgust as she quietly closed the door and went to the kitchen.

It wasn't the first time she'd discovered him in that condition when she arrived for work. She was relieved that he was in his bedroom and fully dressed. Usually it was the lounge and once, naked on the floor of the bathroom.

Senka preferred to work around him, rather than wake him. He could be very bad tempered and was often abusive if she disturbed him. He made her very nervous, especially when his wife was not at home.

An hour later, the sound of the floor-waxing machine moving slowly up and down the hallway outside his bedroom door penetrated Jack's brain. He rolled off the bed onto the floor mumbling incomprehensibly as he struggled to his feet, squinting at the alarm clock.

'Eleven o'clock? Shit, how did that happen?' he moaned hoarsely as he staggered towards the bathroom, narrowly missing a large, blue plastic box filled with cleaning materials.

Senka watched his erratic progress anxiously. Most men she

knew liked a drink, but not like this one. She lowered her gaze as he passed.

Jack showered and dressed quickly before taking a cup of black coffee back to his desk, where he discovered that Senka had already left the post.

He went through it impatiently, discarding all the junk mail until he came to an envelope with the name of a law firm in the City printed on the back. The name looked familiar but he couldn't recall where he'd seen it before. He ripped open the envelope with the colour draining from his face.

Maggie had instructed her solicitors to bring another civil action against him for harassment and threat. She was also requesting that a restraining order be served.

The implications of the civil action were described in alarming detail. If the civil court found him guilty of harassment and threat, he would receive an injunction. If he ignored the injunction and persisted, a breach of the injunction would be regarded as a criminal offence and he would be summoned to the criminal court. If he was found guilty of a criminal offence, a prison term was a possibility.

Jack reread the letter more slowly. He was having great difficulty in comprehending the contents. Beads of sweat began to break out on his face.

What's got into the mad bitch? Why does she always take everything so fucking seriously? Why can't she see that the messages are a joke? All I want to do is to talk to her, for fuck's sake. What is wrong with that?

He grabbed the phone and punched in the number at the top of the letter. There was no signature. He recited the reference number and waited while the receptionist located, 'Mr Andrew Bridgeman, who is dealing with this case.'

This case? This case? What the hell is going on? Jack shook his head, which felt as though someone was smashing it against a wall.

'Good morning, Mr Millfield. What can I do for you?'

Jack's hackles rose at the sound of the patronising manner and clipped vowels.

'You can tell me what the hell this letter I received from you this morning is all about. That's what you can do!' he roared.

'Letter? Oh, yes, I assume you are referring to the letter regarding Dr Savernake?'

'Yes, that bloody letter. What the hell is going on? Is this some sort of sick joke or what? Why is she bringing a civil action against me? And what is all this about the police getting involved, as though I am some sort of criminal?'

'I can assure you, Mr Millfield, that this is definitely not a joke. Furthermore, I advise you to moderate your language and stop shouting. The reasons for the civil action and the involvement of the police are set out very clearly in the letter. If you have anything to say, I suggest you put it in writing.'

'This is ridiculous. I haven't seen Maggie Savernake for months. All I want to do is to talk to her,' Jack was almost incoherent.

'I advise you to instruct a solicitor if you wish to challenge this action, Mr Millfield. I'm afraid there is nothing more that I can say at this time. If you have any other queries, please don't hesitate to contact us. Good morning.'

There was a decisive click and Jack threw the phone down, panting with rage and frustration. She's not going to get away with this. I won't allow it. How dare she try to deflect attention away from herself by pointing the finger at me? This is all her doing. She killed my child, ruined my life and she's going to pay for it. End of story.

His eyes fell on a photograph of Ana on their honeymoon, head on one side, smiling seductively at the camera.

'Look at her, look at my gorgeous, sexy little Ana. Where is she now?' Jack kicked the desk viciously.

'None of this would have happened if Maggie hadn't done what she did. That evil bitch is not getting away with it, police or no police.'

42

Two days after his first phone call, Andrew Bridgeman called Maggie to tell her that he had arranged a meeting in his office with the police for the following afternoon. He asked her to prepare her personal statement.

'Go as far back as you like,' he advised, 'the more evidence we have the better.'

Maggie told him that more suspect email messages had arrived in her inbox, but she hadn't opened them.

'Put them with the rest of the evidence, we'll let the police deal with them. I'm afraid that Mr Millfield doesn't seem to understand the seriousness of what he's doing. I advise you to make your new employers aware of the situation, Maggie. The police will want all your personal details and they may want to speak to your employers as well.'

Maggie's stomach lurched.

'Do I have to? I can't bear the thought of having to talk about any of this to other people, Andrew. It took me long enough to contact you.'

'I know. But I honestly don't understand why. You're not guilty. You are the victim, Maggie,' he said

'I am so ashamed.' Her voice was barely above a whisper.

'You really must stop thinking like that. You've been the victim of a very unprincipled individual. You need to grasp that fact and take control of the situation. Now, go and speak to your employers and I'll see you tomorrow afternoon here in my office at 3pm.'

It was seven o'clock in the evening when Maggie heard Rob and Saz arrive back at the flat. She was still editing her statement. As she expected, it had been very difficult to write. Not only because she had been forced to relive the whole story, but also because she was now faced with the prospect of having to confess to Rob and Saz that she had misled them.

Maggie could hear them moving around in the flat next door and her heart sank. It was time. She dialled Saz on the Team Hunter mobile.

'Hi Saz, I wondered if I could have a quick word. I know you're busy. It won't take long.'

'Where are you?' Saz sounded irritable.

'I'm here, in the flat.'

'Why the hell are you phoning me? Come in, for God's sake, Maggie. The door's not locked.'

Rob stood in the lounge doorway in his shirt sleeves with his tie hanging loosely around his neck. His feet were bare, as usual.

'Hi, we've just got back. Want a glass of wine?' he said with a warm smile.

Maggie shook her head, unable to meet his eyes.

Saz was sitting on the sofa reading a document, with her laptop open on the seat beside her.

'Christ! Whatever's the matter, Maggie? Sit down. You look terrible,' she exclaimed when she saw Maggie's bleak expression.

Maggie perched on the edge of a chair.

'I've got to ask you both something,' she said in a low voice. 'Someone I used to know has been harassing me, sending threatening messages. Emails and texts. I reported it to my solicitor and he suggested that we get the police involved because some of the threats are… serious.'

She paused, avoiding their shocked faces.

'I have to give the police what is called a victim's personal statement before they will issue a restraining order against him. Which means that I have to give them details of my present occupation and address. So, obviously, I need to get permission from both of you before I can do that.'

Saz glanced at Rob, but he was staring intently at Maggie.

'I think that Rob has already guessed a lot of this,' Maggie said, 'the emails I received at the weekend were very... unpleasant. I phoned my solicitor on Monday and he told me that we should start by threatening him with civil action, again.'

'Again?' Saz echoed incredulously.

Maggie nodded.

'I had to do the same thing nearly two years ago, and it stopped him. So Andrew, my solicitor, suggested that we repeat it, only this time he wants me to make the victim's personal statement as well.'

'Has he attacked you physically?' Rob's expression was grim.

'Not this time. He's just threatening it.'

'Are you saying that he's attacked you in the past?' Saz looked dumbfounded. 'What kind of a monster is he? What's his name?'

'Jack Millfield. It's a long story. Too long to go into now. My immediate problem is that the police will want to know where I live and work, and obviously I must have your permission to give them that information. I've already told my solicitor that I will only do so on the understanding that the police give you a written undertaking that all the details are kept out of the public domain.'

'I need to talk to one of our legal guys.' Saz was scrolling quickly through the contacts list on her phone. She looked up at Maggie. 'When's the meeting with your solicitor and the police?'

'In Andrew Bridgeman's office tomorrow afternoon. He said we must move quickly.'

Saz was dialling and waving her hand for silence.

On the edge of her field of vision Maggie could just make

out the long line of Rob's thigh where he was sitting on the sofa near her. She could almost feel the tension radiating from him.

'Paul, it's me, Saz. We've got a little problem. I need someone from your office to be at a meeting tomorrow afternoon. Yes, here first and then at the offices of a law company called…?' Saz looked expectantly at Maggie.

'Bridgeman and Co, they're in the City,' said Maggie.

'Bridgeman and Co. Oh you know them? Good. Well, this is about Maggie Savernake, the girl we employed to look after the flat and the house for Rob. She's having a lot of trouble with an ex-boyfriend and the police are involved. Maggie's solicitor said the police will need her address and work details. As you know, she lives in the flat next door to Rob. So we need to be very careful. What? No. I don't think so. Oh, and I can't be there tomorrow. Rob and I are with the press all day long. Right, you'll meet her here at lunchtime. Great! Thanks, Paul.'

She turned to Maggie. 'Paul Drake's coming himself. He'll be here at lunchtime. He's the top man, a nice guy, very professional. You can have a chat with him before you go to the meeting. Unfortunately, Rob and I will be tied up all day, otherwise I'd come too. Anyhow, you won't be on your own. Team Hunter to the rescue, eh Rob?'

'Are you OK with that, Maggie?' Rob looked worried.

Maggie nodded and got to her feet.

'Thank you. You're both very kind. Thank you. I'm…sorry.'

Saz followed Maggie to the door between the two flats, closing it firmly before she returned to the lounge where she found Rob staring at the floor.

'What do you make of all that, then?' she hissed.

'I don't know. I can't understand how a girl like Maggie could get involved with such a character. Who the hell is he?' Rob muttered.

'Jack Millfield.' Saz was tapping the keys on her laptop. 'Let's have a look… oh, needless to say there are quite a few of them.

Hopefully not all like this one. Wait a minute, Jack Millfield, Director, Millfield Advertising, Knightsbridge. Look there's a photo.'

She swivelled the screen towards Rob.

He glanced at it and stood up abruptly.

'Not interested. Paul will deal with him. Let's drop it. We've got an early start tomorrow.'

Saz raised her eyebrows, surprised by his untypically terse reply.

'Fine. I'll be here tomorrow morning at eight o'clock then.'

Rob didn't hear the front door close when Saz left, nor did he notice the rain when he went outside to stand on the balcony. He was shocked by the fear he'd seen on Maggie's face.

43

After reflecting on the contents of the letter from the solicitor, Jack realised that he would have to move quickly. He took a cab into the office and told Catherine that he had to prepare a new campaign proposal and didn't want to be disturbed.

He scanned the list of sites featuring Rob Hunter's name, ninety-nine per cent of which were obviously created by fans and the usual celebrity trolls. Eventually, his attention was caught by the title of the film mentioned on the TV programme. It was a press release announcing that Rob was expected to make a personal appearance at a press conference which would be held at a hotel in Park Lane.

Jack gave a whoop of triumph and punched the air. All he needed now was a press pass. Shouldn't be too difficult, he thought as he flicked through his long list of contacts. After many years spent buying space in newspapers and magazines for his company's clients, he was spoilt for choice. He grinned, perhaps his so-called 'career' hadn't been such a waste of time after all?

He selected an old drinking pal who had just been appointed show business critic for one of the more insalubrious men's magazines. It was perfect. After listening to Jack's elaborate explanation about having promised a fictional god-daughter that he would get Rob Hunter's autograph for her birthday, the friend suggested that he would tell his editor that, as a personal favour, Jack had offered to write a report on the press conference for their magazine.

Jack was delighted and offered to take his friend to an exclusive restaurant in Chelsea as a thank you.

Half an hour later, he received an emailed pass to the press conference which was scheduled for the following afternoon.

'Sorted,' Jack screamed exultantly as he printed it off.

Catherine stuck her head around the door. 'Did you call, Jack?'

'I thought I told you that I didn't want to be disturbed? Get out!' He flung a magazine at the door, without a second thought for the tearful girl trembling on the other side.

Jack swivelled his chair to stare unseeingly at the panoramic view beyond his window.

He had attended many press conferences over the years; listening to endless presentations in the company of bored, hard-bitten journalists was usually very tedious. This time it would be different. This was his last chance. This would be his *coup de grace*, his golden opportunity to destroy Maggie's chance of happiness once and for all, as she had destroyed his.

Tonight I'll go to bed early, he thought. No food, no wine, no emails, no TV. Nothing. Just sleep.

44

The following morning, Jack took a cab from his flat to the hotel in Park Lane, wearing his pale silver grey silk and linen mix suit with a navy blue shirt and matching tie. Designer sunglasses, in spite of the heavy skies, completed his somewhat clichéd impression of a film critic.

He sat in the back of the cab, briefcase by his side, feeling confident and pleased with himself. Eight hours of uninterrupted sleep had done their work; he felt better than he had felt for months.

As the cab passed Admiralty Arch, he looked across at Hyde Park, where the branches were drooping under the weight of their sodden leaves. There were a few hardy joggers, splashing through the puddles and dodging the pedestrians' umbrellas. Jack hadn't walked through the park since the day he'd had lunch with his mother. He remembered the baby he'd laughed with and the backs of his eyes burned with unshed, angry tears.

As the cab drew up outside the hotel, a commissionaire stepped forward to open the door with a salute and Jack blinked and paused to compose himself before stepping onto the pavement.

Inside the hotel foyer, he scanned the large cardboard posters for the film outside the double doors leading into the large conference room. Life-size cardboard cut-outs of Rob Hunter, brandishing a pistol, were everywhere.

Several rows of gilt chairs, some already occupied, were facing a long table covered with a dark blue cloth and microphones with wires trailing along the table. There were five chairs behind the table.

Jack searched the room, calculating where he should sit. At the front? No, too difficult to make an escape, if he needed to. In the middle of a row? Best place to get lost in the crowd, but again too difficult to escape from.

He finally settled for a chair at the end of a middle row. Visibility is important if you want to get the attention of the chairperson, he thought as he checked his watch. There were ten minutes to go.

He sat with one leg jiggling nervously as he glanced around the room which was filling up quickly. He had forgotten that he was still wearing his sunglasses.

The buzz of conversation was increasing and the temperature in the room seemed to be rising. Jack ran a finger around his shirt collar and dabbed his face with a handkerchief. There had been a moment when he had nearly chickened out and asked his journalist friend whether he would go in his place. But it was only a moment.

Jack knew that it would be too risky and complicated. He would have had to answer too many awkward questions.

No. If you want a job done properly, do it yourself, he told himself as he saw a movement behind the silver curtain behind the chairs where the film people would sit.

The theatrical atmosphere seemed to increase the suspense. Jack's heartbeat accelerated and small beads of sweat broke out on his upper lip when the spotlights clicked on and a pool of light was focused on the long table.

The buzz of conversation faded as a young woman appeared from behind the silver curtain with a clipboard on her arm and a biro tucked behind one ear. She tapped the microphone with a long painted fingernail and a toothy smile. After introducing herself, she called out the names of the various members of the cast and crew who appeared one by one from behind the shimmering curtain, shading their eyes from the spotlights.

Rob Hunter, who was the last, took his place at the end of the row, dressed in a black sweater and jeans. Jack was surprised, the actor was much taller and thinner than he looked on the posters.

Rob raised his hand to shield his eyes again as he scanned the audience. He whispered something to the girl sitting next to him and they both laughed.

Pompous prick, Jack thought as he took out a small pad and a ballpoint pen.

After the introductions, the director and the producer spent a lot of time answering questions about the casting process, particularly why they had chosen a relatively unknown actor like Rob Hunter who had limited experience of cinema. Jack scribbled on his pad, ostentatiously flicking over the pages and glancing sideways at the girl sitting next to him, who was tapping her notes into a laptop.

Finally, the young woman presenter turned to the audience.

'Now it's your turn, and we would be grateful if you would please restrict your questions to the film. Thank you.' She said as she winked at the two actors and sat down.

Jack swallowed as hands shot up around him; he was counting, judging his moment, estimating that it would take him less than ten seconds to reach the exit doors. He raised his hand and waited, with his heart leaping in his chest and his mouth as dry as sandpaper.

After what seemed like an eternity, he heard the girl say, 'Yes, you, the man in the grey suit and the shades, your question please?'

Jack stood up and looked straight at Rob Hunter.

'Thank you. This is a question for Mr Hunter. I want to know if Maggie Savernake has told you the truth, Mr Hunter? Has she told you about the baby?'

Heads turned to stare, first at Jack and then at the table. Jack could hear loud intakes of breath and excited whispering. The actor sitting next to Rob was looking at him with an amused grin. Rob looked as though he was cast in stone, his grey eyes were boring into Jack like lasers.

A couple of voices in the audience yelled, 'Who's Maggie Savernake, Mr Hunter?' 'Who's Maggie Savernake?' 'Whose baby is it, Mr Hunter?'

The producer had got to his feet, speaking urgently into his mobile and the girl with the clipboard had disappeared behind the curtain.

Jack's legs felt like water as the adrenaline subsided. He was half sitting, half standing when he felt large hands seizing him roughly from behind and frog-marching him down the aisle and out of the room.

Cameras flashed in his face as he was pushed into a small office at the back of the conference room and surrounded by four burly security men.

Jack looked up at them as his rage returned. He struggled to get to his feet, ramming one of them in the solar plexus with his head and throwing a wild punch at another, all the while yelling and swearing profusely. It took three of the security men to hold him down after he landed a vicious kick at the groin of the fourth.

He watched the man doubled up on the floor as he heard a desperate female voice shouting in the foyer, 'OK, no more questions, please. No more questions. The conference is over.'

Jack stopped struggling and his mouth twisted into a rictus of a smile. Mission accomplished, the media fallout from this will finish Maggie Savernake for good, he thought.

45

Saz pushed her way through the crowd of chattering journalists streaming out of the conference room with phones clamped to their ears. She could just make out the back of Rob's head at the far end of a corridor. He and his colleagues were being jostled into a room by a wall of security people.

The door was slammed shut as she reached it and two security men took up their positions, facing the crowd, arms akimbo, biceps straining the sleeves of their jackets.

'I need to speak to Mr Hunter,' she said.

'That's not possible, Madam.' The man said as he stared over her head.

'But I'm his agent. I must speak to him.'

'Nobody in, nobody out.' The man's mouth had set in an obstinate line.

'You're Rob Hunter's agent?' said an incredulous voice. Saz spun around to see a young woman, staring at her admiringly.

'Fuck off!' growled Saz. Somebody sniggered in the crowd behind them.

The girl didn't blink. 'Do you know who Maggie Savernake is?'

'Which bit of fuck off don't you understand?' Saz yelled.

Her face was almost touching the girl's.

'Can I quote you?'

Saz read the identity tag suspended around the girl's neck.

'Jenny Faber, Film critic?' she hissed. 'Is that what you are hoping to be when you grow up? A film critic? My advice to you, love, is think very carefully before you quote anybody or anything today, or you'll end up frying chips. I'll make very sure of that.'

The girl shrugged nervously and rolled her eyes at the man next to her.

Saz turned and pushed her way back down the long corridor to the main entrance of the hotel and out into the roar of the Park Lane traffic. She slumped against a wall, struggling to regulate her breathing before she dialled Rob's mobile.

'Saz?' His voice was low and urgent.

'What the hell is going on, Rob? Was that who I think it was? And what's all this about a baby?' She couldn't keep the suspicion out of her voice.

'I think it was and I don't know what he was talking about or why. They're going to take us to a hotel outside London, I'm not sure where. Dave Masterson, the film company's publicity guy, is apparently organising something that will smother this. Divert the public's attention. I'll ring you when I know something. Have you heard from Maggie or Paul?'

'No. They ought to be back from the solicitors by now. God, Rob, what a ghastly mess. We'll have to get rid of her.' Saz's voice was rasping with anger.

'No. Absolutely not. This isn't her fault.'

'Don't give me that. She must have told Millfield about you. She's been lying to us from the start. Maggie's a liability.'

'No. Don't do anything, please. I've got to go. They're moving us now. I'll call you later. Don't say anything to her, Saz, not yet. Wait till I'm there.'

Once she was settled in a cab, still seething with anger, Saz pulled out her mobile again. Maggie's name must have been typed into search engines all over the world as soon as that idiot opened his stupid mouth, she thought. It'll have to be a big diversion to bury this story. But if anybody can do it, Dave

Masterson's the person to do it. Her frown faded as she dialled his number; Dave was an old friend, they'd worked together on several assignments over the years and got on very well together.

She wasn't disappointed. Dave told her that after making a few phone calls and paying an exorbitant sum of money, the film company had managed to purchase several incriminating paparazzi shots showing a very well-known veteran Hollywood actor, a British government front bencher and a couple of international politicians, skinny dipping with a group of pubescent girls off a huge yacht moored off the coast of Corsica. There were even a few fuzzy pictures of some of them playing naked volleyball on a beach.

'It's dynamite and it's going viral as we speak,' said Dave, with a hoarse laugh that quickly dissolved into a heavy bronchial cough. 'Believe me, Saz, the Maggie Savernake story is already buried and forgotten.'

'You're a genius, Dave.' Saz was uncharacteristically close to tears.

'It wasn't that difficult, darling. At this time of the year, they're all at it on the beaches of the Med. You just need to know the right people to call and have enough ready cash to pay them. It's paparazzi heaven out there. Everyone's got something to sell.'

Dave gave another chesty chuckle.

'The arrogance and stupidity of some of these people is mind boggling,' Saz said. 'They've got everything, looks, fame, money and power, and it's still not enough. They have to go that extra mile and get themselves involved in these tawdry little exploits. It makes you wonder whether they're doing it on purpose, sometimes. You know what I mean? Attention seeking.'

'Sex, drugs and rock and roll, with a bit of spicy political scandal thrown in. Who cares why they do it? It's a magic formula for the press and guaranteed to make headlines all over the planet. Anyhow, my boss is a lot happier now that his investment is safe and I hope yours is too. It will certainly help me get some decent shut-eye tonight,' said Dave.

'We're all due to fly to the States tomorrow. I'm on my way home to pack. Do you know what time Rob will be back in London?' asked Saz.

'The boss wanted them to stay out of sight until this new story peaks. We've already got it onto all the social media sites as well as the newspapers. The TV companies have snapped it up, they're gagging for news at this time of the year. So, barring an earthquake in central London or a royal baby, we should be home and dry by tomorrow. I'll call you when I know that they've been let out. So to speak!'

They both laughed with relief.

'Thanks Dave, I owe you a drink. I'll give you a buzz when we get back,' Saz gasped when she had caught her breath.

46

Maggie's meeting with the two solicitors, Andrew Bridgeman and Paul Drake, and the police officer had gone much better than she expected. They were just about to finish when her new personal mobile signalled the arrival of a text message from Rose Cooper, asking to speak to her very urgently.

Maggie's stomach lurched. Had something happened to one of her children? She made her excuses and went to another room to take the call.

'What's happened, Rose? I can't talk for long, I'm in a... meeting.'

'I thought you ought to know that one of the secretaries at college has just phoned to say that a journalist has been asking about you. Apparently he's got your name off the internet.'

Maggie began to tremble, 'Why?'

'You're listed as a former member of staff.'

'No! Why was the journalist asking about me?'

'Jack Millfield went to a press conference for Rob Hunter's new film this morning and he was shouting about you and a baby, if you can believe it. I think he's having some kind of mental breakdown. Dominic told me that his wife has just had a miscarriage,' Rose added.

Maggie steadied herself on the back of a chair. She could hear Rose calling her name.

'Maggie, Maggie, are you still there?'

'Rose, what did the university say to the journalist? What did they tell him?'

'Nothing. They sent him off with a flea in his ear. Apparently Jack was arrested at the press conference. He had a fight with the security people. They took him away in a police car. The last thing the university wants is that kind of publicity.'

Rose's voice was shrill with excitement. 'What on earth is going on, Maggie?'

'I don't know,' Maggie whispered as the door opened and Paul Drake appeared, staring at her ashen face in consternation.

'What's happened?' he mouthed.

'Who's that? Where are you?' Rose said.

'I can't talk now, Rose. I'll ring you later. I'll explain it all later.'

Maggie put the phone in her pocket and turned to Paul.

'Jack Millfield was at the press conference, he's been arrested,' she said.

Paul sighed and rubbed a hand across his face. 'Right. We'd better go back to the meeting, they're getting impatient.'

He took her arm and led her back to where the others were still talking in low voices.

'There's been a development,' Paul announced as they sat down. 'Millfield interrupted the press conference this morning. He's been arrested and taken in for questioning.'

Andrew Bridgeman handed Maggie a glass of water.

'I'd like to know how he got access?' Paul said angrily.

Maggie put the glass of water down. 'Jack Millfield runs an advertising agency. It would have been very easy for him to get hold of a press pass. The letter from Andrew warning him that he would be served with a civil action must have provoked him,' she said, 'My friend has just told me that his wife has recently had a miscarriage.'

'That's no excuse for barging into a press conference and punching people,' muttered the police officer, 'The guy sounds as though he's unhinged.' He stood up. 'I better go.'

He picked up the large brown envelope on Andrew Bridgeman's desk. 'Now I've got the personal statement, we can get the restraining order sorted out straight away. The next time Mr Millfield steps out of line, he will be committing a criminal offence. Don't worry, we'll make that very clear to him.'

He smiled at Maggie, shook hands with everybody and left.

Paul Drake's mobile sounded.

'I'd better take this,' he said as he went to stand outside, while Maggie and Andrew glanced anxiously at each other, wondering what was coming next.

In a few minutes Paul returned, grinning broadly.

'Don't worry, it's not bad news. The film people went into major damage limitation mode as soon as it all kicked off at the press conference. Their PR people are in a league of their own. They were on top of it like a ton of bricks. They've just broken a story that has pushed the names of Rob Hunter and Maggie Savernake right off the front pages. They are also trying to take down any stuff that got onto social media. That's more difficult, but I'm pretty sure that the other story will monopolise everybody's attention for weeks.'

He grinned at their dazed expressions. 'Everything and everybody has a price, at the end of the day.'

Andrew Bridgeman stood up with a loud groan of exhaustion.

'Well, I don't know about you, but that's more than enough excitement for me for one day, thank you very much. It sounds like we've sorted the problem out, Maggie. I don't think you'll be hearing from Jack Millfield for a long time after this. And even if you do, he will be committing a criminal offence and the law will deal with him.'

Maggie found it impossible to smile. How was she going to face Saz and Rob now?

*

Saz let herself in through the communicating door soon after Maggie arrived back at her flat in the late afternoon.

'Hi Maggie, how'd it go at the solicitors?' she said brightly.

'Jack was at the press conference,' Maggie said, putting her bag down.

'Yes, I know.'

'I'm going to leave, Saz. I can't stay after this. I'll never forgive myself,' she said, 'I know that you're going to be very busy for the next couple of weeks and it's the worst time for me to go, so I've decided to wait until you've found someone suitable to replace me. I don't want to leave you in the lurch, on top of everything else.'

'Don't be silly. We're not going to find someone like you. You've got to stay. Rob will be very upset.'

'I doubt that somehow. He'll be very relieved,' Maggie replied.

'Ray Brookes has buried the story. It's finished. Over. It never happened,' said Saz.

'But I know it happened, you know it happened and worst of all, Rob and the rest of the film crew know it happened. I can't face him after this.' Maggie's voice broke.

Saz put a hand on her arm. 'Don't cry, Maggie. Rob is due back in London tomorrow. We'll have a chat before we go to the airport. We're off to the States for about ten days, remember? Listen, I'm going to leave the keys to my place with you. If you could just go in and cast your eye around: windows, power points, etcetera. This little kerfuffle has taken up a bit more time than I can spare at the moment.'

'I am so sorry. I feel terrible. This is the very last thing you need, or deserve. You have both been so kind.'

Maggie's voice was thick.

'Stop it, Maggie. Just make sure that I've switched everything off in my place after we've gone. Now, go and have a hot bath and go to bed, you need your sleep and so do I. I'll go and get my stuff from Rob's flat and go home. Don't forget to lock up before you go to bed!'

Saz laughed as she closed the door between the two flats again.

47

Rob arrived in St John's Wood just after seven o'clock the following morning. He acknowledged the man behind the desk with a perfunctory nod before racing up the stairs and was startled to find that the front door to his flat was double locked and all the rooms were in darkness, with all the blinds and curtains tightly closed.

There was no sound coming from Maggie's flat.

He phoned Saz.

'Rob? What's happened now?' Her voice was slurred with sleep.

'I think Maggie's already left.'

'That's impossible. I spoke to her yesterday evening. What's the time? Oh my God, it's only just gone seven.'

'What did you say to her? I'm worried, Saz.' Rob said urgently.

'I told her we want her to stay. Listen, calm down. I'll be over as soon as I can. Start packing.'

After making himself a cup of coffee, Rob went to stare at the contents of his wardrobe. It was the first time in a very long time that he had felt so unenthusiastic about going anywhere.

When Saz arrived just after eight, she found him scratching his head and staring stupidly at the clothes which were now piled on his bed.

'Do you really need to take all of that? We're only going for ten days,' she said crossly.

'I haven't heard a sound from Maggie's flat,' Rob said.

'What? Still nothing? That's odd, she usually gets up very early.'

'I know,' Rob opened a drawer and closed it.

Saz held out a suit on a hanger. 'This one will be OK, won't it?' She laid it on the bed. 'Put that in the Yes pile, while I go and get a cup of coffee.'

'I made the coffee an hour ago. It's probably cold.' He said.

'I'll make some more and try the communicating door while I'm waiting for the kettle to boil.'

Thirty seconds later, Saz was back. She took a key off the hook inside one of the units.

'Is it locked?' Rob stood in the kitchen doorway with a shirt in his hand. 'The front door to this flat was double locked when I arrived,' he said, 'Do you think that Maggie is worried about the security? We ought to sort it out before we leave. I'm going to ring her front door bell.'

He threw the shirt on the worktop and went out onto the main landing, pressing the doorbell and holding it down with his finger until he finally heard the key turning on the other side.

Maggie's eyes didn't rise beyond the middle of his chest.

'Hi,' she said.

Rob took a step backwards to look at her. 'You OK?'

'Fine. You?'

'Fine, now that I've seen you,' he said. 'Saz is here and we wondered if you would give us a hand with the packing?'

Maggie followed him into the other flat without speaking.

Saz was talking on her mobile phone in the kitchen. She raised a thumb in greeting to Maggie as they passed.

'I hate packing, I always have,' Rob said as he unzipped a suitcase, 'I don't know why I can't take a rucksack.'

Maggie began folding the clothes and laying them neatly inside the case.

'Hi Maggie, did you sleep well?' Saz was holding a steaming mug of coffee. Maggie nodded.

'Lugging a huge case around with us doesn't make any sense. Why can't we hire or get stuff from the wardrobe department?' Rob grumbled as he handed a shirt to Maggie.

'Because this is a PR exercise and you're supposed to look your best and you paid a fortune for some of this stuff. Please hurry. We must leave by one o'clock and we ought to eat something before we go. Airport food is dire.' Saz said.

'I could make sandwiches while you finish packing,' Maggie suggested, without looking at either of them.

'Done,' Rob and Saz said in unison.

Half an hour later, Maggie had prepared a small selection of sandwiches and fruit and laid them out on the kitchen table.

'I think this merits a small glass of wine, don't you?' Rob put three wineglasses and an open bottle on the table.

'I was beginning to think that I'd have to buy some Dutch courage in the departures lounge,' Saz said with obvious relief as they sat down.

Rob filled the glasses. 'To Team Hunter,' he said, clinking his glass against the other two.

Saz took a long gulp and put her glass down. 'Rob said that the front door was double locked when he arrived this morning, Maggie.'

'Yes.'

'Is that because of what happened yesterday?'

'Yes.'

'Surely you don't think that, that lunatic will risk breaking the restraining order after all his antics yesterday?' Rob said incredulously.

'I feel safer when the doors are locked.' Maggie said as she pushed a sandwich around her plate.

'Talking about yesterday, why did he mention a baby? Is he mentally disturbed or something?' Saz's words hung in the air and Maggie could feel their eyes boring into her. They were waiting for answers.

What was the point of going on with this charade now? She looked at their expectant faces.

'It's difficult...' she said. 'It's very difficult.' She sighed and took a deep breath, 'I met Jack Millfield when we were students. I think he was my late adolescent rebellion.' She gave them a desolate smile. 'We broke up after a few months. Jack was sent down for punching a tutor and we lost contact. We met briefly again at a reunion dinner at the end of 2006 and after a couple of dates, I went back to his flat. We were very drunk.' Maggie's mouth was dry. 'A few weeks later I discovered that I was ... pregnant. When I told Jack, he said he couldn't deal with it and told me to get rid of it.'

'Bastard,' whispered Saz.

Rob stood up and went to stand in front of the window with his back to the room.

'I don't know why I told Jack,' Maggie said as she glanced at the tense set of his shoulders. 'I'd already decided that it was a terrible mistake. Jack wasn't the man that I remembered,' she hesitated, 'To be fair, I had changed too. I think we were both trying to relive our youth.'

She swallowed with difficulty. 'I don't remember much about what happened after we went back to his flat. I've never been a drinker. I must have passed out or something.'

'My God, did he give you that date rape drug?' Saz looked horrified.

'No. I don't know. I don't think so. I don't think Jack's that evil.' Maggie took another deep breath. 'I arranged to have a termination.' She began to stumble over the words, close to tears. 'Jack began harassing me, telling me that he'd changed his mind. When I told him that it was over, he wouldn't leave me alone. On the night before the termination, he attacked me when I was walking down Gower Street.'

'Attacked you in Gower Street?' Saz echoed incredulously. Rob remained motionless with his back to them.

'It was just before Christmas, it was raining. I tried to fight him off and I fell over. I had a miscarriage about fifteen minutes after I got back to my flat. I was in hospital overnight.'

This was followed by a long shocked silence.

'I thought it was over,' Maggie said at last, in a dazed voice, 'but it wasn't. He began phoning and texting me several times a day. The messages went on and on and on. They were full of threats and abuse and eventually I had to take time off work.'

She saw Saz's outraged expression.

'Jack was threatened with a restraining order and it stopped for a while. Then I lost my job and had to give up my flat and went to live with Rose and her family. And then I found you.' Maggie smiled through her tears. 'Jack thinks that I had a termination, that's why he keeps saying what he says.'

'But why didn't you tell him the truth? Why didn't you tell him that it was him that had caused the miscarriage?' Saz looked indignant. 'He should be told.'

'I don't know. I think I wanted to punish him. Instead of which he's been punishing me. He got married three months ago and Rose told me yesterday that his wife has just had a miscarriage.'

Rob turned to look at the two women. His face was grave.

'They've let him off with a caution, apparently interrupting a press conference was not a good enough reason. But it's not all bad news. After they saw all the stuff from the solicitors, they have issued a restraining order and if he breaks that he'll be arrested again and charged with committing a criminal offence.'

'The police officer explained all that at the meeting yesterday,' Maggie said, 'But how can I be sure that it will stop him?' She looked desperate.

'I don't think we can ever be sure of that, but if he's a director of an advertising agency, surely he won't risk getting arrested and going to prison? It would ruin him,' Saz said.

'Jack Millfield has been a blight on my life since the day I met him at the Reunion,' Maggie said. 'The only difference now is that he has involved you two as well. That's why I must leave. It's not fair.'

Rob crossed the room. 'Of course we're involved. You're working with us and we want to help you. We can give you the security you need.'

He sat in the chair next to her. 'Listen to me, Maggie. Saz and I don't want you to leave. We need you. I agree with Saz; I don't think that Millfield will break this order. I'm sure it's over. And, as Saz said, we could always ask the solicitor to write to him and tell him that he caused the miscarriage. The hospital will have medical reports; we could get copies.'

'You've done enough already,' Maggie said with an exhausted smile.

Saz stood up. 'We'll keep that bit of ammunition in reserve. I'll talk to the solicitor on the way to the airport. The cab is booked for one. It's nearly that now. Are you packed, Rob?' She glared at him over the top of her glasses. 'We've got a plane to catch and a film to sell.'

Maggie followed them out to the top of the main staircase and Saz hugged her tight, pressing her cheek against Maggie's.

'Guard the camp while we're away. We'll be back before you know it,' she called over her shoulder as she descended the stairs.

Rob's took Maggie's hand and his lips skimmed lightly across her cheek. 'Promise to call me if you need anything,' he said.

She nodded.

He lifted her chin, searching deep into her eyes. 'Say it, Maggie.'

The colour rose in Maggie's pale cheeks. 'I promise,' she said with a sudden, dazzling smile.

Rob blinked and stepped backwards, holding a hand over his eyes, as though he had been blinded and they both laughed as he walked down the stairs and disappeared from her view.

Maggie closed the front door, still smiling and went to the window to watch as their cab turned into the main road. She remembered the day when she drove to Heathrow to meet Rob. It seemed like a very long time ago.

As she cleared away the remains of the lunch, she realised with a small shock that she felt calmer and more at ease than she had felt for two years; it was as though a huge weight had been lifted from her shoulders. Finding the courage to tell Rob and Saz had changed everything; the haunting, nightmare fear of discovery had evaporated.

It's over, she thought. It really is over. It's time to move on.

She went into Rob's bedroom to put away the discarded clothes spread across his bed. I'll finish the book and start another one. I might even collaborate with Rob on a play one day, she thought, he said something about wanting to return to the theatre.

Without realising what she was doing, Maggie pressed one of his shirts against her face. He would be wonderful in *Coriolanus*.

Just then she heard the insistent ringtone of her new mobile sounding through the open adjoining door from somewhere inside her own flat. She went to pick it up, stifling the instinctive flutter of anxiety.

'Hi.'

'Well?' Rose made the word sound like a severe reproach. 'I've been waiting for your call for hours.'

Maggie pictured her friend's pixie face, the inquisitive, knowing dark eyes and cheeky smile.

'Hi Rose, I'm really sorry. It's been a bit hectic. Look, I'll meet you at the cafe on Hampstead Heath in an hour and I'll tell you everything.' she said.

'What? Absolutely everything? Every single little detail?' Rose was almost inarticulate with excitement.

'Yes, everything.' Maggie said.